DEAD GODS

DEAD GODS

CHUCK LANG

Cursed Dragon Ship
PUBLISHING

For my wife, Michal, and my sons, Julian and Elliot, with love

CHAPTER ONE

"Christ, another Saint," Eddie said as milky smoke snaked from his mouth. He took another drag from a roach pinched between fingers and pulled his black '75 Chevy Vega onto the rural road's shoulder. The ditch was clogged with grass where a plywood sign stated in the red-run of weathered paint-brush script *Welcome to Saint Andrew!* A boat floated under the greeting, loaded down with a Rockwellian family. The mother opened paper-wrapped sandwiches, and the daughter spread a checked cloth on the boat's bench. A grinning son reeled in a fighting fish while the vested father clenched a Peterson briar pipe between his teeth as he held out a net. "Jesus." Eddie shook his head.

He shifted back into first and released the clutch with herky-jerky laziness. In the passenger seat, Rhea's head lolled, and her red curls swayed against her neon-spattered Pet Shop Boys T-shirt. She still slept.

He looked in the rearview mirror more out of habit than caution. It wasn't the traffic that made him step on the brakes. He hadn't seen another car for miles. It was the back of the billboard lit by the late morning sun. Black and red spray paint blotted and drizzled the plywood. Some professed love with initials, a plus sign, and dates: '75, '77, '82, with '86 the most recent. Another asked if Sharlene wanted to go steady. There was the typical 666, inverted pentagrams, and horned goats next to an order to die and someone who wanted to say *I hate you*. Eddie didn't stop for all that. He stopped for the limp, orange tabby nailed by the paws to the bottom corner. The red there wasn't paint. Eddie's empty stomach turned. He looked at Rhea, accelerated, and left the sign behind.

After taking another long, shaky drag, he switched the radio on. Through the car's remaining speaker, a disc jockey nasally announced what everyone had been waiting for, the day's top-of-the-charts song "Amadeus" by some German dude named Falco. The singer nudged out a series of *oh*s and chanted that classical artist's name to electric strings. Eddie loved it and cranked the volume to the number eleven he'd gouged into the radio's black corrugated face. The filler vocals turned to a hot bacon spatter of static.

Rhea lifted her head and said with a mousy squeak, "Jesus Christ, Eddie. Open the fuckin' window. I can't see. And turn that shit down." She waved her hand too emphatically for Eddie's taste. He could fuckin' see, which meant she could damn well see. Eddie huffed and, with a convulsive jig, spun the chrome window crank.

He'd have told Rhea to open her own window, but he had broken and duct-taped the crank days ago after losing a piss-em-off match: a game they mastered over the years. Hours in the car together had led to many games, but Eddie's record wasn't good. Besides, Rhea would be groggy, so he laid off. He flicked the roach onto the tar where spring runoff quenched its showered sparks.

The chill wind buffeted the smoke from the cab and

tousled Rhea's curls. A lock caught the corner of her mouth, which she pulled out with a yellow-polished pinky nail and twist of her head—once again, too emphatically for Eddie's taste yet alluring like a Harlequin cover harlot. Rhea groaned and palmed saliva from her freckled, seatbelt-hatched cheek. She wiped the spit on her ripped and dusty Girbaud jeans. "Where the hell are we?" She leaned forward, twisted the volume down, and squinted out the smudged windshield.

"I dunno. Another town. *Saint* something again," Eddie said. Under the brake pedal was a roadmap stamped with the mud chevrons of Eddie's sneaker soles. Rhea wasn't stupid, but that didn't stop him from footing the wadded map under his seat, coughing to cover the crumpling paper.

Rhea leaned back and held a limp hand below her straight nose as if thinking. Eddie gritted his teeth. Next, she'd flourish and wag her finger for emphasis.

"But," she said, "you know where we are."

Yep, there it was, the swirl and wag. Her fingernails coated in chipped polish made it worse, like she was taxiing him into an airport terminal labeled *I win*.

"Yeah, Minnesota. I think. It's on the—" He stopped. "Anyway, who cares. It's just another town."

"You could check the map." She looked out her own window, tapped her temple, and shrugged.

He'd been taxied. There was no winning. "All right, next town. Besides, we're low on gas."

She turned and smiled with lips that were dry yet inviting and ran her fingers through his black curls and blond roots. He shivered, relaxed, and closed his window. They'd been in the car for over twelve hours since leaving some small town lost in the flat wastes of Montana. Now they wandered through a part of the Midwest that named towns after dead-man saints. Each town had a church, a bar, and sometimes—if you were lucky—a gas station.

The Vega choked on a black clot deep in its workings and jerked Eddie and Rhea with mechanical epilepsy. Eddie stomped on the gas pedal and strangled the steering wheel. The car pissed itself, soaked the gravel that crackled under its tires, and listed on the shoulder where it stopped. The two stared through the windshield in silence. Eddie set his forehead on the horn and let out a long and breathy "fuck."

"The town's just up the road," said Rhea. "I see a church."

Eddie ratcheted the parking brake, shouldered open the driver's door that gave a hoarse screech, and walked toward Saint Andrew.

Rhea got out with a similar protest of hinges, threw her hands up in the air and squealed, "Where are you going?"

"Uh, duh! I'm walking to town." He fish-hooked a single finger in the corner of his mouth, twisted his head, and pointed at the crucifix-crowned steeple. He was being an ass yet didn't want to lose another pissing match, so he took his spit-wet finger out of his mouth and swooped it low toward the town, shoulders limp and submissive. "Come on, Rhea. We gotta get help."

Rhea slung her acid-washed denim jacket over her shoulders and slammed the car door. Squinting with hurt, she stamped toward Eddie yet still held his hand as they headed into town. "You're an ass," she said.

"I know." He didn't say he was sorry, which was another moment in time he knew she'd enter into her inventory of the unforgettable.

It didn't take long to reach Saint Andrew. It was a lucky town: had a church, had a bar, had a gas station. Signs labeled each building. The spire and crucifix belonged to the Immaculate Conception Catholic Church. The bar was called Frank's, and the gas station, The Store. Further down the highway was a schoolhouse and someone's home. A gravel road branched west just before the gas station but was quickly lost in leafless trees and needled pines. They stood near the station's pumps, and Eddie asked, "You wanna come in with me?"

"No, I'll stay here. You go in." She shrugged. "I could use the air."

The Store had a sidewalk running its entire length that became a porch of sorts with a deep, overhanging roof. The siding was cedar, painted brown. The corner near the pumps had a few windows and a solid door with security glass. Brass bells clattered as Eddie opened the door. Turning back, he could see Rhea leaning against the brushed metal of the Amoco gas pump, still picking and chewing the polish from her nails. She looked up at the church, and the late morning sun caught her face, highlighting scattered freckles and silver wisps of frozen breath at her lips. He ducked into The Store.

Behind a low glass cabinet displaying hand-made lures was a man whose ass consumed the wood stool on which he sat. His head was wrapped in goggles that magnified the tweezers clenched between sausage fingers as he spun filament around white feathers half-swallowed by alligator clips. Beyond the counter droned the electric hum of bait vats tagged with damp cardboard warning NOT FOOD 4 PEOPLE in black marker.

The fat man interrupted the hum. "Need help?" The gullet beneath his chin—speckled by black thistles of whiskers—weighted down the corners of his mouth. A cracked, red name tag was pinned askew and punched with the white letters JOSH. The man ogled Eddie then stood. A stench curdled the air. His tent of a T-shirt curtained over the counter in pools of threadbare blue. He crutched himself up on Michelin Man meat hooks and asked, again, "Help you?"

"Uh, yeah. I need this." Eddie fumbled over rust-pocked shelves and grabbed a bag of Wonder Bread. He held the polka-dotted bag of fortified fun before him, warding off the man. "And I need a tow. My car's a mile north of here."

The man wheezed between each word. "That's Josh. He's out back. In the garage. I can show you."

"Nah—no," Eddie said too urgently. He pointed at the man's name tag but stopped. "I'll find him. Josh. Out back you say? Got it. Thanks." He placed the bag filled with little slices of America back on the shelf and Charlie-Chaplined out the door. The bells clattered.

Outside, Eddie opened his mouth then pointed toward the back of The Store. This was enough for Rhea to smile and nod. Eddie could feel her eyes on his ass packed into black jeans as he descended a short hill. He turned and grinned. She rolled her eyes then went back to picking her nails.

Behind The Store leaned a pole barn. The garage door was dented at bumper level but open enough for Eddie to see a short man in a soiled green mechanic's jumpsuit hunkered under a pickup raised on a greased pillar. Metal clanking metal echoed deep inside the garage. Under the truck's chassis, strobes of light popped, and sparks that fell to the concrete danced and died. One of the brightest sparks landed on the man's green-sleeved wrist; a thin pillar of smoke twisted up from the fabric. The popping and sparking were interrupted with a *hah* and *hoo* trailing into a string of *fuck*s as a greasy hand smacked the spark.

A welder's helmet clacked on the floor, and the mechanic strut from under the truck. Sweaty black hair caged his blue eyes set in a face rutted with lightning bolt scars. Still spouting strings of profanity, he looked up and caught Eddie's eyes.

"What?" said the mechanic, palming his burnt wrist near his breast where his tag clearly read *OWEN*. His voice was like the hiss of greased hydraulics, fluid yet sharp-edged. Metal on metal clanking continued within the garage.

"My car . . . Are you Josh?"

"Yep." Tonguing a piece of meat and bread from his teeth, Josh snorted the remains to the back of his throat and spat it on the gravel. He swiped his bangs aside, smudging more grease across his forehead, and tapped the nametag.

"Yeah," Eddie said and buried his hands in his pockets. "My car. It broke down about a mile north of here. I need a tow and someone to check it out. It's in bad shape."

The metal-on-metal clanking inside the shop stopped. A man who resembled a blond, balding weasel came out of the dark garage with a stonemason's hammer in his right fist. Josh shook his head. The weasel's name tag read *CAL*.

"You get done what I told ya'?" Josh said.

Cal sucked on chew behind his lip and spat out a black glob and said nothing as he eyed Eddie. Eddie took his hands out of his pockets and took a step back. Josh smacked Cal's chest.

Cal eyed Josh. "Fu—what?" he said, his brow furrowed.

Josh stepped forward, spread his arms, and like fingers over stubble, said, "Did you get it done?"

"Nah."

Josh trembled with half-fists held at his sides. "Get it done."

Cal, head hung low, kicked a rock. Hammer swinging heavily at his side, tight in his fist, he limped back into the shadows.

Josh turned back to Eddie, shook his head, said, "Good help and all," and shrugged.

"My car," said Eddie.

"Yep. Let me shut this shit down." He pointed at the welding mess on the garage floor. "And I'll get your car." He pulled a red rag from his back pocket and wiped his hands and face.

Slightly less greasy, he was either pissed or surprised to see Eddie still standing there. Josh pointed at himself, Eddie, The Store, and finally the pickup behind him, and said, "*I'll* pick *you* up *front* then take a look at *your* heap of *shit* after *I* get done with *this piece*."

Eddie shook his head and walked back to Rhea.

CHAPTER TWO

By the pumps, Rhea laughed as Eddie filled her in on the *JOSH-OWEN* tag swap and Owen's stench, when over the hill growled a goliath, fifties tow truck. The truck's grill was a rusted, chrome-toothed grin between lazy-eyed headlights that ogled the ground and sky. Josh was at the wheel. A cigarette hung from his mouth. He ground the truck's beaten brakes and stopped next to Eddie and Rhea, leaned across the cab, and opened the passenger door with the dull echo of empty metal. Josh coated a layer of lust so thick over Rhea's body that she nearly wiped the perv-paint from her chest but folded her arms instead.

"Hey, I'm Josh." His upper lip did its best impression of a pubescent Stallone with an added stroke of pasty child molester.

"Yeah. Hi." Rhea reverted to gum-chewing valley girl and shielded herself behind the gas pump. She had dealt with dicks like this before, but this dick had a special flare of asshole in him that seeded her belly with sick.

Eddie severed the space between Rhea and Josh and said,

"Uh, yeah, so, where can my wife hold up while we—you and I —get the car?"

That word, *wife*, tensed Rhea's chest as it slid easily over Eddie's lips. She looked at Eddie and held his arm just below the shoulder. He touched but didn't hold it. They weren't married, yet she wouldn't mind that word being his until she croaked. But Eddie wasn't ready. There was a little too much loser left in him. She tried to erase that from his mind, but it never ended well: yelling, tears, a shrug, and limply retreating like the defeated goth-boy he once was and still wanted to be.

Eddie had been talking; she hadn't heard the words. It was Josh's voice that became clear when he said, "She'll be *fine* at Frank's." He craned over Eddie's shoulder and, with more perv than Stallone this time, jerked his head at the pole barn saloon across the highway.

Rhea huffed in disgust yet turned. Frank's haunches were covered in tan, corrugated metal pocked with nails that leaked rusty tears. Its façade, however, enjoyed greater care. Blanketed with rough-sawn lumber stained an earthy red, it sported a balustered balcony and four windows curtained with yellow-flowered bedsheets. White-framed French doors split the windows into pairs. Screwed into the balcony's railing was a white sign with the bar's name painted in black. Under *Frank's* was the red shadow of the previous name: *Sam's*. Under *Sam's* were the scrolling lines of *Lou*. Under *Lou* were the ribs of what may have been a *D* and *C* and a large-lettered *AL*. A concrete porch hid under the balcony with steps on the north end.

The building was a story, a story she wasn't sure she wanted to hear. It seemed old. Stuck. As though it'd been there longer than possible. Unchanged. Maybe unwanted? But grudgingly cared for by whomever was within and simply accepted by those without as a thing that just existed.

Eddie touched Rhea's hip, kissed her long and light then said, "See ya in a bit."

She smiled, eyes on his, her lips wet with Eddie, which she let last. Eddie mounted the Buick tow truck and slammed the door. Rhea leaned languorously against the gas pump's cool metal and nipped off more nail polish. Through the truck's oval, rear window, Eddie blurred.

Josh ground to the next gear, and the truck belched inky smoke from rusted pipes. The orphan exhaust crawled along the broken road where it wrapped Rhea's body then curled over The Store's roof and Josh's shop. In that smoke was a piece of home, a piece of California baked in the summer heat where smog dyed the skies purple, obscured skyscraper peaks, and clouded the shores of Coronado.

She shook the memories aside and simply listened. Listened to the cool breeze that kicked up dust at her feet and bent leafless trees. Listened to distant boat motors and the shivering calls of songbirds. Listened to the town itself as if it and its people shared a hidden voice. Listened to the children who giggled and screamed just beyond a hill which she crested. It was there that a Brownstone schoolhouse sat.

It was an ugly thing that slumped like a grave's monument on a slab of concrete. Its brickwork was patched with a cream resin turned yellow like wads of fat. A white picket fence studded with bent nails did a meager job guarding it. Metal swings screeched while children kicked themselves higher and higher. Others in a game of tag hounded a little blonde girl near a tree-choked slough. Some boy with a dull splat of brown hair clipped the blonde girl's foot, sending her tumbling in a flurry of dead grass.

She brushed off her white dress, wiped away tears, and pointed at the boy. "No fair! No tripping." She screamed, "Teacher!"

On a park bench painted green dozens of times, a gray-haired woman in a pink, brocade dress sucked on a cigarette.

"Teacher," the girl whined. "He tripped me."

The gray-haired woman took the girl in her arms and thumbed away muddy tears, pulled out a crumpled tissue, and dabbed the girl's runny nose. "Look at you, my little sweetheart. It's okay. You're okay. You're okay." Her voice turned husky, and her steel-gray eyes twitched. "He'll get a lickin' for this. You sit here." She set the girl on the bench and stomped toward a clot of boys who wrestled in a cloud of dust. She stabbed a fist into the fray and dragged the boy by an ear into the schoolhouse.

"Teacher, what did I do?" the boy yelled. Through open windows his squeals echoed like hammer strikes on metal as the teacher smacked his bare ass behind brick walls.

Numb needles pricked Rhea, too, except it was her dad's palm, years dead.

The boy's squeals became dry laughs.

Under an open window, all except the blonde girl gathered: a solemn congregation, fearful yet reverent.

On a swing, the blonde girl's shoulders rose with every smack and a grin razor-slashed her face. Behind her, in a white gown stood a sickly boy with black hair like greasy feathers.

Smacks echoed.

The black-haired boy touched the girl's shoulder, leaned close, and pointed at Rhea.

The boy's dry laughs were cut by gasps.

The girl nodded, released the swing's chain, and bent her fingers in a lazy wave. She whispered to the black-haired boy and giggled.

Something inside the beaten child broke, hacked out by the teacher's palm and silenced.

Rhea clenched fists at her sides, shook her head, and said, "Stop."

The teacher smacked.

A cotton-stuffed hush covered the slough.

A bell rang.

The children filed into the schoolhouse.

The little blonde girl followed. Her eyes on Rhea, she massaged the smile from her pudgy face.

"My god," Rhea said, longing for a smoke yet not wanting to break her week's long end to that habit.

The school's doors closed as a black Cordoba, pinstriped red, rolled by on the highway. The driver, smeared by the window's bowed glass, pulled up to The Store's pumps. Owen lumbered from under the awning, filled the car's tank, and squeegeed the windshield. The car pulled away, and Owen stuffed a wad of bills in his pocket. Looking at Rhea, he stroked his gizzard.

Rhea folded her arms over her chest and crossed the road where, just south of Frank's and sharing a gravel parking lot, stood a yellow-bricked church. On a granite dais was the church's name and a faded Virgin Mary, who offered open palms. Rhea mouthed its name in disbelief: *Immaculate Conception Catholic Church.* Cracked concrete steps led to crucifix-etched doors and, through skeletal trees atop the steeple, loomed a silver cross. She abandoned the church and headed to Frank's.

Owen's eyes were still on her. No longer at the pumps, he stood with his face near the security glass for a moment then receded. Rhea relaxed yet held her shaking palm to her churning stomach. Why had she let Eddie go without her? She shook her head and breathed. Frank's polished rail and uneven steps had a rhythm carved by time. Behind the weathered front door's tinted window, a woman rested her chin on a mop. The door's handle was cold brass that pulled with tempting ease.

CHAPTER THREE

AN UNCOILED SPRING dug into Eddie's ass as the Buick tow truck bounced down the highway. Two speakers strung up with bailing twine clacked on the truck's metal frame. Speaker wires dangled from the rearview mirror to a cassette radio bolted to the dash. Josh shook a cassette and shoved it in the slot. Mid-song, Billy Idol crackled to life professing his soul to an angel.

Josh pounded the steering wheel as he sat spread-legged, one foot on the gas, the other thumping the greasy mat. Banging his head on the off beats, he crinkled his nose and bit his lower lip like a rabid chipmunk. He stopped, grinned at Eddie, said, "Good shit, man," and went back to his lonely dance. He sniffed through empty nostrils every time the truck trundled over a lump in the road. And then, the ass spoke, again. Eddie was hoping to avoid this, but the idiot had to talk —yell, in fact—over Idol. "So, where'd you find a sweet piece like that?"

"Jesus Christ," Eddie said as he held his hand over his mouth and looked out the passenger window like Rhea had in

the Vega. He shook his head; he was turning into her, and this
ass caused it.

Eddie looked at Josh.

Josh looked at Eddie. "What, man? Come on. Can you
blame me?"

This man *was* an ass. Eddie could say her name, say something like, *It's Rhea, ya fuck. Not sweet piece.* Then give him a
couple quick pops in the face like smacks of punctuation. But
that'd just turn into something Eddie didn't want. Anger and
busting ass were weak, and Eddie didn't need that, didn't need
what he once was.

He'd play this one safe. Guys like this needed someone like
them, maybe someone a little less than them. It'd be the only
way he could get through this, so he put on his best I-don't-
give-a-fuck and fuck-the-man attitude. "Shit, man, her
name's Rhea." He softened his voice, just enough to show
fondness, maybe weakness in Josh's eyes. He looked at his feet.
"You're right though, she's fine. And I'm luckier than I
should be."

Josh grinned. "Yeah, that's what I thought. I see you got no
ring."

"Yeah, we eloped. Can't afford it."

Josh sniffed then tugged on a pack of smokes caught on his
name tag. He pulled the pin, tossed it on the dash, and said,
"Jesus Owen, quit taking my shit ya' fat fuck." He offered the
pack of Camel Unfiltered to Eddie. "Smoke?"

That smoke was a handout. Eddie was an alley beggar, and
Josh was the ass who'd tell the bum to get a fucking job. That's
what Eddie wanted, so he took a smoke and patted denim for
his lighter left in the Vega. This would mean he needed
another handout: all the better.

Josh held out a Zippo. Eddie took it. He lit his smoke and
snapped the lighter shut. Its brushed brass was etched with

Semper Fi on one side and embossed with the US Marine Corps logo on the other.

Eddie picked at the eagle's wings caked with red grease or dirt and said, "Marines. You?"

A silver crucifix swung from Josh's right lobe, and his upper lip twitched. He held out a rigid palm. "Nah. Dad."

Eddie gave the lighter back. "Tell your dad, thanks."

"For what?"

"Serving."

"He's dead."

"War?"

Josh tucked the lighter back in the pocket of his overalls, turned his eyes back on the road, and said, "Nah, in my—his home."

"Sorry to hear that."

Josh shrugged.

"How?" asked Eddie.

Sidelong, Josh looked at Eddie. His cigarette hung like a dead limb from wet lips. Eddie picked stuffing from the oil-spotted upholstery. Something wasn't right. Something was missing. Eddie needed to keep the conversation going, not let it end with the death of Josh's dad. He'd pushed too far, pissed him off. It couldn't end there. Angry Josh meant Eddie was in control. Josh needed control. He knew something about Josh, something personal. Josh needed that on Eddie, beyond Rhea. He was running out of time, so he started with her, with what was easy. "Rhea and I . . ."

Josh perked up at the mention of Rhea. Eddie sighed. Of course that's all this guy needed.

"Yeah?" said Josh.

"We, Rhea and I, been on the road for a while." What next? He could talk about her dead family. About the night they left her El Centro house in the Vega. About the diners and bars they'd worked since. None of that was what this ass wanted, so he came clean. "I was a dealer."

"Dealer. Like Vegas and cards?"

"Nah. Drugs."

"No shit," said Josh in what verged on a question.

Josh had something personal, but he'd need a bit more. "My family, my dad. It's what he did. What we did. I couldn't do it. So we ran."

"Rhea went with you? A drug dealer."

"Yeah, can you believe it?"

"What'd you deal?"

"Everything. Whatever came up from Mexico, Cuba, further south."

"That's some Miami Vice shit."

Eddie smirked. His eyes grew dry and hard. Anger twitched inside. There was too much of that old Eddie left in him to control it sometimes.

Josh said, "Chicks, man. They dig the assholes."

Sure, Josh wouldn't let her go. Eddie relaxed and ran the back of his hand across his chin. "Who knew, man. Who knew. I'm as surprised as you."

"Your family know where you are?"

"Nah, haven't for nearly three years."

"Cops?"

"Dunno."

"Speaking of cops," Josh said. "Looks like the chief's takin' an interest in your car."

Behind the Vega, a black-and-white Crown Vic's bubble lights pirouetted. The chief sat in the Vega's driver's seat clutching a gold-corded cattleman hat. His face was obscured by the sun visor. A twisted baggy filled with weed was on the dash.

Eddie closed his eyes and shook his head. "Jesus Christ," he said as he shrugged. If this was the place the cops caught up with him, this was the place.

Josh slung the truck around and reversed up to the Vega. He said, "Stay here. I got this, man." He smacked Eddie's shoulder, opened the door, and jumped onto the highway with a solid thud of boots.

Eddie did as he was told. In the side mirror caked with dust, he could see Josh and the cop like a sepia-toned peepshow. The cop got out yet kept the Vega's open door between him and Josh. The cop had a nest of hair and a thick, auburn beard. His uniform hung from his shoulders like a towel. His jacket was unzipped. The cop's black name tag sucked in the sun and made the white letters glow *AMOS*. Not a single person here hadn't worn a tag: Josh, Cal, Owen, now Amos. Josh and Amos's conversation droned like children yelling under water, so Eddie cranked down the window until it squawked.

Josh spread his arms like an angry gull and jabbed a thumb over his shoulder. "Look, Amos, the Old Man said to get 'em. I'm gettin' 'em."

"Them?" Amos asked.

"Him and a girl," Josh said.

"Well, this says he's mine. Maybe her too." Amos spit toothpick pulp and held up the baggy.

"That don't mean shit here."

"That's up to me." Amos tapped his badge.

"That badge don't mean shit neither. You sure as fuck don't listen, do you?"

"I choose when to listen. One of these days, you'll get it." Amos scratched his beard. "You're too much like your dad. He didn't get it neither."

Josh stepped toward Amos. "You know shit about my dad."

"I know enough."

"Yep, and you stepped in just right—right when he'd pay for the shit he'd done."

"Son, you're lucky he ain't here no more."

"And I am, ain't I. Suppose I should thank you for that too?"

Amos knuckled his nose and said, "I can't . . . There ain't nothin' I can do, son."

"Don't call me that."

"Then I'm sorry."

"Sorry? You ain't sorry." Josh's shoulders rose and tightened. "Every god damned time I do the shit I'm told, you gotta get your fuckin' nose dirty. Like I said, you don't listen and didn't. Better yet, you listen when it fits you. I had it figured—"

"Ain't nothin' you say that'll make me listen now, Josh."

Josh raised a fist.

Amos crossed his arms on the door frame. "This ain't goin' nowhere, son. They just got here. I'm takin' him in. Maybe get her. After that, I'll do what I can."

Josh dropped his fist and said, "Fuck you, Amos." Eddie shut the window before Josh climbed into the wheelhouse. Josh pulled the choke and cranked the key. The truck heaved. "That's right, bitch," he said. "You know you want it." He spat, pumped the gas, and the engine roared. "The chief says you're his. I get your car."

Eddie nodded, tossed the Vega's keys onto the seat, and resigned to whatever the cop had in store.

CHAPTER FOUR

RHEA OPENED the door to Frank's and was hit by the scent of pine and stale beer. The freshly mopped floor was gold wood abused by boot heels and booze. A slump-shouldered woman, hardened with age, leaned on a mop. Her hands were callused and dusted with dead skin.

She wore a blue hoody pulled over gray mom-hair and a braless, barrel body. Her blue jeans were clearly men's. The zipper opened to the right, and the waist and legs were cut square but fit her body. Neon yellow flipflops clung to her feet. A galvanized bucket perched next to her like an obedient dog.

It took a few seconds for the woman to rouse, but when she did, she patted her apron, and in a baritone voice shredded with smoke, said, "I didn't unlock . . ." She looked around the bar, shook her head. Her desert-cracked face softened with a slight smile. "Hey, hon'. You look like you could use a drink and breakfast."

Those words betrayed her smile, countered it with oily sadness. Or was it sympathy? Rhea couldn't tell.

"Yeah, that sounds good." Rhea usually didn't drink in the

morning, but somehow this woman knew that she needed it. She gave in to temptation and took her first steps inside. The woman pushed her mop and bucket behind the bar. Wet flipflops smacked her heels.

"Come in. Choose a seat," said the woman.

It was an odd way to offer a seat—choose a seat, not take a seat. Yet, it made sense. No one took the seat. Seats were chosen. And that seat became home for an hour or two while a surrogate family coddled with food and drink, and maybe, if they were willing, conversation. Rhea wasn't sure if she wanted that, but she needed something in her stomach to deaden the young day.

The bar was lined with nine stools upholstered in green vinyl and studded with brass tacks like squat pyramids. Rhea chose the third stool from the door and settled with a sigh. The mahogany edge of the bar, stained dark, was carved with sense for Rhea's contours—anyone's contours, probably. She kicked off her high-tops and massaged her sockless feet on the brass rail.

In front of a beveled mirror were shelves stocked with a world of booze: Russian vodka, French liqueurs, German beers, Scottish whiskies. Rhea imagined the rest of the bar looked like others she'd worked: twisted keg lines like veins feeding customers and—on occasion—the bartender.

The woman dumped the mop water into a utility closet's deep sink. Next to the closet was a paneled door open on loose hinges where sunlight washed a set of steps. Whatever lay above the bar was hidden. Only the balcony doors and windows covered in floral sheets were firm in Rhea's mind.

"So, what can I getcha, sweetheart? By the way, I'm Ruth." She straightened her shoulders and offered her cracked-clay hand, which Rhea took. Ruth's hand was like Rhea's grandfather's, powerful and abused by labor, yet warm with empathy or uncertainty—she wasn't sure which. It was a grip that didn't know its own power and therefore never fully committed to the bond. But it was kind and knew many others.

"And you're?" asked Ruth.

"Rhea. My name's Rhea. I just got here."

Ruth gave a thin-lipped smile that crackled her cheeks and the edges of her eyes like fall leaves. "I figured, hon'. We don't get many strangers here. Everyone knows everyone. Breakfast? Bloody Mary?"

"Yeah."

Ruth retreated to the kitchen and returned moments later with a stocked condiment tray that latched onto the bar. Her bartender's dance produced a Bloody Mary crammed with olives, celery, a pickle, probably more on a red plastic sword and a chaser of light beer. Confident in the cocktail, Ruth leaned against the counter and supported her weight with her elbows. "The grill's gotta warm up. Food'll be out in a few." She paused and looked at a rag bent in frozen resignation over a steel sink. She pried the rag free and said, "Sorry, Frank."

"Frank?" Rhea sipped her Bloody Mary.

"Sorry, Frank's the only one I got. I live alone, upstairs."

"I was wondering about that. Nice sheets."

"Sheets?"

"The windows on your balcony."

"Oh, yeah. That. I just haven't gotten around to it."

Above Rhea, the ceiling sagged, and in every corner, shadows fed off what light there was. What she said next came out all wrong, and yet everything about the bar seemed like a judgement waiting to happen, so she returned the favor. "You love this bar?"

Ruth's eyes hardened. She tossed the rag in the trash and said, "I'm careful who I love."

"I'm sorry. I didn't mean anything." Rhea sipped a finger or two of the Bloody Mary and hid behind the glass.

"You're not like most." Ruth scratched up a few quarters' worth of tips. "Usually when I set a cocktail like that in front of someone this early, they down it like Dixie-cup-Kool-aid. What brings you to Saint Andrew?"

Rhea forced a stiff smile and chewed on an olive. "Our car broke down about a mile north of here. We're from California. Left a while back. Been traveling ever since." The night she and Eddie had left was still fresh, but something forced the memory aside. Someone behind her glimpsed in the mirror. Someone had been there.

"If you need a place to stay, down the road are better ones," Ruth said.

Rhea stiffened and couldn't will herself to turn. A weight pressed upon her shoulders. No, not a weight. Hands, thin and frail yet firm.

"You okay, hon'?"

"I . . . Is there?" Rhea rolled her eyes to her shoulder where there was nothing. She gasped. "No, not now."

Panic set in like it hadn't for years. Her chest heaved. One frail hand—her hand?—moved from her shoulder to her throat, stifling the words to mere crackles with cold fingers spare on flesh. The other hand slipped with satin slowness into her fingers like Marilyn seducing an evening glove. That same hand pulled the plastic sword from her drink and slid the remaining vegetables into the glass. It twirled the sword, spinning the fruit with the vodka.

Her jaw moved, and with a hiss and flick of her tongue, she said, hollow and slow, "Stay. Yes, we'll stay."

No. That isn't—

Yes, it is.

"I can't," Rhea said to those words, that voice like warm honey wine in fields of flowering thistle.

Ruth moved toward Rhea and asked, "You can't, what, hon'?"

You can.

Rhea sat straight and held her jaw. Her throat was tense. Each breath heavy. "We can't find a home. We're looking"— she pulled the tiny sword from the drink and stabbed and stabbed—"for a place to stay."

For good.

"I can't."

Say it.

"For good. To stay, for good." Rhea ran the plastic blade across her tongue, licking it clean.

Ruth paled, somehow broke. When she said, "Not again," she withdrew, shrunk, turned into another Ruth, one who'd seen more in her decades than possible. She shook her head and mouthed words only she knew. The sagged ceiling groaned. The shadows swelled.

Look.

The bar's mirror hung heavily. Patches of the silver plating had flaked away clouding the rest of Frank's that plunged darkly. The jukebox, bubbling neon gold and red, scratched a record to life with static pops. Patsy Cline's slow polka-country beat and chipper strings slurred to life as she announced she was back in her baby's arms. Rhea turned. The jukebox was dead, cord and plug coiled, outlet empty on the wall. Cline groaned to a halt.

Say nothin'.

Rhea stammered and turned back to the bar. She gulped her drink, liquor drowning what she had seen, felt, and said. Yet, it wasn't enough. She shuddered. Fear surged. Panic's black haze returned. The hand around her throat tightened. Or was it Rhea being Rhea again? Like when her dad pointed a thick finger at her as she sat crying on her bed?

Yes.

The frail hands left. Her throat eased. Her breath settled. It was her. Just Rhea.

"Who's the other one with you?" Ruth's bartender tone hid behind sadness.

"What?" Rhea slurred like she had just awoken.

"You said *we're* looking for a place. Who's the other?"

Rhea shook aside the black haze. "Eddie, my boyfriend. He's with Josh getting a tow."

Ruth turned, her eyes stone. "He'll be all right."

"Yeah, he'll be fine." Rhea downed the rest of her drink and chased it. "He's an ass."

"Your boyfriend?"

"No, Josh."

"Well, hon', you hit the nail there. Sometimes I think it ain't his fault. Other times?" She shrugged, regained her voice. "Eddie'll be all right. For Josh, work comes first. After that, he needs care."

"Typical," said Rhea. "May I have another?"

"What?"

"Bloody Mary."

"Sorry, no. You said *typical.*" Ruth mixed another cocktail.

"Oh. Typical, Josh needs care."

"More than you know, darlin'. You never answered my other question. Why here?"

Rhea lifted the sword from her drink as if to parry Ruth's question. A question that seemed personal, accusatory. Silly. She shook her head. Silly Rhea. "I dunno. We're just looking. Trying to find a place. This was next on the map."

"Really?" The word lingered. Ruth strangled the bottle of vodka. Her knuckles whitened. Her hand shook. She gaveled the bottle on the bar and said to the walls in staccato beats, "Like I said, better ones . . ." then winced and clenched her hoodie over her chest.

"Are you—" Rhea began.

"Sorry, yes," Ruth said through clenched teeth. "Heart ain't what it used to be."

Rhea slid her hand toward Ruth as if closeness would heal.

Ruth eased her shoulders. "California, you said."

Rhea pulled her hand back to her drink. "Y-Yeah, Imperial Valley. I had a house. We left it."

"You just left?"

"Yeah, crazy." Rhea closed her eyes. "It wasn't a good place."

"How?" Ruth slid the second drink and chaser toward Rhea.

"Well, Eddie and I, we . . . I need food, Ruth."

Ruth unfolded her arms and pointed at Rhea. "Right. Any preference?"

"Anything but pancakes. And sausage. No bacon. How about, anything but breakfast."

"You got it." Ruth walked into the kitchen set between the utility closet and stairs. "What if that bacon's on a burger?"

"I'd take it." Rhea spun on her stool. Across Frank's, a dozen tables seemed randomly placed, but she could see Ruth swaying among them, tray hoisted over her head. A pool table dusted with pretzel salt took up a swath near the juke box. Another pool table and more tables hid around a corner.

"Here ya go, hon'," said Ruth.

Rhea took a bite of the burger. Daubs of melted fat and cheese glazed her lips. She chewed slowly, letting the rich moment last. "Thank you, Ruth. How much?"

"On the house."

"Thank you. You're the only one who runs this place. Got help?"

"No, no help right now."

"There's a lot of tables. They ever get filled?"

"Some nights, usually Thursdays and Saturdays."

"You need help?"

"Maybe. You know what you're doing?"

"Mostly. Eddie and I, well, we work diners and bars while on the road. Last place was somewhere in Montana."

"That's a haul to get here."

"Yeah, we mostly sleep in the Vega, our car."

"Your family know where you are?"

Family.

That word was heavy like mud and oil. Numbness crept into Rhea's fingers. Tears burned. She fought the returning haze. Ruth said something, but it was like wet cotton filled Rhea's ears. She pulled hair from her cheek. She hadn't showered in days. It was oily like her sister's hair sprawled on the broken concrete of the basement. A red and black ant twitched on her eye.

Sister.

Her parents were twisted in a knot, together, in their bed like they never did when they were clean.

Parents.

Rhea looked up at Ruth who held a napkin. She sucked ice from her cocktail and took the napkin. "Thanks. Ruth, I—"

The front door opened. Josh swaggered in like a comical Wayne, bootheels smacking. He swung his leg over the stool closest to Rhea and touched her shoulder. "Sweetheart." He grinned and sucked at his teeth then grabbed a toothpick from a shot glass near Rhea. Pit-rot curdled from his body and lingered.

Ruth grabbed a bottle of Jim from the shelf, slapped a rocks glass on the bar between him and Rhea, and filled it half full. "You need this, Josh. And she ain't yours."

"The Old Man said as much. Said they need a place." He took a few swigs, lit a cigarette, and blew smoke like an arcing Vegas strip fountain.

"No, Josh, that can't . . . The Old Man. They just got here." Ruth slid her hand toward Rhea then clenched it into a fist.

"Old Man?" Rhea asked Ruth.

Ruth looked at Rhea and shook her head.

Josh eyed Rhea. "When the bait's juicy, the fish bite. Amos got other ideas, but you know how that goes. Speaking of which, where'd I see him last? Amos, that is. Oh yeah. Ain't he up the road a few? Found a car. Right, Rhea?" He dragged her name out like he had finished a drunken afternoon quickie with her bent over an alley garbage can. "Turns out your boyfriend . . ." He let that last word stick.

In the mirror, Rhea's eyes met his as he swiped away a curl blocking his view, and she whispered, "Yeah?"

He smiled. "Boyfriend's bad. Somethin' 'bout drugs and dealin'. Chief locked him up."

Rhea searched the bar for answers. Her arms tensed. Her lungs seized. The mirror's silver cracked then spun into a gaping horror.

Josh leaned closer. "Turns out Chief'll see you too. Unless ya ride to my place. It's safe, real safe." He sucked in deep through his nose at her shoulder.

Other words echoed, words that weren't Josh's. *I'll keep you safe.*

Ruth stood back. Or was she held back? Rhea's stomach twisted. She kicked herself from the bar and stumbled. Her feet slapped the floor. The stool hinged on two legs and hit with a double thud of vinyl and wood. The hands from before pushed and touched like a sick uncle. Eyes blurred with old tears, she pulled groping hands from her body, but they weren't there. She twitched her eyes from Josh, to Ruth, to the bar, to the jukebox then viced her head between her hands.

Safe.

Josh thumbed his nose. Ruth clutched a rag and swung around the bar, free from what may have held her. Rhea turned to where the jukebox flared neon, and Patsy Cline was again embraced by her baby's arms. Someone had been there, someone by the box, deep in the corner. A dark something slender like a coffined corpse, sweeping and gowned with flecks of yellow. The music became louder, painful. The sick touch bore down, grew heavier, pressed her lungs with pops of pain. She stumbled and clutched the totem machine that cut out then belched static.

"Make it stop," Rhea said through breaths, but her voice fell flat, overrun by noise.

Ruth turned from Rhea, pointed at Josh then the door as she yelled, her voice now garbled like cries of the drowning. Josh kicked the stool against the bar and strut through the door where a shard of light cut the gloom.

Ruth's mouth formed words yet was mute, as she rushed toward Rhea and fell to one knee. Ruth clenched fists above her heart, shook her head, and yelled a silent, *No.* Impossible wrinkles branched across her face as she shook her head defying the pain she must have felt then gave in and nodded.

Rhea rested her head atop the humming jukebox. At her touch, the white noise slid down from chaos to a mourning chorus of thousands.

Ruth stood, grabbed Rhea's shoulders, and wrenched her from the juke box. Her words cut through the static. "Rhea, he's gone. You're okay."

"I'm sorry." Rhea shrugged off Ruth's hands, shook her head, and balanced herself on the jukebox's cool glass. Its lights were out. The record spun to a halt. Her legs and chest burned with embarrassment. "I just . . ." There were no words. It was just Rhea being Rhea. She rubbed her temples and focused on Ruth's maternal gaze twisted with worry.

"Did you . . .?" Rhea said. No, Ruth hadn't heard, hadn't seen. Rhea was certain. Just Rhea. The groping hands fled, and she took a long drag of the pine-scented air. Her chest ballooned as if she'd surfaced from deep waters. Just Rhea being Rhea. Fear poured out her legs as though the floor itself drank it deeply. Tension fled. "Your heart. You okay?"

Ruth looked at her chest. "Yes, honey. I'll take you to Eddie."

Rhea nodded. Her dirty curls swung.

"Lemme close up, and we can head to the station."

Rhea let Ruth usher her to her stool, which she brought to its feet.

"Finish your drink, hon'. I've got no car, but the station's just down the road." She flip-flopped to the door and locked it with a clatter of keys.

Rhea knuckled away tears. "You said you had a place."

"Yeah, that's right."

"We need it."

Ruth closed her eyes and mouthed words almost as if in prayer. She nodded and said, "Sweetheart, I got a place if you need it. It ain't much, but it's cheap and comfortable."

CHAPTER FIVE

EDDIE STOOD next to the west window of Chief Amos's smoke-dusted headquarters and rubbed his uncuffed wrists. The window's panes were licked by cream paint that covered its frame. Eddie had a clear shot down to Lake Andrew because Amos, or someone, must have cleared down a few hundred trees. Eddie had taken Anatomy in college, and the lake reminded him of a cancerous kidney he'd seen during a longwinded lecture by a professor who probably put on his lab coat just to take a piss. Fog clung to the water and hid the western shore and most of an island. On the south shoreline, a dark-angled roof poked above the trees. Somewhere on the lake, a boat motor echoed with tinny coughs.

Amos grunted and hung up his rotary phone with a plastic clatter, pecked at his typewriter, and slammed the platen home. Eddie turned as Amos swiveled in his chair and thudded his heels on his oak desk. The boot's black leather had peeled like sunburned skin, and steel glinted through the toes.

"You look like a young and alive Boris Karloff," said Amos in his lazy voice that bordered on a drunken slur.

"Who the fuck's that?" said Eddie.

"Jesus, kid, that mouth."

"I've been told. Fuck's Karloff?"

Amos shook his head. "Actor. Seen the old Frankenstein black-and-white?"

"Yeah. In college. Cinema class."

"Karloff's the creature."

"You mean Frankenstein?"

"You don't pay attention. Frankenstein's the doctor. The creature's the creature. You look like the actor, not the creature. You got longer hair though. He's got a few inches on you height-wise. But this thing"—he flicked Eddie's license onto his desk where powder-sugar-dusted file stacks slid—"makes you look like you belong on the cover of some crap band's record where the guys look like dead girls."

Eddie smiled. Take the bait? What the hell. Cops loved talking shit. "And your stacks of dusty flower-power LPs last got you laid a few decades ago, I'm sure. Besides, that was then. All the rest can get fucked. So what's next?"

"What's next." Amos rubbed a nostril with a knuckle, pulled out a tweezer from a desk drawer, and plucked a tuft of nose hairs. He chucked the tweezer—hair and all—back into the drawer and wiped tears from his eyes with a hanky. "Well, you don't seem to give two shits about nothin'."

"You do?" Eddie sat in the wood chair in front of the desk.

Amos tapped Eddie's ID. "Your license expired. Your car's registration is years overdue. Your plate stickers say otherwise. And county records got nothin' on you but said they'd get back to me, which means they won't."

Eddie shrugged. "Like I said, what's next?"

"Well, paperwork's not my thing today. Ever, really. And your car is as good as impounded with Josh and Cal on the job." From a black boat of an ashtray, he picked up a smoldering Camel, took a drag, and tamped it out on Elvis's face. He chased the smoke with coffee from a diner mug stamped with *Lou's Lounge* and the outline of a spoon and martini glass with spiked olives. He picked up the twist-tied baggie filled with weed. "And this shit, I'm keepin'." He tossed it in the trashcan filled with cigarette cartons and dead pens.

"So all that shit you said on the highway?" Amos had ripped Eddie a few new ones while Josh dicked with the Vega. Eddie took it. Why not? Podunk police and all.

"I can't have Josh thinkin' I've gone soft. Besides, you've got time on your hands."

"Time? What makes you think that?"

Amos shook his head. "You're here."

"Jesus, Amos—"

"Chief."

"Does anyone give it straight here?"

"I'm as straight as they get," said Amos. "You got a home?"

Amos wasn't Josh. This man spoke a new language. Some sort of half-give-a-shit talk that meant he could deny *and* confirm.

Sympathy? Dead end.

Honesty? Trouble.

Half-n-half spiked vodka was the way to go. "No, left it a few years back. Haven't seen it since."

"You need one, though."

Eddie shrugged, crossed his legs, and picked at his shoe. "We're looking."

"Lookin' for what?"

"A home, like you said."

"Are you? And who's we?"

"Rhea, she's my damn . . ." Amos was balls-old. He wouldn't horn in on her. Couldn't, in fact. "She's my girlfriend. At Frank's, right now. I guess we're looking for a place to stay."

Eddie looked out the window. The fog still hung low over the lake. Fog that never happened in the desert. It clung to the lake like frayed ropes. "We can't keep moving. Something's gotta be done. We gotta do *something*."

"Lookin' for a home. Been years since you had one. Your movin' sounds more like runnin'."

Eddie smelled blood yet said nothing.

"What from?" asked Amos.

Eddie's shoulders shivered. A black seed of anger tumbled in his chest.

Amos continued. "No words? Lemme fill you in."

Jesus Christ, he knew it'd come. Just like fucking Rhea when she dropped the shit, Amos would layer every sentence on another. Wouldn't stop. Eddie would open his mouth, and Amos would raise one of those sausage fingers. Eddie'd shut his mouth, let Amos have his spotlight even though it'd be easier to wrap his fingers around that hairy fucking neck of his, crush his throat with his thumbs. Better yet, slice that gizzard with his blade. Let the blood run while he coughed out a new hole.

"You left California, what, three years ago? That about hits it going by your car's papers."

Eddie nodded, bit down hard.

"Your plate's stickers are up to date, which means you skim them off others."

Eddie shifted in his seat, twitched his head just a bit hiding a good old, *fuck off*.

"Those blankets in your car mean you ain't settled, spent nights in that thing probably. Again, what you runnin' from?"

Those blankets were perfume and exhaust, Rhea's hair touching his cheek. He was able to get out a slight, "Family," even though his lips refused to move, had seized and shook.

"Family? That's it." Amos shook his head. "Yep, ain't nothin' special 'bout you."

Eddie's shoulders drooped. Amos must've seen.

"Nothin' special. Not one bit. Just a bitchy goth boy runnin' from family that took your allowance. So you ran. Jesus. Kids're full of shit, all of 'em."

Eddie's shoulders rose, tensed. He strangled the chair's arms until they creaked like those stairs into that old cellar stained with blood.

Amos leaned forward on his desk and spoke quietly through years of smoke and liquor that covered bad shit no one should see. "Don't know what to say? Don't know if you can say it? Wanna hit me? Beat me? You think I don't see the shit you're shovelin'. Look at you. You can hardly stay in that seat. I ain't stupid, son. Take a breath before you do somethin' stupid. I seen what I wanted. Besides, most are lookin'. Especially here."

Eddie's heart spun. He breathed. Through his teeth, he said, "You still haven't answered my question. What's next?"

"Yeah." Amos got up from his chair and looked out the window. "Well, first thing, stay away from Josh. He'll do a piss poor job fixin' your car, and given your record with me, I'll make sure he don't get to it."

"What's with Josh?"

"I think you know."

Eddie nodded. "I got a taste of him."

"That's enough." Amos pursed his lips, scrubbed his beard, and said, "Now, Eddie, I'm taking it easy 'cause it comes down to me not giving a shit on what I got on you. But know this. There're things I'll end if needed." Amos met Eddie's eyes. "You got me?"

"I got you, Chief." California cops weren't like Amos, but

what he did back then was one of those things the chief would end.

"You said your girl, Rhea?"

Eddie nodded.

"She's at Frank's with Ruth. That's good. Maybe Ruth'll hook you up with a place. She got plenty. You got money?"

"Nah, a few bucks from slinging dishes and booze."

"That's all right. We'll work something out."

"I don't get it," said Eddie.

"Get what?"

"We roll in. You take me in. You hook us up."

"Your car's dead. Ain't got much choice. And I don't like leavin' newcomers in the breeze. Besides, somethin' about you—"

The front door opened, and the screen door smacked shut. "Ruth." Amos nodded. "This must be Rhea. Eddie mentioned you."

Eddie turned with a thin smile. "I'm free." He rubbed his wrists and fluttered his hands. Rhea stood with fists at her sides. Some curly-haired bitch that made a good stand-in for an oversized Oompa-Loompa walked in behind her like Bono's bodyguard on a bender. Rhea's forehead messed into lines deeper than her age should allow, which Eddie knew she hated. This was a familiar scene for her. She'd be pissed for a few hours then bring it up months later.

But there was something different this time. Her tears were angry, but she wouldn't let them wet her cheeks. Eddie walked toward her and laced his fingers through her red curls. Her freckled face was warm. She looked into his eyes. Eddie tilted his head and softened his gaze. He let the corner of his mouth twitch then shrugged. It was the best he could do for an apology. Afterall, what the hell did he do? It wasn't his fault the Vega broke down. "You okay?"

"No," said Rhea

"What—"

She pulled her head away.

"Okay . . . Is this Ruth?" He pointed then held out his hand.

"Yeah. Ruth, this is Eddie." Rhea said every word through her teeth.

Ruth shook Eddie's hand. She was firm yet dry when she said, "Pleased." She released Eddie's hand, but he held it a bit longer, clenched like he owned it then let go like he'd sold a used car. Her eyes twitched before she turned toward Amos and asked, "Whatta we got?"

"Well, I don't know 'bout her, but this boy stays," said Amos. "Got a place?"

"Of course," Ruth said. "Rhea and I just got done talkin' 'bout that."

"They don't have money," said Amos.

"Don't matter," said Ruth. "Rhea says they've got experience that'll work at Frank's, and I've got a cabin for them."

"You sure about that?"

"I am, Joel. They can't leave," said Ruth to Amos. She shook her head.

Amos scratched his beard, pulled a smoke from a pack kept in his chest pocket, and lit up. "I got you," he said as he bit down on the filter. He nodded and blew smoke into a slow-turning ceiling fan, offered a smoke to Eddie, which Eddie took, and said, "Remember what I told you."

"Yeah." Eddie leaned into the lighter Amos lit for him.

"There's an end, son."

"I can go?"

"Yeah. Ruth will care for you now."

The screen door smacked. Rhea was already out the door. She always waited but not today. She pulled from his hand too. He looked at Ruth, who stood with her arms crossed.

"Well," Ruth said. "I've got that place for you. Let's get to it." She walked out the door and caught up to Rhea.

Eddie turned to Amos. "Thanks."

Amos nodded. "You better go, son. She's not happy."

Eddie didn't know if that meant Ruth or Rhea, so he just nodded and stumbled out the door where last year's wet leaves covered a gravel driveway that curled through tall pine and white birch. He looked up through the limbs. Wisps of clouds cut across the blue sky. He took a deep drag from his smoke and closed his eyes as he shook his head and exhaled. She, Rhea, needed him. He was sure of it. He opened his eyes. Rhea and the woman were nearly to the highway when Rhea turned around.

"Eddie," she said as she raised her palms. "What are you doing? Come on."

Yep, she needed him. "I'm coming, sweetheart."

Rhea's arms dropped limp. Eddie jogged up to her.

"Rhea says you're from California," said Ruth.

"Yeah," said Eddie. "So where's this cabin you mentioned?"

"On the lake. Down the road. It's rented most in the summer, but it's yours for now. I'll cut ya a deal. It's private, nice. Heat's woodburning, but there's plenty dead timber needing cutting."

"Labor for rent?" asked Eddie.

"If you'd like, sure. But you gotta stay warm."

"Eddie," Rhea said. "Ruth's looking for a short order cook, maybe bartending and waiting."

He put his arm around Rhea's shoulder. "All right. That offer include me?"

Ruth smiled and looked at Eddie. "You've got a job if you want it." She broke her smile. "Don't let this place take you in, though."

"We've seen plenty places. This'll be no different," Eddie

said as Rhea leaned her head on his shoulder. Her hair lashed his face and smelled like road dust. "Cabin got a shower?"

Ruth nodded.

Just short of the hill before Frank's, Eddie looked back down the road. From a yellow cottage next to the church walked a man in black who locked the door and let the rusted screen door smack shut. Smeared behind a dusty picture window stood a boy with black hair in altar boy robes who faded deeper into the house. The man in black waved.

"Who's that?" Eddie asked but saw the clerical collar lapping like a dry tongue. "Ah, priest."

"Yeah, that's right. Town's only one. Saul."

"Huh?"

"His name. Father Saul."

"Never much liked priests." Eddie's throat dried.

Saul stopped and kept his eyes on Eddie. Or were they on Rhea? He couldn't tell. Saul scratched his throat, lazily pointed at Eddie, mumbled something, and went back to scratching. Eddie's lip twitched. He turned and followed the Oompa-Loompa motherfucker past the bar and gas pumps. There was something about her. How she walked. How she talked. How she looked at him. How she looked differently at Rhea that made something hot inside him burn. It burned like the desert rocks of Anza Borrego and the fire that lit Rhea's face on a night filled with her tears, death, and sweet satisfaction.

As if galloping from the lake, a breeze chilled his knuckles, and a voice like razers through ice inside and around him said, *Special.*

CHAPTER SIX

RHEA, Ruth, and Eddie passed Josh's garage where the Vega sat. A green and black puddle soaked the gravel below its engine. Eddie pulled the map from under the driver's seat and grabbed their duffels from the back seat. Rhea smirked. Eddie shrugged and stuffed the map into his duffel. Josh welded under the stilted pickup.

The gravel road to the cabin slithered down a hill where the lake hid behind trees. Rhea could smell it, the lake. It filled the air, but she hadn't noticed until now. And yet she recalled it at The Store and inside Frank's. The rot of fish, weeds, and rain clung to her. At the bottom of the hill, she caught her first glimpse of Lake Andrew beyond a landing scattered with blue-gray chips of granite leading up to the water.

A red-sided and white-trimmed ballroom-once-a-barn sidled up against the shoreline. Its windows were curtained and dark. Just outside the ballroom's front doors, a dock jutted into the waves. At the end of the dock, a man in overalls stooped over a tacklebox.

His face sagged like a wet rag, and tufts of white hair stuck out the back of his red and white seed-cap, its logo long since peeled and faded above the bent bill. He licked his line with a lazy tongue, threaded the hook and knotted it. After baiting the line, he adjusted his cap, cast, and took a slow swig from a bottle of beer stashed in a foam cooler.

As they continued, a single pickup crackled by on the gravel road, squeaking under the weight of a round bale loaded in its bed. A tired boy at the wheel lifted a single finger when he saw Ruth. Ruth nodded.

"Not much happens here," Rhea said.

"Not if you're passin'. Just passin'," Ruth said.

"And that man on the dock, who's he?"

"Alphonse. Al Jones. Farmer. Lives up the road. Those silos." Ruth lifted her head toward a distant hill coated in the late morning sun where two gray silos stood with black and white checkered caps. "That's his. Wife's dead, heart attack. Son died in a grain bin. Pulled him out, mouth stuffed with corn, eyes red and packed with dust. He'd have been back with Mrs. Kraus's third graders." Ruth shook her head.

Rhea grimaced, held her hand over her mouth, and said, "When was that?"

"Oh, forty years or so."

"Mrs. Kraus or the son?"

"The son. Kraus been gone just over ten years now. All Al does is fish and drink. His daughter's married to Richardson across the lake." She pointed past Al where a heavy house clung to the opposite shore as though it wanted the waters to take it. "Richardson the butcher lives beyond the shore in those trees along with a few others."

Eddie looked at Al, whose pole bent and jigged, and said, "Butcher?"

Ruth laughed. "Sausage, roasts. You know, butcher."

Eddie chuffed a laugh. "Rhea, I like it. The mechanic, not so sure."

"Well, just do your business. It's best to stay away from Josh. Let's just say he ain't got a dad no more. Mom though. She's a piece a work."

"So I heard," said Eddie.

"Heard?" Ruth's question was calm, one that hid another beneath the actual words.

Eddie shrugged.

"Cal," Ruth continued, "he's different."

"Wait, Cal?" asked Rhea.

"Yeah, he works with Josh."

"Eddie, you said nothing about a second mechanic," said Rhea.

"Yeah, so? He's an idiot. Blond, slack-jawed."

"Don't be so sure, Eddie. Those two boys, Josh and Cal, that is, had it rough. Both lost their dads. There's a lot of that here."

Eddie shook his head. His lips moved, but like Ruth in the bar, no words came out. His forehead knotted. The corners of his mouth sank. His shoulder slumped like he'd gone back to his California goth ways. And his eyes faded, almost glaucomic as if he'd just woken from a midnight dream. "Got it," he said to no one. He looked past Rhea at Ruth. "So . . ."

Rhea said, "Eddie, who are—"

"Ruth, why are you here?" Eddie forced out the last word and looked at the silos.

Ruth hit a stone with her toe. Rhea caught Ruth's elbow. Ruth knelt and tore a broken nail free as she sucked air through her teeth. "Saint Andrew, I take it you mean," she said looking up at Eddie. She wiped blood on her jeans. "It just worked out, what needed to be done. What needed to happen. There ain't much to it, really."

Eddie grunted something through his nose like *hm* or *huh*.

Whatever he wanted to say was cut off by him biting down and keeping his mouth shut while shaking his head.

Rhea smacked Eddie's thigh then helped Ruth up. After Ruth was on her feet, Rhea touched Eddie's shoulder hoping he'd turn. He shrugged her off and left the conversation at that. Typical. She needed something, wanted something, but Eddie was long gone or something else was in his head. His mind was somewhere Rhea had never seen, and she wasn't always sure she wanted to see it. She shook her head and dropped back next to Ruth.

They passed the landing to a swamp pocked with kinked cattails soaking in the lake where pads of ice refused to melt. New tails began to take the old's place. Black birds with flecks of red in their wings landed on the rushes where they bobbed close to the water. The closest bird trained its twitching eyes on Rhea and stuttered what sounded like *over here* or *okay leave*. Past the birds, a tiny Al cast his line.

"Ruth?"

"Yeah, hon'?"

"Did Al ever own Frank's? I mean, the bar?"

"Not sure. I bought it from a guy, Frank. Frank bought it from Sam, but Sam called it Sam's. Sam bought it from a guy named Lou, but it was called Lou's. See?"

"Clever," said Rhea.

"Yeah, I broke tradition." Ruth shrugged like tradition was an afterthought and breaking it was expected. "Before Lou there was Dave and Charlie and others, but their names got smudged by water. It's been here a while."

"How long?"

"Indenture says 1832. Others been here since the 1600s. Fur trade and such." Ruth clenched her chest and eyed the Manor. "I can't image being here since . . . back then."

Days. Weeks. No longer than that was she in one place

since California. And that place? She closed her eyes and shook her head. "Three hundred years."

"That's 'bout right."

"That's—"

"Old?"

Rhea nodded and opened her eyes.

"Not compared to some. The Dakota stayed close for thousands. This place might be that old too."

"They stayed just close?"

"Yeah, nothin' shows they been right here." She jabbed her finger at the ground. "Seems they stayed away."

"From Saint Andrew?"

"Well, what'd become Saint Andrew."

"Why?"

Ruth shrugged. "Some places are just bad."

"Bad." Rhea touched her own hand. "Ruth, at the bar I had . . ." She looked at Eddie who eyed the distant silos. "Never mind. Maybe later."

Ruth looked at Eddie then Rhea. She limped a bit on her toe, slowed even more. Eddie kept walking.

"Hon'," Ruth said. "Talk if you need to."

Rhea looked into Ruth's eyes. She knew. Somehow, she knew. Knew there were years on the road with Eddie but nothing that moved forward. Nothing that moved forward but that stupid Vega down the road. But who was this woman? "I'm fine, Ruth, really."

Ruth wilted and said, "Here's our turn. Eddie, take this road."

They veered onto a driveway parted by a line of brown grass. Ruth's flip-flops kicked up dead blades. Rhea stayed next to Ruth. Eddie lagged like someone refused to let him go.

The path skirted the swamp just short of half a mile then back to the shoreline where, beyond budding trees, waves washed over the rocky shore with a radio-static crackle. More than a mile into the woods, the path curved east onto a peninsula where six cabins sat, empty and dark.

Each cabin was nearly identical, large enough for two, maybe three rooms. The chinking between the logs, once white, had darkened with dirt and lichen. Cedar shingles sweatered in moss covered the roofs from which sprouted charred, metal pipes topped with dunce-cap cones. The screened porches faced the lake, and the front doors landed smack in the center of the same wall.

A pile of split logs had been stacked between two trees near a shack further from the shore. On the logs, a gray squirrel stood tall, sniffed the air, then spiraled up a tree and into its branches.

"Well, here they are. Have your pick," said Ruth. "None are taken."

Eddie went for the first cabin that gave a full view of the lake but stopped short. "Holy shit," he said, stuffing his hands in his jean's pockets. "That's a house." He nodded his head north across the lake. "Check it out, Rhea."

Ruth said, "The Manor," as frigid wavelets lapped her toes.

Rhea bit off more nail polish and spit it into the water. "I saw it when we passed Al. But, well, I didn't ask."

A third of a mile across the tiny whitecaps was an island near the east shoreline, separated from the rest of Saint Andrew by another swamp. On that island hunched a house with yawning windows and steep roofs shingled dark and pocked with dormers and turrets of little use other than to impose rigid lines. Facing the lake was a ground-level porch and second-story balcony that spanned the side fully and were caged by spiral balusters and thick banisters. The house's white paint had all but flaked away, the siding turned black and mold-green. Rhea forced her eyes from the Manor to a second island from which a tree, now dead and white, sprouted.

Ruth said, "Come on. Let's get you settled. You wanted to shower?"

Rhea inhaled the lake wind and followed Ruth. Eddie stayed behind. The porch door's spring crooned as Rhea pulled it open. On the porch was a simple wood swing chained to the ceiling.

Ruth twisted the cabin's key from her ring and gave it to Rhea. "Owen'll make you another copy. For Eddie."

Rhea looked back at Eddie, who nodded and said something quieter than the waves.

"Go on in, hon'," said Ruth.

A lace curtain covered the door's window. Rhea unlocked the cabin and entered. The interior was simple and musty. The living room formed a tiled L with the dining room and kitchen. Next to a plaid wool couch sat a Zenith television on a TV dinner table, unplugged cord curled on the floor. An amber ashtray sat on top of the Zenith's plastic wood. In front of the couch was a cedar steamer trunk belted in leather. The carpeted bedroom took up the rest of the cabin, along with the bathroom. The walls were covered with pressed paneling, and an iron stove stood on a granite pad; its potbelly held charred logs.

"There's power. Breaker's in the bedroom," Ruth said as she entered the room and clacked switches, sparking lights the previous tenants hadn't turned off. "The wood stove's the heat. You could use the oven, but that's trouble, gas and all. Refrigerator works with the icebox up top. Drawers got dishes, forks, knives, spoons. Move-in ready, they say. Could use a wash." She dragged a finger across the counter and pinched the dirt with her thumb and let it drop to the floor. "Open the windows, and the must'll leave."

"It's great, Ruth. Thank you. Is there a phone?"

"People come to get away. No phone. There're canoes in the boathouse if you don't want to walk, or Amos might lend you his johnboat. He ain't been fishin' lately. It's got a motor."

Eddie entered rubbing his forehead. "Nah, we'll be fine. Getting away is what we need. Besides, we've never driven anything without wheels. Say, you said that house—"

"Manor," said Ruth.

"Yeah, that. No one lives there." Eddie dropped his hand yet kept his eyes on the floor.

"Empty," Ruth said. She reached toward Eddie. He took a step back. She lowered her gaze and cocked her head to the side like will alone would force Eddie to look at her. "You doin' all right?"

"Eddie?" Rhea said.

"Yeah, fine," said Eddie who waved them both away.

"Well, I'll leave you to it," said Ruth. "Say, when're you lookin' to start?"

"Start." Eddie looked at Rhea with eyes dulled like a kid without hope.

"At Frank's, Eddie," said Rhea. She shrugged and smiled and pulled a curl behind her ear which brought Eddie to as she'd hoped.

"Heck, it's almost noon," said Eddie keeping his eyes on Rhea. "What is it, Thursday?"

Ruth laughed. "Saturday. Last of March."

Eddie shook his head and looked at Ruth. "Busy day at the grill?"

"Can be," Ruth said.

"Need me?" Eddie asked.

Ruth shrugged. "I didn't expect you to start so soon."

"I'd like it."

Ruth looked at Rhea, her head tilted just enough to ask permission.

Rhea pursed her lips, gave a slight nod, and said, "But I need to wash up. And, some time to . . ." She swiped her hand toward the cabin and lake.

"Tell you what, Rhea," Eddie said. "I'll head to Frank's, get the grill started, set up the kitchen." Eddie looked at Ruth.

"If you're up for it," Ruth said.

"I am," said Eddie. "I need it."

"Yeah, all right." Ruth dug into her pocket for the keys. "I don't usually . . . That'd be fine. Lock up when you get in. Fire up the grill, set up how you like, but don't let customers in 'til I get there. Put up the be-back clock in the window." She threaded off another key and handed it to Eddie.

"Got it." He squinted and smiled with a nod. "Trust me."

Rhea asked, "Is there a shower?"

"Of sorts," Ruth said. "Showers are communal. Over there." Ruth pointed through a window at the shack beyond the log pile. Pinecones from a nearby tree covered the corrugated tin roof. "No community right now, so they're all yours. We'll fire up the water heater. Besides, looks like you need more time than him."

"Join me at Frank's later," said Eddie to Rhea.

It wasn't a question, more something he expected. Rhea had grown tired of expectations. She needed time. Time alone, and if that cabin was what she had, then it'd do. "I don't know. I might relax. Rest for a bit. Work's not my thing just yet." She looked at Ruth. "That okay?"

"Sure, hon'. Take your time. I'll send Amos with food. You can work it off."

"Thanks, Ruth," Rhea said. "We haven't had a place since, well, just since."

"It's okay, sweetheart," Ruth said. Rhea tensed. "I know it

can be hard. I'll help you get this place up and running while Eddie does his thing."

Eddie nodded and let the screen door slap shut behind him. Framed by a cabin window, Eddie walked along the road, said something, shook his head, and looked at the sky.

As if chanting, Rhea said, "What is he—"

"He do that often?" Ruth asked.

"Hm?"

"Talk"—Ruth placed her hand over her heart then bunched her hoodie inside her fist—"to no one."

Sure, there were times in the past. But didn't everyone? And the bar. That was . . . That was one of her times, right? Just Rhea being Rhea.

"Hon'?"

"Water heater. Shower?"

Ruth nodded, but it wasn't as simple as that. She nodded more like a shrink that'd given up. Let the patient leave knowing something terrible was coming. All she said was, "This way."

CHAPTER SEVEN

Gravel crunched under Eddie's feet as he headed to Frank's. He palmed the brass key. Around him, the frigid voice said, *Yours.*

"No." Eddie shook his head then looked through the trees toward the sky. He'd been stripped by the voice that poked, jabbed, explored like a clumsy surgeon since that priest. Sure, he had voices before. He would talk himself through the terrible things that had to be done while he hid in his little black room. But *this* voice could not be silenced. A lake breeze scattered dry leaves across the road. One leaf caught his leg. He picked it up by its stem and spun the fat spade between his fingers. Only brown veins remained.

Go.

He did as the voice said and carried that leaf along the swamp and highway, past the ballroom and Josh's garage, and finally up Frank's steps. The key slid over the lock's tumblers and twisted like fingers over oiled skin. He wanted it. He wanted inside. Whatever was there was a home he'd never had before, and his knuckles that were once cold somehow took from Frank's the warmth he needed. Or was it that Frank's offered him that warmth? He shook his head. How stupid. It was a place. A place like all the others they'd had since California. And yet?

"One second, son." The man's words were a record scratch of cigarette phlegm. Eddie froze. The cops in California had taught him as much. The man grabbed Eddie's shoulder and tugged him around. The priest. The hell's his name?

You know it. Wait.

Eddie tapped his temple.

Old skin sagged over the priest's clerical collar that strangled his throat. He pursed his lips and pushed black-rimmed bifocals up his nose with a finger bulging with arthritic joints. He held a lit cigarette between yellowed fingers and chuffed smoke as he spoke. "You're the boy on the road with Ruth and Red." He swung his cigarette to the south where Eddie had walked with the others. "Welcome, son, to Saint Andrew."

"Rhea," said Eddie.

"No, I don't—"

"No, you said Red. Her name's Rhea." The priest took a half step. Eddie didn't move. "People like that word here, *son*. You always call people that?"

"Just the boys. Old habits. I'd tell ya tending flock and such, but that got nothin' to do with Peter. And you're?"

"Eddie. You-You're Saul."

Saul nodded. "You got Ruth's key."

"I work here." Eddie stuffed the key in his pocket. He still held the leaf.

The priest gunslinger-squinted bloodshot eyes. "Strange. Care if I come in? I'm dry."

Eddie held the door.

The priest. Let him in.

The door's trim creaked as Eddie tightened his grip. "I can't. Ruth said—"

Let him in.

Eddie's grip failed, and he released the door. "Sure." He exhaled and relaxed. Inside, pine, beer, and smoke lingered in oily darkness. Eddie plugged in the jukebox's braided cord. Bubbles stumbled through neon tubes that pooled red on the hardwood floor and Cline returned to her baby's arms.

Saul straddled the stool furthest from the door, and the door closed behind him with a click. He laid his forehead on folded hands as if praying. Cigarette ash flittered to the floor as he spoke. "Light switches are in the utility room."

Eddie tossed the leaf on the bar's waxed top and brought the house to life with the clicks of a dozen switches and the buzz of yellow fluorescents. He stepped up to the taps where a honeycombed rubber mat, wet with disinfectant, covered the concrete floor. Saul rested.

Feed him.

"Poison?" Eddie asked.

"Vodka. Top shelf. Absolut. Three rocks."

Eddie clacked in three cubes from the rolling freezer, poured a swift double, and slid the glass toward Saul on a white cocktail napkin. He leaned against the glass-doored beer fridge. Hidden from Saul, pinned to the bar's mahogany, were brass plates etched with names. The plate near the ninth stool was engraved with *Saul*. "Reserved stool?"

"Yep," said Saul.

Eddie pointed at the next plate. "Amos."

Asshole.

"He is," said Eddie.

"Sorry?"

"He's an ass."

"Yeah, the chief you mean. Part of my penance to sit next to him, I guess you could say. I heard you met him."

Eddie nodded. "There's no plate next to the chief."

Saul took a swig and sucked air through his teeth. "The Old Man. He lived in the Manor more than a hundred years ago."

"The Manor—"

Yours too.

Eddie looked up at Saul. "—across the lake from the cabins. No one's taken that seat since?"

Saul's lip twitched into a grin behind his glass as he took another pull of vodka before setting it down. Grin gone, eyes on Eddie, he said, "Nope."

"This bar hasn't been here for more than a hundred years, has it?"

"Parts of it. See the shit everywhere?"

Close to the bar, the walls were covered with old rifles, steering wheels, decades-old beer cans and whiskey bottles, a child's dress that had once been white, and a tiny tricycle. Hung from the trike's handles was a heavily wired bra that was more like a lace-trimmed horse harness. Like the dress, it too had been white but had seen fire. The metal had heated to an iridescent sheen of blues, and the lace went from an oily brown to melted black. Photos steeped in sepia speckled the walls while others looked more like clouds of gray where ghostly men held firearms on an unrailed boardwalk next to women and children hardened by dust and death.

Eddie looked back at the brass plates. "Cal and Josh got their own, closest to the door. These others had names, but I can't read them."

"Yeah, Frank's works that way."

"Fuck's that mean," Eddie said, thin and even without a hint of question, more like an order.

"You need manners, son."

"I've been told."

Saul took another swig. "Fuck's that mean? I ain't figured it out."

"What's to figure out? Ruth takes the plate down, carves the name—"

"Nah. You know that ain't the truth, which is somethin' you won't get from most here. Least not the whole truth."

He may have been a priest, but he didn't talk Amos's shit. "Well then what's the truth?"

"Most don't give it straight. They're afraid. Afraid what'll happen."

"Happen?"

"This place has its ways. People don't get messed up in other's business 'cause they don't want trouble. At least not until they think it's worth it. Me? I don't give a shit. I been through, seen, and heard too much to care."

Eddie shook his head. "You're—"

Feed him.

"Food?"

Saul drained his vodka and spit a cube back into the glass then tapped it with a gold pinky ring. "Nah."

Eddie poured. Saul drank.

"You lost, son?"

"Don't call me that."

Listen.

Patsy Cline scratched and stopped short of being here to stay. The box pulled the record and clacked on another but didn't spin. From behind the pool table, a rusted radiator hissed.

"I ain't changin', son. You lost?"

"I'm not lost. Just moving."

"Right. Rhea, she lost?"

"Maybe. But being with me means she's not."

"That's a stretch."

"The hell's that mean?" Eddie pulled a bar rag from a drawer that made sense and twisted it between fists.

"You like that word, *mean*. I *mean*, know your place, *son*." Saul wiped the vodka from his lips, took a final drag from his cigarette, and smothered it in a black plastic ashtray worn dull by scouring.

"You looking for a—"

Shut your mouth.

"I ain't lookin' for nothin'. Not from you. You're the one who's lookin'."

"Who the hell are you to tell me what I'm doing. This is temp—" Eddie stepped forward but was stopped by a cold hand on his chest.

Learn.

"Anyone who gets that key ain't lookin' for temporary. Let me tell you somethin', son. Ruth don't give out those keys to anyone." Saul stabbed a gnarled finger just short of Eddie's chest where only the memory of the hand that held him back remained. "Special. That's you. Special."

"Special, shit." Eddie fended off a smile and dusted his chest with the towel he'd been twisting. No, this wasn't a game he'd play. But the voice. Special. The bar. His.

"Son, you don't know it yet, but you've got a place here, and I'll help you find it." Saul drank then set his glass on the bar. The folds under his eyes reddened.

Could he trust him? "You're a priest. God and I don't—"

Saul pounded his fist on the bar. Vodka jumped from his glass and beaded on the polish. "God ain't got shit to do with this place or you."

Eddie laughed and waved the priest off. "You're mad."

Through wet, red lips Saul said, "Maybe, but I know me. I've known others. And you're lost. Look in that mirror, son."

Saul inhaled through wide nostrils and nodded toward the wall of booze. Eddie turned and looked at himself in the bar's silver-flaked mirror. Saul pulled out his pack of Marbs, lit a smoke, and dragged in deep. "Whadda ya see?" He blew out the smoke with indifference.

Eddie turned back toward Saul. "I'm not here for some psycho-bullshit, father."

Saul's lips sagged into wet twigs. Tendrils of smoke curled from his mouth. "Turn, son."

Eddie turned.

"Whadda ya see?"

Eddie saw himself, cloudy and yellowed in the old mirror. Where the silver cracked, his face was cracked. Where the mirror was beveled, there were more Eddies. He shrugged. "I see my face, you, and the bar."

"Right, and there ain't need for much more." Saul sucked vodka from ice cubes.

Eddie turned back to Saul. "So what." He shrugged.

"You got yourself, son. You know where you are." The juke scratched Cline back to life, this time with a piano swing and Patsy's cotton-soft voice touting new love in another's heart. "You know who you are. But you need purpose." Saul dug into his pocket and pulled out a wad of bills and coins. He counted out five singles and tucked them under his empty glass. From the coins he picked out two silver dollars. "Here, son, this one's for you." Outstretched eagle under his finger, he scratched the coin across the bar top. He held up the second coin. "This one. This one's for Red." He flicked it with a finger and walked to the door. "You know where I live. When you need me, come get me. And son, Amos don't know shit."

Eddie picked up his coin, looked up and said, "What—"

The door closed on Saul's heels. Through the door's glass, Eddie saw the priest shuffle down the road trailed by cigarette smoke. On the bar, Rhea's coin skittered and stopped. Eddie held his face against the cool glass until the priest was out of sight, locked up Frank's, and turned the be-back sign without changing the clock. The speakers on the jukebox crackled, the music stopped, servos wined, and the jukebox glowered red in the corner where a shadow stooped.

You did well.

"I did well."

You'll do well.

"I'll do well." Eddie stood behind the bar.

Listen.

Eddie nodded.

Get the bar ready. Customers need you.

"I'll get the bar ready." He fired up the grill and left Rhea's coin and the leaf on the bar.

CHAPTER EIGHT

THE SUN CRESTED and began its descent when Rhea tossed the last log into the showers' boiler. Kneeling, she closed the iron hatch with a broken broom handle the way Ruth taught her. Through a window stained orange, flames curled around logs that quickly charred.

"Well, that's that," Ruth said. "I've been long enough. Eddie's alone, and Frank ain't easy." She smacked the dirt from her jeans. "Part of me hopes he opened for customers, but that might be askin' a bit much."

Rhea looked up at Ruth. The light of the flames flickered across Ruth's face and tinted her red hair like late fall leaves. "He'll be fine," Rhea said. "Eddie knows what he's doing. A couple hours running Frank's should be nothing." She stood and nodded toward the boiler. "When will this be ready?"

"'Bout half an hour or so. Heck with how long it took us to get going full blast, it might be just right for one. The rest will have to wait."

A boat sputtered past the cabin, and its wake curled on the

shore. Its fisherman made his way to the distant dock where Rhea could barely make out Al, still casting and pulling in fish. "Ruth, this place. I want to like it. But . . ."

Ruth reached out, held Rhea's shoulder, and said, "Be careful what you like, sweetheart."

Rhea shrugged off Ruth's grasp. "Please, stop calling me that."

"What?"

"Sweetheart. I ain't . . . I'm *not* any of that." Rhea shook her head and stood.

"I'm sorry, h-Rhea. That's just what I call . . . Well, I'm sorry."

"My dad called me that."

"Where's your dad? California?"

"Sure."

"Meaning?"

"He's dead. Mom too."

"I'm sorry, hon'. Any other family? Sister?"

Rhea's face bunched up. She palmed tears from her eyes. "Dead too."

"My god. I-I'm sorry."

Why sorry? It was a stupid thing to say. She'd heard it so many times from everyone except him. There was a long silence as the heat from the boiler warmed Rhea's back and legs. But it was what people said. Well, most people. What else could they say? Rhea crossed her arms over her chest in a tight knot and shivered. "I guess I forgot how cold I was." She toed a twig that hadn't made it into the fire.

"Let's get you inside. Grab a couple logs. Warm up the cabin."

Ruth and Rhea made their way to the cabin with logs and kindling. Ruth shoveled charred logs and ash from the potbelly stove. They stacked new logs on the granite pad and placed the kindling in a brass basket that looked like something a fairy-tale sister would carry. The fire started quickly and in minutes heated the cabin enough for Ruth to crack two windows, airing out the must. Ruth took out a bucket and bleach and wiped down the cabin with rags from a linen closet.

"You don't have to do that, Ruth," said Rhea. "Eddie and I can clean up later."

"No, that's okay, hon'," Ruth said as she rung the rag into the bucket.

Rhea sat on the wool couch and slid her hands over the rough and ribbed fabric softened by years of use. She unlatched the steamer trunk and opened it. Inside was a crocheted blanket that was a patchwork of blues and grays matching the couch. She draped it across her legs. The blanket hid stacks of Time magazines. Kennedy, Nixon, the Pope, and other men's faces clogged up the covers. No copy went beyond the sixties. Deeper in the stacks were a few Playboys from the same decades.

She looked over her shoulder. Ruth had made her way into the bathroom, so Rhea pulled out a copy that had a young woman lifting her white shirt. Her blonde pigtails lapped her shoulders. On her belly was painted a white bunny, and in red jersey letters were the words *student power*. She paged through the naked bodies and pretentious articles then tucked it back when she heard the toilet flush and Ruth flip-flop into the living room. Rhea latched the steamer.

"That'll take care of most of the cleaning, hon'," Ruth said. "I made your bed too. The sheets were fine if you don't mind smelling like mothballs for a night or two until I can get you cleaner sheets. Find something?"

"Just some old magazines." She toed off her sneakers and pulled the blanket over her legs and shoulders.

Ruth patted Rhea's blanketed knee. "I'm sorry about your family, hon'."

There it was again, *sorry*. But Rhea didn't flinch at Ruth's touch, nor did she mind it. She just shook her head slowly as though her neck was stone. "It was hard." Another stupid thing to say. What else was there to say though? Jesus, her thoughts were broken like some kid playing the same few measures of a song they loved, over and over until their parents told them to turn that shit down.

Ruth was silent. It was best Ruth hadn't asked, but Rhea felt she wanted to know. It was there, in her eyes. No, not her eyes, her mouth. It was the corners that were turned down just enough, twitching just a bit, thinly pursed. And then it was her eyes, glazed soft by old tears, marbled green and blue like the lake. Rhea looked at the lake through those eyes and cleared her mind. "Ruth?"

"Yeah, hon'," Ruth said.

"How long have you been here?" Rhea asked. Eddie had asked *why* she was here. Not everyone had a *why*. Everyone had time, knew how long.

Ruth pulled a soft pack of Camels from her pants pocket, tapped out a lighter and smoke, and after a few scratches of the flint, gave up. She walked to the potbelly, lit the smoke on the stove plate, then sat back on the couch and offered Rhea a smoke.

"No, thanks. I quit weeks ago."

"I wish I had your will." Next to Rhea, Ruth took up a whole couch cushion. Curled up as she was, Rhea's toes touched Ruth's thigh, so she edged closer to the arm to give Ruth space.

"I put in an all-nighter at a diner and chained through a carton. Walking to work the next morning, I lit a smoke and threw up. I crushed the pack and tossed it in the ditch. I haven't had a smoke since. That pack's probably still sitting there in the tall grass."

"Hard?"

"Sometimes. Inside, I tell myself I hate it. I hate it. I hate it. Seems to work."

"I've been here a long time, Rhea."

"Saint Andrew?"

"Yeah."

"What made you stay?"

"A boy and a baby. And it's not what you think." Ruth pulled long and hard from her smoke.

"Did you love him?"

She exhaled plumes that settled on the ceiling. "Like I said, it's not what you think."

"Sorry." Rhea curled her toes and looked at the steamer.

"No, it's my story to tell." Ruth kicked her flipflops off and crossed her legs at the ankles on the steamer. Her heels were callused dusty white, and her jeans hung loose.

"Are those men's jeans?"

Ruth scratched out a laugh, coughed, and took another drag. "That's part of the story, I suppose. Men's sizes are just easier to shop, and my body don't have the curves of youth." Rhea shook her head wanting to counter what Ruth had said, but Ruth continued with a wave. "I don't need no random number that tells me I'm fat."

"You're not—"

"My story." Ruth smacked Rhea's leg with the back of her hand. "Let me finish."

Rhea nodded and looked out the porch window toward the lake. Ruth did the same. Al still stood on the dock, and shadows started stretching east over the waters. The Manor's patches of white paint glowed.

"I don't wear bras no more neither. The last found itself in a fifty-gallon oil drum filled to the brim with other A to multiple-D cups belching inky smoke at the stars."

"Did that really happen?"

"Not like most think, but it did. At least for me. I was there. And so was that boy. Really, that night's a blur. I remember feelin' old. In my late thirties those twenty odd years ago, it was the young dolls around me that did it. He didn't look at them. Flames licked his face as he watched me strip my bra under my peasant blouse. I had a silver peace sign 'bout the size of a grapefruit. Nice and heavy. It pulled the chain tight and that blouse against my breasts. The fabric was thin, even for then, embroidered with yellow flowers. I'd wear it for another half decade at draft-card burnings. Most everything was about fire back then." She shook her head as if she had or wanted to say other things. "Anyway, I was all but naked to him. I took that boy that night, aborted his baby, and he returned to the states in a casket, a bullet through his pretty face."

Rhea held the blanket against her face. There was comfort in the darkness, but there were also half-open eyes, dulled by death. Eyes and bodies that returned so many times over the past years and, of course, in Frank's. Yet that dark voice, those sick touches hadn't returned. It was just her. Just Rhea being Rhea. But now there was only Eddie to tell her that. Lonely tears soaked her cheeks.

"It's okay, hon'. That was a long time ago." Ruth rubbed Rhea's back with her palm.

Rhea jumped and pulled her head from the blanket.

"Rhea," said Ruth clutching Rhea's shoulders as she eyed Rhea's neck. "I'm sorry. None of my business and all, but Eddie? Has he done somethin'?"

"I'm sorry. Since I got here, I had these . . . Eddie's good. He saved me."

"Since here, you had what?"

"I-It's stupid. So much of this is stupid. I'll tell you later."

"Tell me what?"

Rhea shook her head. Finally, she had a place to stay. It was a home. Temporary, yes, but still a home. She didn't want misery. And she didn't want to share that just yet. If ever. No one wanted to hear her shit. And then there was this woman. Ruth. There was something else in her Rhea loved. Something behind those soft eyes: a mind or soul that saw more than spoken words. She may have even loved Ruth herself. And it was that love that ultimately stopped her from telling her all she held secret.

So Rhea said, "I can't. Not yet."

"All right, hon', your story. But I'm always here."

"I need time," Rhea said. "You should go."

Ruth stood stoop shouldered. Rhea thought of a time to come where she'd return to her seat at the bar after pissing Ruth off with drunkenness and poor tips the night before. When she returned, this woman, Ruth, wouldn't shame, wouldn't accuse, wouldn't hate. She'd be there for her and them, all those who lived in Saint Andrew, with stern comfort. Always listening. And that was something to love, something Rhea never had.

"When you need me, you know where I live," Ruth said and walked out the cabin and down the gravel road.

Rhea slept, yet she did not remember dreams. When she awoke, the trees' shadows stretched across the lake's sullen waves like groping fingers. She fed the potbelly stove another log and found four bags of groceries and two cases of Blatz beer sitting on the kitchen counter. A note was attached to the beer that read, *Your groceries. More in the fridge. —Amos.*

In the fridge were a couple stacks of meat and a carton of milk. She opened the icebox and found a square bottle of Smirnoff. The vodka had already congealed to syrup. She unpacked the rest of the groceries, placing everything where it felt right.

Rhea undressed and wrapped herself in a towel and made her way barefoot to the showers with a grocery bag holding soap, shampoo, and a washrag. On the shack, fat squirrels scratched across the tin roof foraging pinecones and nuts. Each shower stall was separated by corrugated fiberglass. Iron stains trailed from the showerheads to the floor drain. In the corners and between each shower, spiders spun thick webs. Rhea sighed, grabbed a broom from the cabin, and cleared the webs from a single stall close to the door.

The water was hot and hit her like an angry masseuse, which was strange comfort given their time on the road since Montana. When the water grew cold, she dried herself off, tossed a couple logs into the boiler, and headed inside.

In the cabin, she unpacked her white baby-doll gown, a black hoodie, and a pair of gray sweats. The sweats and hoodie were wards against the dusk. The gown she saved for nights with Eddie in a room rather than the Vega. She hoped this'd be one of those nights, yet Eddie hadn't returned from Frank's. Nothing new. Saturdays were busy everywhere. For good measure, she threw on her jean jacket over the gown and hoodie.

She stacked up a sandwich, pulled the vodka from the icebox, and headed to the dock held above water by two metal pipes. She pulled up her sweats, sat down, and swirled her feet in the numbing water. She ate and drank as the dying sun lit the Manor orange and called out the black rot outside veins of peeled paint.

Even across the lake, she could make out the French doors

at the center of both balconies. Her own bedroom in California had French doors and a balcony. At night she'd walk through those doors onto the terracotta tiles still hot under her feet from the day's sun and look down on Wensley Avenue lined with dwarf palm trees and the blades of the agave plant that took up half her yard.

But her house was just as rotten as the Manor. Ugly things happened there. What ugly things made the Manor what it is? Or was it just a forgotten home, abandoned and unloved?

Sandwich gone, she took a few pulls from the bottle. The sky had turned into a smear of stars like Rhea hadn't seen since the days she and Eddie fled from their families into Anza-Borrego east of the Laguna Mountains. Saint Andrew was different. The Imperial Valley always had insects. Here, winter had yet to set the bugs free and held spring at bay.

A light wind rolled through budding branches and interrupted the quiet with a boney applause accompanied by waves that soaked rock and sand and lapped her white calves. The waning moon cast paper-rips of silver along the tips of the waves.

"Beautiful, isn't it?" The voice was young and light with a hint of Alabama.

Hot fear hit Rhea's heart and legs. The vodka plunged into the lake as she scrambled to her feet and scraped her thigh on the dock's planking. She wobbled and held out her hand in weak defense while choking on her own breath as her shoulders heaved.

A woman in a flannel nightgown peppered with yellow daffodils stood on the dock. She held up her hands and said, "I'm sorry. I didn't mean to scare you." She stepped forward. "I won't hurt you."

Rhea found the dock's edge with her heels and choked the

metal pipe to avoid joining her vodka. Her knuckles flared white.

"I live across the lake," said the woman, palms open. "Really, I saw the cabin lights. My name's Deirdre." She offered a limp hand and dropped the other. "Didi."

Rhea released the pipe and clenched the jacket at her chest. She breathed. "You—god."

"I know," said Didi as she pulled red curls from her cheek and locked them behind her ear, exposing her nightgown's collar buttoned tight around her neck. "I'm sorry about your vodka."

"It's okay. I didn't pay for it—yet." Rhea released her jacket. "Deirdre?"

"Didi," she said. Her touch chilled Rhea when they shook. Didi was pale, and goose bumped. She had no shoes, and her feet were wrinkled like they'd soaked for hours.

"You shouldn't be out like that," said Rhea.

"That's what the Old Man says, but I don't listen, don't mind. There's another bottle in the cabin near the showers." Didi shrugged and smiled. Her eyes were dark, shadowed from the sun that set behind her, but there was a little girl in those eyes that smoked with defiance in greens and blues. She couldn't have been older than Rhea. Another gust kicked up from the lake and billowed her nightgown, which she pressed against her thighs like that old Monroe flick.

"Aren't you too—"

"I know. Too young," Didi said. "Law says I'm good. Besides, I'm older than most think."

Rhea shook her head and shrugged. "Laws don't mean much to me. I've been drinking since junior high. So how about the cabin?"

"Would you mind? I could use the company. The Old Man's terse tonight."

It'd been far too long since she'd had a night with anyone other than Eddie. Rhea nodded, turned, and looked past the Manor where Frank's and Eddie were hidden by trees. "Why not? I've got time."

"I'll get the bottle." Didi headed toward another cabin, and Rhea entered her own.

Rhea's cabin was hot, but she threw another log into the stove and cracked the windows just a bit more. The lake had filled the cabin with its green scent, but the hot iron of the stove and the light haze of wood smoke that seeped through the burner plate were stronger than the lake and the must. Even the blanket had lost its scent as Rhea curled on the couch.

The screen door creaked and slapped shut. Didi entered, held up a frosted bottle of Smirnoff and two glasses, and said with a smile, "When," as she poured. Rhea stopped Didi at a few shots.

Didi poured just a bit longer, poured her own, set the bottle on the floor, and asked, "Just got here?"

"Yeah, today. Our car broke down. Josh is fixing it."

Didi laughed. "Yeah, they'll fix it."

"What is it with those two? No one has faith—"

"Faith?" Didi downed vodka like water.

Rhea shrugged. "Sure, why not?"

"Some people don't deserve it."

"They don't?"

"Not a bit," said Didi. "You heard 'bout their dads?"

"Ruth said—"

"Whatever she said was too nice. Those boys don't deserve nice." Even in the light of the cabin, Didi's eyes were stained dark. Mocking Ruth's scratchy, baritone voice, she wagged her finger and held her other hand like a big belly and said, "They deserve better. They deserve love." She stopped mocking. "What'd she tell ya?"

Rhea tensed and pulled a hair's distance from Didi. "Their dads are dead," Rhea said, as if mourning someone close.

"Did she, now?" Didi's voice guitar twanged like the deep South.

Rhea thought back. Dead? Maybe not. She took a few sips of vodka. "Lost, maybe? I don't—"

"That sounds more like her," Didi said. Her tone had been flat until the last word, which was spat out. "Josh's dad's dead. Cal's dad's in a chair. He don't leave it much. Don't speak neither. Got a tube in his throat and two in his stomach: one goin' in, the other goin' out if you catch me. Josh's dad fell off a ladder in his kitchen. He and Josh were fixin' a light. Josh clicked the wrong breaker. His dad weren't nothin' in his older years, took a tumble from the ladder—aluminum, I guess— after gettin' a shock, and fell on a screwdriver that went clean through his ear."

"God," said Rhea.

Didi shook her head. "No, Amos." She tapped a fist on her knee then pointed across the lake toward Amos's office. "He got the call. Said it was an accident. Thing is, I don't get how the screwdriver was in his left ear when he fell on his right. That's what they say, at least. I didn't see it myself." She shrugged and took another pull of vodka.

"Josh was there with his mom?" Rhea shook her head with her mouth open, realized she probably looked like the valley girls she hated, and downed some vodka.

"Well, I guess his mom saw it happen. Josh was downstairs by the breaker box. Tell you what I did see, though: his grad party, Josh's, that is. His dad bought a keg—before his dad was dead—and stuffed it in a trashcan with ice and a stack of cups in the backyard. All the *in* kids"—Didi quoted with her fingers —"were out back with the keg. I was on the deck and could hear his mom's bit-pillow squeals and his dad snortin' like a ruttin' pig grindin' their bedsprings to dust. I'd have spewed if I didn't want to lose the beer in my belly." Her smile blazed.

"Later that night she—Josh's mom, that is—was by the keg. His dad snored on the floor by the TV that blared the anthem then that dead-air tone. His mom was on the deck's steps. Her face was twisted ugly. She tugged dirt-blonde frizz from her mouth and cheeks already wet with tears and mascara. She sucked on the keg line through slack lips like a sad clown or one of them cartoon hobos. Beer foam—tinted red with blood from her fat lip—curdled out her mouth like she was havin' a seizure. Pathetic." Didi emptied her glass and swung it like futile punctuation. "She told Josh to leave. Leave home and Saint Andrew, I guess, and he just said, 'No ma, I ain't leavin',' like he had a choice or somethin'."

"He couldn't leave?" Rhea asked.

"He coulda, but the Marines wouldn't have him. Neither would the Army. So he stayed. Loser." She uncapped the vodka and poured another half-glass for both of them.

"Thanks," Rhea said. "Saint Andrew is small. No one helped?"

"Like you said, this town's small. Small means folks mind their own. Maybe that's why Amos said what he said—that it was an accident. Maybe that's why he ignored how Josh's dad had jigsawed his son's face with his fists the night before he fell off that ladder. Josh died that night. Well, he shoulda."

Rhea closed her eyes. She was warm. The vodka numbed her face and legs. Every breath was liquor. She regretted laughing about Josh when Eddie told his stories at the gas pumps. She now knew why Josh needed care and got where Ruth was coming from. "My dad . . ." Drunk tears streaked Rhea's cheeks. "He did things too, but he's dead. So is my mom. And sister."

Didi set her glass on the floor and wrapped an arm around

Rhea's shoulders. Rhea turned toward the lake, away from Didi, who massaged Rhea's shoulders in waves. Her hands smelled of the lake and were still cold, but it was comfort against the fire's heat.

When Rhea spoke, she spoke to the Manor. "I remember the ant most. My sister was in the basement, curled on the cracked concrete next to the drain. The ant crawled across her half-open eye. Or tried. One of its feet was stuck in her mascara while the others dragged on her iris. Vomit and foam twisted into the drain. My parents were on their bed, holding each other naked. They never did that, not that I saw. They were purple like they'd been there for days. I'd run off for a while."

"What killed them?" Didi said.

"Drugs. I muled. It's how I met Eddie."

"Muled?"

"I'd drop dope in a stump or dumpster for another to carry until it got to the user. It wasn't like the Miami cop shows. Dealer and wasteoid didn't meet unless there was a debt."

"Did you? You know . . ."

"Use? No. My dad did." Rhea clenched her fist. "He must have gotten my mom into it. I don't know. Maybe she used and I never saw. Users and addicts are good at hiding. Families don't want to believe. My sister, though. She didn't. I know that. And yet, there she was on the concrete."

"That's horrible," said Didi. Her voice was distant, hollow, almost bored.

Rhea shrugged off Didi and turned. Didi looked down at her lap and hid in the kitchen.

"Didi," Rhea said. "I'm sorry. I don't know why I told you all that. Really."

"No, I wanted to hear it. I didn't stop you." Her voice stretched thin like a thread strung between two cans. She turned on the faucet and splashed water. "Did you mule those drugs?"

"The ones that killed my family?"

"Yeah."

"I don't know," said Rhea. "Maybe. I may have touched them."

Rhea looked at her hands and shivered with hate. Hate for herself. Hate for her dad. Hate for her mom for doing nothing. Hate for her sister for not . . . No, that's not true. Love for her sister, hate for her loss. The loss of her young and smiling on swings then years later next to public pools under the desert heat.

Rhea wasn't a pool-side princess. She didn't dare. But her sister, with her red hair pulled tight in a pony, was. Her sister would slow-mo saunter in her white two-piece while self-centered prisses whispered *slut*, and their douchebag boyfriends gaped.

Rhea's face bunched into a nest built from that same pain she held inside, and more tears fell.

"You weren't like your sister," Didi said from the kitchen. "You aren't like your sister."

"How do you . . . know?" She must have said those things. Her body hummed with heat and seemed to float above the couch. She'd had enough vodka but wanted more. "We weren't alike," she said, all inhibition and uncertainty gone. Her guard was down. It was rare, and Rhea embraced it.

"Where was Eddie?"

"College." Rhea choked on tears, poured a shot of vodka, and downed it. "LA, I guess. He left me and got away from his family. He came back. I was on my balcony. It was night. The insects came back, migrating south, flying thick like how the snow is up here. As a kid, I was told those bugs would live in lungs and plant eggs. I held my breath in those clouds.

Anyway, I was twenty. My family had been dead for a couple weeks. I threw a party. I could hear *Sisters of Mercy* thudding through the floor in four-four telling me everything would turn out right. I stood on that balcony looking at the flagstones below, knowing that if I hit it just right, I'd split my skull, crack my spine, bleed out. I wouldn't scream. I'd had enough. Then Eddie ducked through those French doors, lounged there like an overexposed polaroid and said, 'Wanna get the fuck out of here?'"

Rhea closed her eyes. Spots from the ceiling light bled into the dark behind her eyes in a multi-colored glow of melted faces. "He was different back then, and I loved him for it. White, pancaked face, black number-one-dyed hair framing his swimming eyes, black jeans, and army surplus boots with tongues that lashed out like Gene Simmons on stage. There wasn't much to say except, 'yeah,' and Eddie took my arm. We stuffed a duffel and walked down the steps, past heaving junkies snorting dust, through the noise, out the front door, and across the crunching brown lawn to Eddie's Chevy Vega.

"That was three years ago. There were other towns, but we left each as we headed east, gassing up when we could. We'd cobble together diner wages and leave smelling of bacon and twenty-four-hour pancakes only to spend the night kinked together like abused sock dolls in the Vega's back seat. There were nights where I'd peer at the stars through the bowed window, cracked just enough to keep the cab cool. Eddie's breath would wash across my neck, and I'd hold him tighter. He'd stir, and I'd release him. During those moments, life is simple, free of what we once were."

"Rhea, you can have that here. In Saint Andrew," said Didi.

Rhea opened her eyes. Didi was standing above her, pale and cold. Her frame had changed though. Her shoulders were square and steady. Her hair was wet to the scalp and lapped her shoulders, soaking her gown that clung to bare skin. There was a puddle at her feet.

"I have to go," Didi said. "See you soon."

"But—"

The screen door slapped shut. Didi walked past the windows and from Rhea's sight. Rhea dropped her glass of vodka on the floor and looked at the ceiling blurred through tears. The room spun.

CHAPTER NINE

EDDIE WRANGLED A PACKED Frank's that reeked of the gutted fish hard-knuckled anglers had butchered. Pool balls clacked, and a clot of the fishermen whooped like fat seals when the eight-ball sunk early. Ruth checked in just after three o'clock and thanked Eddie for opening even though she'd warned against it then headed to Amos's office.

By four, loud-mouthed customers flooded the recesses of the bar, and heavy-footed farmgirls strutted to a base line that bounced from the jukebox while Kristofferson graveled on about chilly winds, guitars, and people who don't listen. The old Regulator clock mounted to the wall read 4:13 when the church bell rang once then dribbled dead. The Regulator's pendulum swung on.

Five rolled around, and Josh with Cal swaggered in smelling of old oil and orange soap. They took their seats at the bar. Two whiskies in, Josh wrapped his knuckles on the bar, and Eddie slid him another. Cal took a fourth Blatz. The other stools were empty.

Eddie stepped into the kitchen and slung rows of burgers bubbling in their own fat and slapped on fluorescent orange cheese. He stacked grilled buns and the dripping patties into red, paper-lined baskets, slapped a fried egg on each, and piled on hand-tossed fries. It was an easy order, not that there were any hard ones that night. Everyone took it easy on Eddie, even Josh and Cal, who stuck to liquids until Eddie hit a lull.

"Mind gettin' me one a them?" Cal asked as he wiped foam from his upper lip dusted with a blond stash and thumbed toward the table Eddie had just served.

"Me too," said Josh. He twisted his glass of whiskey on its white napkin and watched the ice swirl when he held the glass still.

"Ya bet," said Eddie without giving them a glance. He slapped the order together and skidded them their baskets with a condiment tray.

Josh twisted the glass again and said, "Isn't that somethin'. Just keeps goin' after I stop."

"The ice?" asked Eddie more graciously than Josh probably deserved.

"Yep," said Josh. Cal leaned over and snorted a laugh.

"Tends to do that," said Eddie. He'd done the same thing after having a few in Mexicali meat market clubs. There was a trance in that glass where the liquor and ice water swirled like oil that deadened the strutting-cock-show on the club's dance-floor where even the men wore less than what Eddie was comfortable with.

Josh dug into his pocket and tossed a five onto the bar then said, "Get yourself one."

"Nah, working," said Eddie.

Josh looked up from his glass. "It's a tip. Take it and drink."

Eddie took the money and poured himself a scotch. He

grabbed a pack of Marb Reds from under the bar, lit up, blew smoke, and took a swig. Josh twitched his fingers in a silent gimme-one, and Eddie tossed him the pack and lighter. Josh gave a smoke to Cal and took his own but lit both with his own red-crusted lighter.

Smoke seeped from his mouth as Josh said, "Frank loves you."

"What?"

"Frank, the bar. Hasn't been like this since Ruth first stood where you are."

"When did Ruth start?"

"A while back," said Josh. He shrugged and chewed on half a fry and used the other half like a pointer. "Like she's been here for forever." He waved the fry around then tossed the other half in his mouth and chewed wetly.

The bar burst with late afternoon sunlight when Saul entered. He sat on his stool and rubbed his neck where his clerical collar was cinched tight then said, "You haven't moved Rhea's coin."

"It's not mine," said Eddie. He backed away from Josh, who had buried his face in his basket of food turning more toward Cal as Saul looked his way. Josh leaned toward Cal and whispered something. Cal laughed; his shoulders jumped ever so slightly.

Saul snatched Eddie's pack of smokes and lit up with Eddie's lighter. "Vodka," he said, his voice was wet like gravel under a truck's tires. Eddie poured Absolut over three rocks and set the glass in front of Saul on a napkin. He kept the bottle under the bar. "That's service. Busy bar. Just you?"

"Yeah," said Eddie. "Just me. Ruth's with Amos."

"That'll happen." Saul reached behind his neck and unbuttoned his collar. He sighed then hacked like a rasp scratching iron. He ripped out his clerical collar, specked with blood, and set it on the bar. "Speaking of service. Mine's on Sundays. But I'll give you a special one. You ain't visited me yet."

"I just got here," Eddie said. "No time."

Saul leaned toward Josh and said, "I've got service to tend to."

Josh nodded and nudged Cal, who'd finished his pilsner. Cal wrapped his knuckles on the bar and followed Josh to a pool table.

"Serve 'em," said Saul, who took a drag then snubbed out his smoke.

Eddie poured a beer and whiskey then brought them back to where Josh and Cal stood by a cocktail table. Josh sneered at Eddie and tossed him another five. Cal chalked a pool cue and eyed Eddie, who returned to the bar where Saul downed his glass of vodka with full-throated ease. Above his Adam's apple, Saul's neck was hatched red and blistered. A raw line of angry veins curled toward his shoulders and jaw. From the corners, Saul's eyes met Eddie's. He set his glass down, pulled his collar closer to this neck, and said, "I'll take another. Get yourself one."

Eddie poured while he said, "Your neck."

"Long story. One you'll know."

Listen.

Eddie shook his head and looked up at the burned bra that hung from the tricycle. "All ears."

"Not yet," said Saul. "I ain't ready. I said I'd give service. You willin'?"

Take it.

Eddie closed his eyes and nodded, slowly, like a drunk staving off sick.

"Good," said Saul. "What brought you here?"

Eddie opened his eyes. Saul's eyes were like yellowed porcelain crackled by red veins. "Rhea. Rhea brought me here."

"That so?" Saul leaned forward and pulled another smoke from Eddie's pack. He lit up. Behind him the bar customers eddied between tables, and their voices washed over walls and drowned the jukebox.

"Yeah," said Eddie. "I'd gone to college. Art major. Cinema."

"Graduate?"

"Nah, left well before I got close. I left for Rhea." Eddie looked back at the pool table. Cal had just sunk a couple balls and pumped his fist in victory. Josh leaned on his stick and looked at Eddie. He had that Billy Idol sneer, and the crucifix hanging from his earlobe shivered. "Who's the Old Man?"

Saul looked up at Eddie, who kept his eyes on Josh yet could still see Saul's face had sagged, become slacked and rutted like a limp rope. Saul said, "Not yet. Why college?"

"Get away from my family. Amos isn't the Old—"

"No!" Saul pounded his fist on the bar then pointed at Eddie. "I heard 'bout the drugs."

Eddie laughed and shook his head. "This town. Where'd you hear?"

"Don't matter. You left college for Rhea."

"Yeah, like I said."

"Why? When?" Saul pressed in on Eddie, not physically but with straight shoulders like he was chained to a wall and a craned neck pricked with blood.

Eddie pointed. "Your neck—"

"Tell me," Saul said.

Tell him.

The razer voice cut deep. Eddie stumbled and leaned on the beer fridge. "Her father . . . Nah, that's not it." He looked down at the rubber mat that now reeked of wet bread. Spilled beer foam hugged the inside edges of the mat's hexagonal pools. Eddie stabbed at the bubbles with the toe of his sneakers. "I hoped college would get me away. Away from my dad, his business. I was wrong. I was in a cinema class in the campus theater watching a French film starring an intelligent balloon and this friendless kid." Eddie shrugged. "Some jerk kids murdered it—the balloon—with rocks and slingshots."

"What's this gotta do with Rhea?" Saul asked.

Eddie clenched his jaw, and his head twitched as if bit by a hot needle, but he swallowed the anger. Saul needed to shut his face. "I'm getting there. The music and screaming kids— the ones who killed the balloon—squelched when the professor stopped the reel and asked what the balloon's death meant. He was a Californian leftover of the sixties. His hair was a giant cotton swab that stuck out between paisley collars." Eddie held his hands above his head measuring the professor's substantial hair. "Some dweeb in a baggy sweater pressed up his glasses and gave a bull-shit answer that had nothing to do with kids being dicks. The movie started again before a leather jacketed greaser in chains slumped in the chair next to me. He smelled like this beer. And his jeans were more dirt than denim. 'Hook me up, man,' he said. He had a lopsided sneer like that dick, Josh. Junkies can be dangerous, but this was some college flunky, Billy Idol wannabe, looking to score points with chicks. Long story short, I told Billy-bread-boy to go fuck himself. On the screen the French boy was hugged by dozens of other balloons. I left the theater and took my Vega south to Rhea. She was standing on her balcony."

Liar.

Saul elbowed up on the bar and took a drag from his smoke and said, "You sure that's how it went?"

"What do you—"

Liar. The voice came on strong, became harsh, abusive, as though it was raising a thick fist above a crouching child. Eddie clenched his eyes, held his forehead between his thumb and middle finger. *Tell him.*

"No. I can't," said Eddie.

Tell him.

"You can't what?" asked Saul who grinned as if Eddie's confession was already laid out before him like a shitty poker hand.

Tell him.

The fist dragged through his face like a frozen wind, forcing Eddie to look at the kitchen. "No, no, I came back early."

Wrong.

The fist shoved Eddie's head back so he could see the jukebox. There, next to the jukebox that bubbled red, was a black horror hunched like an anorexic ape. "No," Eddie whispered as he held his jaw and tongued a tooth where blood seeped. "I mean, I came back." His voice quavered, had become hoarse, dry. "I came back earlier."

Better. The ape stepped behind the jukebox. Fishermen sunk pool balls.

"Two weeks before the balcony." Eddie downed his scotch and poured more.

Saul leaned forward and nodded. There was a thin smile on his face, and the whites of his eyes, once yellow, had cleared and grown wide. Then his brow twisted, and his face lifted as though he was eager for what Eddie had to say next. "And?"

Trust.

"I had a goon send her on a run. Delivery. Drugs. I went to her house. Her dad took the drugs. That was easy. He used. Her sister was weak, young. I hid her in the basement. Her mom fought. But I got her too. I stripped 'em both and laid them on their bed."

Murderer.

Eddie knuckled tears from his eyes, poured more whiskey, and washed down the clot of guilt.

Never, murderer.

"My God, son. You're—" said Saul.

Eddie held up a finger, stopping Saul before he could say more. "Yeah, murderer. But . . . I can't."

Speak, murderer.

"I pulled Rhea from the run. Told her the cops knew about it, and we ran to Anza-Borrego. There, we fought over her dad, how he was bad for her, how she needed more, needed me. Primo acting." Eddie smiled. "I left her there. That was hard, but I had to be an ass for everything to work as planned. She got back home, somehow. I gave it a couple days then saved her from that balcony. She'd have jumped. We left and made our way here."

"Son, come get me after you lock up."

"I ain't—I'm *not*—Where's Ruth?" He looked up at the bra.

Saul pursed his lips into a crooked twig. "Never mind her and remember what I said about Amos." He flipped Eddie a few bills and left.

Good.

Returning to the kitchen, Eddie leaned over the stainless sink, wretched, and washed the vomit down the drain like liquid rust.

Weak.

The voice was close. He splashed his face with cold water and ran his wet fingers through his hair. There was no mirror, but he knew how he looked. He'd felt this way far too many times while standing behind palm trees and fences watching cops and paramedics pull white-sheeted bodies from trailer parks and rotted shacks.

They need you.

It was beside him, black and decrepit, yet it rose, thin and dreadful, leaking black at the edges like blood from wrists in bath water. It held a cane and smelled sweet and green. Eddie gaped yet couldn't breathe. He shook his head, and the beast nodded then grabbed Eddie's shoulder with slender fingers like broken twigs. It turned him toward the bar and pushed.

They need you.

Eddie walked to the till where customers had lined up. Each step was bound to the floor by an invisible band that snapped only when it wanted Eddie to move further. The bills Saul had left were still there, next to Rhea's coin and the leaf. He put the bills in the till and pocketed Rhea's coin. He tucked the leaf under the bar between napkins. Al nodded grimly with downturned lips. Eddie mixed him a stiff white Russian and waved away his money. He poured and mixed and ticketed short orders. One of the fishermen pumped coins into the jukebox, and Ozzy cackled as millions of people boarded his train.

Ruth returned just before six. She stopped at the threshold of the door as smoke and quick guitar riffs rushed out with the heat into the early spring air. It was still light outside, but the sun was low and lit the porch orange. Outside, Owen gassed up an RV. Ruth shook her head. Eddie elbowed up on the bar, chin in palms. He wrapped up his conversation with a fisherman, and Ruth joined him.

Ruth looked across Frank's. "My god. You've packed him. Frank." She looked at Eddie. "Had I known, I'd've come back."

Eddie shrugged. "I handled it."

"Here comes Josh. He give you trouble?"

"Nah."

Josh and Cal bellied-up. "Eddie had a visitor," said Josh. "Had a good gab."

Ruth looked at Eddie. "What? Who?"

Eddie shrugged. "No one. Saul. He drank. No food. Paid well."

Ruth held Eddie's arm and turned him toward her. "What'd he say?"

"Nothin'." Eddie pulled away. Ruth cocked her head. "Nothin'. Jesus, lady, I took care of Frank for you. What do you want?"

She let Eddie go. "Sorry. Saul's not the kind of—"

He poured the usual for Cal and Josh. "Yeah, I keep hearing that about people. Like you said 'bout Josh, here."

"Jesus, Ruth," Josh said and washed those words down with liquor. "You're in everyone's shit. Learnin' ain't your thing. What'd she say?" Josh looked at Eddie.

"Nothin' you don't already know, slick," Eddie said. He shook his head. "Nothing."

"I bet," said Josh. He ran a knuckle under his nose.

Push him.

Eddie looked at Josh. His nails were ribbed with grease and oil. "You workin' on the Vega?"

Josh laughed, shook his head, and polished off his glass.

Eddie pushed. "'Cause I heard you ain't shit for fixin' things."

Josh stiffened and wrapped his knuckles on the bar for a whisky.

"Eddie, don't," Ruth said.

Eddie poured. "Ruth here told me you're a little light in those boots. Told me you need someone watchin' out for you."

"I didn't." Ruth shook her head.

Eddie stepped up to the bar between Ruth and Josh. "Told me you're a worthless prick with a dead dad."

Murderer.

Josh pounded the bar, and his whiskey jumped. He shoved his stool that slammed the floor next to customers who shook their heads and kept drinking. "I ain't nothin' like what she says. You'll find that out soon enough." Josh slapped Cal's shoulder, and both walked out of Frank's, beer and whiskey in hand.

"Eddie," said Ruth. "You can't—"

Eddie looked at Ruth.

Apologize.

"Shit."

Sorry.

The voice was right. What the fuck was he thinking? She owned this bar. It was hers. At least, for now. "Sorry, Ruth. I don't know why."

Ruth looked at Eddie. Her eyes watered, highlighting the green. "You lied."

"I know. I shouldn't have. Josh is just . . . Frank's is yours, Ruth." He nearly tripped on her name, but it was time to bring it home. Chicks dug stupid shit, even the old ones. He ran his fingers through his hair again and smiled like a teen flirting with a crush in one of those stupid ass romcoms: just a feather of a smile mixed with watery eyes he'd learned to lure when he needed to cut the shit and get on to fuckin'. Did she buy it? Ruth held Eddie's shoulder. He hated the touch, but she needed it, so he let it happen.

"It's okay, Eddie," she said. "You need a break. This place— There's a lot going on. Take out the trash. There's a bench out back. Take a few. I need you the rest of the night, though."

"Yeah, you're right," Eddie said.

Good.

Eddie tied up the trash and stopped in the hot kitchen. "There's orders that need fillin'," he said and pointed at the notes on the stove's hood.

Ruth nodded and said, "Fillin' . . ."

Fillin', why the hell was he talking like that? And she heard. Did it matter? Nah, hang with people, you start sounding like them. Eddie opened the screen door and headed outside.

Wood steps sagged under his feet. Out back, he slapped open a green dumpster's metal lids and chucked the trash. Bottles shattered with a shrill echo.

"You're out sooner than I thought. I thought that bitch'd be talkin' your ear off 'bout feelings and shit," said Josh who leaned against Frank's.

Cal laughed.

"Fuck you want?" said Eddie.

"Fuck you know?" Josh's half-fists trembled like nests holding hate, and a dance of kickin' ass tugged at his boots. His eyes were wide. And his brow was shredded. Eddie knew the look and had dealt with dumbasses like this before: Be as dumb as the shithead that wanted blood. "I know shit, man."

Josh's shoulders were limp and heaved as he did a one-two farmer's blow on the gravel to prove Eddie didn't mean shit, took one step, and like sandpaper on stone said, "One day. One. He got the keys."

"What're you talkin' about?" Eddie backed toward the door.

"Frank. You don't even. Ruth." His face seized into tights ropes slurring his words. "She forgets."

"Forgets what? I just work here for the cabin. Nothin' personal."

"You made it that in there." Josh stepped toward Eddie and raised a fist. "Frank's never been mine, and you take it. Take it on day one."

Eddie shook his head. Josh made little sense.

"I'm not takin', taking nothing."

Behind the dumpster, a—*the*—hunched shadow shifted. *No. Yours. Kill him.*

"No," Eddie said to the shadow.

Josh glanced over Eddie's shoulder, ran his knuckle under his nose, sniffed, and shook his head.

Do it.

"I can't," said Eddie through his teeth. "Not here. Not now."

Josh said something, but the voice came on stronger. *You will.*

Josh raised a fist, side-stepped, and brought his arm down in a broad arc. It was a wild punch. Eddie cocked his head to the side just enough, so Josh's knuckles swiped short of his jaw.

Kill.

"No. Josh, stop."

"Too late," Josh said as he swung again.

There was a white flash and a crack. Eddie's chin kissed his shoulder. He went down to his knees. Josh stepped forward, reeled his boot back, and kicked up blue granite with his heel before his toe struck Eddie's chin. Eddie fell, balled up on his side. The gravel on his face was sharp yet cool. Josh spun around Eddie and kicked his lower back. There was a spike of pain that melted to a dull ache.

Josh pulled his boot back, but Cal said, "Come on, man, stop. Kill 'im now, and the Old Man'll—"

"Yeah," Josh said and stopped mid-boot. Instead, with a long, hard snort, he pulled everything from the back of his throat and spat on Eddie's head. It was warm and thick and smelled of whiskey and fries as it soaked Eddie to the scalp. Their boots crunched on the gravel as they left Eddie behind.

The hunched horror was icy and close when it said, *Worthless.*

"No," said Eddie. He coughed, and blood ran over his teeth and into the gravel.

Weak, said the voice.

"I . . ." Eddie opened his eyes, yet just one obeyed. Only

cold, oily blackness was there. The pain surged, and he sobbed unrestrained in his loneliness.

Worthless.

"No." He choked on dust and tears. "Special."

The hunched horror laughed, said, *Prove it,* and melted into the dumpster's shadow.

Eddie rolled on his back. The stars above were made liquid by tears when he said, "Worthless," and tires crackled over gravel.

CHAPTER TEN

THE CABIN LIGHTS GLOWED, and Rhea squinted and squirmed. Her body ached. She looked at her wrist where there was no watch. One hadn't been there since she and Eddie paid for showers at a truck stop up in Canada months ago. Some gas station clerk probably looked at it now, counting the minutes to shift's end.

She stood, and her head surged toward a hangover throb. The stove was dark. However long she was out, it was enough to burn logs to embers and ash. She held her stomach made queasy by too little food and too much vodka. Rather than giving up the drunkenness, she stumbled into the kitchen, chewed down potato chips with three aspirin and chased them with foamy beer.

Their duffels were laid on the bed. She unzipped Eddie's and pulled out the road map. Back in the kitchen, she dug out a pencil and sat on—or rather chose, according to Ruth—the aluminum-framed chair that held its seventies, red and white vinyl sheen.

She smiled at the memory of Ruth and her hard,

welcoming hands. She'd had a life Rhea wanted: defiance and love in an age of conflict. The boy with the bullet in his face, the one who died—Rhea assumed in Vietnam—must have been someone to want and Ruth, gorgeous. Rhea shook her head. Ruth had pain too. She'd lost the boy and his baby, and Saint Andrew didn't seem to be a place that accepted choice. Or was it?

Her lips downturned and tight, she leaned on the table and closed her eyes. She'd talk with Ruth soon. An urgency had come to it now, as though Ruth wouldn't always be there to help Rhea, save her from her family, from . . . From what, her?

She opened her eyes. Her knuckles were white. She relaxed and ran her palms where someone had marred the table's creamy, gold-flecked surface with a hot pan's amber crescent. After unfolding the map, she flattened it on the aluminum-banded edge of the table and wiped off dried mud. "Jesus, Eddie, give it up," she said as she traced chevroned lines of his sneaker's soles that would remain until the map was frayed and forgotten. She pulled her curls and yanked them into a neon green scrunchie.

After a swig of beer, she scanned the map's saint-named towns, running her finger along a freeway. Eddie never took freeways, but it was a good place to start since it split the state. St. Paul stuck out, so she started there and moved west to St. Michael, St. Cloud, St. Wendel, St. Anna. Dozens of saint towns dotted the state. Finding the lake was impossible: There were thousands of blue blobs and gashes.

She pounded her fist. "God dammit, Eddie. Where the fuck are we?"

She downed a few chips with beer as she scanned south of the freeway then north, chewing and picking her nails as she went. When she reached Minnesota's stovepipe, there were three empty beer cans and a fourth cracked open but no Saint Andrew.

The forest lit up when headlights bounced through a thin fog. Blood surged through Rhea's veins as her heart beat hard. She stood, shut off the lights, and locked the door. She didn't have time to close the windows before a truck scraped past pine and stopped. She ducked and strained to look out the window. The driver-side door groaned, and the driver's boots snapped twigs. In the truck's sickly yellow light, Chief Amos put on his cattleman hat. Rhea sighed and slid to the floor.

"Rhea," Amos said. "You there?"

"Yeah, I'm here."

"It's okay, hon'," said Amos.

Rhea shook her head. No one could just call her Rhea.

"I've got Eddie," Amos said. "He's hurt."

Rhea's heart surged. She unlocked the door and ran out barefoot to the truck. The rocks sparked pain, but she didn't stop. "What happened?"

"Dunno. Fight he lost, I guess," said Amos as he helped Eddie from the truck.

"Lost." It wasn't a question, but Amos took it as such.

"Yeah, bad, but not too bad."

Rhea had seen Eddie in worse shape: black eye, swollen cheek, and he held his lower back and flinched when he breathed.

"He don't feel like telling me what happened, so I'll just leave him to you," said Amos.

"Sorry," said Eddie. "No break for me." He shrugged and sucked in air through his teeth.

"Eddie, what—" said Rhea.

Eddie shook his head. "I'll tell ya later, hon'. Let's get inside." Eddie slumped to the ground, and Amos caught him.

Rhea swung Eddie's arm over her shoulder, looked at Amos, and said, "Thank you, Chief. I'll take care of him."

Amos nodded. Rhea stumbled to the cabin, but stopped when Amos said, "I'm not sure I like you two bein' out here without anythin' but your feet to get you out. I got a boat." Rhea turned with Eddie and looked at Amos. Amos continued, "I'll bring it in the morning."

"Thanks," said Rhea. Eddie nodded. "We owe you for the food." Amos just tipped his hat and got into his truck. His tail-lights blurred to red cotton in the fog.

"God dammit, Eddie. What'd you do?"

Eddie just shook his head, and Rhea brought him into the cabin and laid him on the couch. He kicked his feet up on the couch's arm, and Rhea put a pillow under his head. She took off his shoes and tossed them by the door. She went to the kitchen, packed ice in a towel, cracked open another beer, and gave both to Eddie.

"Who did this to you?"

"Josh." Eddie iced his eye.

"What'd you do?"

"Nothin'. Just takin' out the trash, and he sucker-punched me."

"You must have said something, Eddie. I know you. You pushed him too far, said something."

"Nah, not really, just somethin' about his dad and fixin' the Vega." Eddie shrugged.

"His dad?"

"Turns out he's dead."

"Yeah, I knew that. How'd you—"

"In the tow truck, on the way to the Vega. He told me."

Rhea sighed and shook her head. "Eddie, we gotta get along with these people. They've done nothing but help. There was a girl . . ." She stopped. Where Didi had stood, the puddle remained.

She tossed a towel over the puddle and looked at the map as she grabbed her beer. "I don't get it, Eddie. Where are we?"

"Whadda ya mean?"

"Where the fuck are we, really?"

"Saint Andrew, really."

"You're an ass. On this map"—she thumped the map with her finger—"where are we? I can't find the lake or the town."

"I don't know. I-I haven't looked at that map for days. I just drove."

"You said you knew."

"I did. Until we got here."

"What town did we pass before Saint Andrew?"

"I don't know, another saint somethin'."

"Why are you talking like that?"

"Like what?"

"Like you live here. Like you're one of them. You've been talking like that since you got back."

Eddie leaned on an elbow and cocked his head. "Sorry, I just spent the day crammed in that bar with stinking fishermen, that shitfaced Josh and Cal, and Ruth. Then I got my ass kicked. It tends to grow on you."

"I'm sorry," Rhea said. "I didn't mean to make anything of it. You want to take the day off tomorrow?"

"What? No. Ruth wants you there in the morning though. I'll work nights."

"Jesus, we can't work the same shift?"

"Nah. You cover days, and I'll take nights. Ruth'll be in and out during the day since it ain't busy, she said, but she'll cover nights with me to keep an eye on things, Josh included."

"I guess. Yeah, that makes sense. I just hoped this place would be different, that we'd have more time together."

"We can. We've got time right now." He slid one foot from

the couch and set it on the floor and patted the couch between his legs. Rhea sat. Eddie said, "I don't feel all that bad. Really. I've had worse."

"Yeah, I remember."

Eddie's eyes lit up. "And I was thinking. Maybe we should stay."

"Eddie, isn't it a little—"

"Just listen. Think about it. Ruth's old, like she's gotta be five hundred pushin' a thousand," Eddie said.

Rhea smiled and looked at the floor where her empty glass still lay.

"My point is, she's old, and the way I ran that bar, we could buy it or be partners or somethin'. You shoulda seen those fishermen. They drank like what they were catchin', and the bills rolled in."

"What about Josh?"

"Fuck Josh. He's a loser with a dead dad. Hell, I don't even know if he has a mom."

"He does." Rhea wished she hadn't said it as softly as she had.

"You shittin' me. You think he's worth somethin'?"

He knew. He always knew but only let on when it was convenient. "No. I . . . He just . . . I don't know. After what he did to you." Rhea touched his bruises.

"Yeah, that's right. He's worthless. A sack of shit. Just like his toady, Cal. He just stood there and watched like some foot freak."

"Eddie."

"I don't know why we're talkin' 'bout those two anyway. The bar, Rhea. Frank's."

"Yeah?"

"What do you think? My plan?"

"We need time, Eddie. We've been here not even a day. It feels like forever, but it's only been short of a day."

Eddie's nostrils flared, and his eyes became hollow like when he first entered the cabin. He nodded then grew limp and breathed, erasing the vacant eyes. He was Eddie again. The Eddie she loved and held in the Vega. "You're right, Rhea. We need to give it time."

She looked across the lake at the Manor. Mist clung to the placid lake. Out there Ruth was serving people. And Didi, well, Didi was out there, too, somewhere. Waiting to be found or to find. Eddie hadn't taken his eyes from her. And in his eyes was hope. She massaged his thigh. "I don't know, Eddie. It's simple here. You may be right. We'll see. Can they find us here?"

"Who?"

"You know. Your dad. Your mom. Anyone. Cops," said Rhea.

"I don't know. Maybe not. Amos said he put in a records request, but they had nothin' on me. I don't know how, but they don't. Said they might get back to him. A longshot, though. Could be my dad coverin'. Covering."

"You remember the last town we went through before Saint Andrew?"

Eddie gave a half smile, shrugged, and said, "Sorry, no. There were a bunch of saints. Then there was this town, the sign with the cat, and the Vega breaking down."

"Cat?"

"You weren't awake. There was a tabby nailed to the town sign, dead."

Rhea stopped stroking Eddie's thigh. "What the fuck. You didn't think to . . ." The cat didn't matter. It could wait. She needed to know where they were. "Eddie, this place isn't on our map."

Eddie shrugged. "Old map."

"No, we bought it in Washington."

Eddie shrugged again. "Small town."

"Maybe. There're others about the same size."

"Does it matter?"

"Not really, I guess."

"It's better that it's not on the map, right? Not on the map means they can't find us." Eddie sat up.

"I suppose. It's just odd."

He wrapped his arms around Rhea and pulled her close. His cheek had become rough with stubble, yet his eyes were as soft as the day he took her from that balcony and had taken on the blue of the landing's granite. His breath was warm and painted with scotch when they kissed long and light. He leaned back and pulled her down with him. On her thigh, she could feel him grow hard.

She stopped and said, "Wait here." In the bedroom, she took off her sweats and hoodie. She looked in the mirror, pulled out the scrunchie, flounced her hair over her shoulders and pulled a curl over her forehead. The babydoll gown clung to her breasts and hips.

He smiled as she pulled him into the bedroom.

After, drunk and tired, she dreamed of Didi—her voice echoing across the lake—then woke to the morning sun. Lifting Eddie's arm, she slid out of bed, stuffed her gown into her duffel, and tossed on her sweats and hoodie. She dumped grounds and water into the Mr. Coffee and snapped the switch that glowed red then stoked the boiler. She fried eggs, bacon, and toast in a cast iron skillet the size of a truck's hubcap, poured coffee, and washed down a double dose of aspirin. At the end of the dock, she dipped her feet in the water and finished her breakfast.

The sun blazed clouds in red and orange but had yet to crest the trees steeping the Manor in shadow. A loon skidded on its belly in the water and called out forlorn yodels near Al, who slowly reeled in his bobber. Next to the dock, Amos backed up his Bronco and pushed a boat from its trailer. He tied the boat to the dock and parked his truck next to the ballroom. The boat's motor coughed to life, and Amos tipped his hat to Al then chugged toward Rhea. She finished her breakfast before Amos drifted next to the dock, threw her a line, and cut the motor.

"Mornin', Rhea," Amos said. At least he'd called her Rhea. "This boat's yours until it ain't. Have a good night?"

"Yeah, thanks," Rhea said. "Other than, you know."

Amos nodded and pulled himself from the boat with an old-man grunt that seemed too emphatic given the size of his arms.

"It's peaceful here," she said.

"Yeah, mostly. You have any trouble last night?" He looked side long at Rhea. "Any visitors?"

"No trouble. Eddie's fine."

"I figured he'd be all right. Visitors?"

"No. Well, a woman." Rhea shrugged. She wanted to see her again, Didi. There was an honesty. Maybe not honesty. Maybe a directness few in this town had. Like Amos. He didn't look at her, didn't turn toward her. Rather, she was a spirit next to him he felt obligated to speak to. "Didi," she said.

Amos ran loose knuckles over his beard. "Did she now?"

Rhea grabbed his sleeved forearm and turned him toward her. She looked in his eyes that were a sickly green. He squinted and pulled his arm from her grasp, but Rhea was tired. "Why don't people just give straight answers here? No one talks."

"Meanin'?"

Rhea sighed and looked through the dock's boards where the lake's water grew restless then at Amos's ragged boots. "Where is this place, Amos?"

"Meanin'?"

"Jesus." Rhea laughed. "I looked at the map. It's new, the map. I can't find Saint Andrew anywhere, and Eddie doesn't know a thing."

Amos stuffed his hands in his pockets, shrugged, and said, "Well, hon', some places just ain't on maps."

There it was again: hon'. She looked up at Amos. "Meaning?"

Amos scratched his chest and flung his other hand as if presenting Saint Andrew to a gameshow contestant. "Some places get lost. The Saint is one of those places."

"Meaning?" She stamped her bare heel into the dock's wet boards.

"Everyone comes here on their own. Meanin' alone." He dug into his shirt pocket, took out a soft pack of Camels, and lit up with a match. He offered Rhea a smoke. She waved him off.

"I've got Eddie," she said.

"Do you?"

"Well, yeah, he's in the cabin, right now." Rhea gritted her teeth. Amos was frustrating. He never tensed and spoke with a lazy mouth, slurred through cigarettes or indifference.

"But do you have him?"

She looked at her cabin. "I don't know."

"That means you don't. You're alone, Rhea. And you're here, which means you need somethin' like the rest of us. You know what you need?"

"Need?"

"You asking that means you don't know what you need. You gotta find it."

"Why?"

"You wanna stay?"

"Stay?" asked Rhea.

"Saint Andrew."

"No. I don't know. We were thinking—"

"No, I doubt Eddie was doing much of that. You were thinkin'. You need to do a bit more of that. Maybe find someone that'll help."

"You?"

Amos laughed and shook his head. "I doubt it."

"Didi? Ruth?"

"Maybe. Be careful around Didi. She's always workin' somethin' one way or another. And take care choosin' who you trust."

Everyone said as much: take care, make a choice. "Meanin'?" Rhea asked with a deliberate twist of Saint Andrew and smiled.

"Meanin'"—Amos smiled—"there ain't a single person out there who ain't got some selfish in them. They all need somethin', and they'll take it where they can. You just need to know which selfish you're willin' to accept."

She looked up. Amos was large, powerful, yet age had settled in, softened the edges, unlike her father. It was a presence that cut through the cold; there was no fear, no danger, only peace. And yet, there was a patina of sadness, of emptiness, of loss. Rhea knew its shade. She touched his bearded cheek. Amos pulled away, pursed his lips, and flicked his cigarette in the lake.

"Come on. 'Nough of this bullshit. Gimme a ride back to my truck?" Amos nudged her toward the boat.

"I've never driven a boat. Boated?"

"I'll teach you. Show you around a bit." Amos held the boat, and Rhea climbed in. "Maybe get some of that thinkin' done."

CHAPTER ELEVEN

EDDIE AWOKE to coffee too long on the burner. He pulled on his boxers, poured a mug, and sat on the porch swing where the screens sagged like thick-lipped smiles. Rhea and Amos stood on the end of the dock next to a flat-bottomed boat suited for the murky waters of a Vietnam river. Amos held Rhea's shoulder. She said something and shook her head. Amos, still touching her shoulder—her fucking shoulder—turned Rhea toward him and spoke. His voice was a mere thread, a base string's electric hum through an overworked amp. She touched his cheek then got into the boat with that bastard. Eddie turned away.

Watch him.

The voice washed over his shoulder. He nodded. The horror hadn't left. There was hope. Eddie's eyes twitched. With a few tugs, the boat's motor growled and whined when Amos goosed the gas. Eddie followed the two as they headed south. He wanted the distant shore to be swallowed in flame and sallow smoke, see their boat lit with rifle fire. He wanted an end. Hateful, his shoulders trembled.

Watch her.

Eddie sipped coffee and watched the show. Amos strained the motor and said something as he pointed to the south with a thick finger. Rhea turned toward Amos and nodded then looked back over the boat's bow where she clenched the rails. She held her head high, her chin thrust into the wind that bucked her hair as Amos picked up speed.

"Happy," said Eddie.

Amos.

Eddie shook his head and clenched his mug. As if pulling a file from her inventory of the unforgettable, Rhea opened her mouth and heaved her shoulders, but her laugh was drowned by the motor and boat skipping over the water. She knew he was watching. She must. She was with Amos because he wasn't him, wasn't Eddie.

Unwanted. Worthless.

No, she was with Amos because Eddie didn't say sorry, because he'd broken the Vega's window crank, because he'd hid the map, because he'd left her in Anza-Borrego. That bitch.

Murderer.

"Jesus, she'll tell him. He'll figure it out. Take away Saint Andrew." Coffee burned his tongue and throat then settled in his stomach where bitterness churned. Amos and Rhea continued south and into the cover of reeds and trees.

Back in the cabin, Eddie topped his mug off with vodka and sat at the table. His stomach churned. His legs shook. She was out there, somewhere, with him. He tapped his finger where Lake Andrew should be, in the heart of Minnesota near snaking rivers, yet it was not there. He penciled in what should have been the lake's shore and where Rhea and Amos ducked into a cove.

Like a fresh IV, Eddie's blood froze and was replaced with

hate, an anger fed to him from the outside, from the hunched horror, that pushed. She was probably there, now, laughing with him, talking about some stupid shit that lured her into his arms. That old fuck. Worthless prick. Rhea's laugh echoed, and Eddie drove his fist into the table.

Saul.

Eddie downed the entire mug and said, "He knows." In the bedroom, he dumped his duffel on the floor. His army surplus boots topped the pile. He tugged on black jeans and boots. The tongues lashed out, the laces noose-knotted around the necks. He pulled over a black T-shirt he'd oil-painted with white letters, *Sisters*, and dragged a wet comb through his blond-rooted black hair. He tossed the vodka and a few beers into his duffel, slung it over his shoulder, cracked open a fresh beer, and headed into town.

All the way, Amos's boat motor ground its teeth in Lake Andrew as Eddie dragged his boots in the gravel. No trucks passed, but Al was at the dock's end where Amos's truck waited. He sat in an aluminum lawn chair as his red and white bobber twitched. Rhea and Amos were a distant stock of green crowned with red floating through the cove.

Josh's shop was quiet. The tow truck leered at the Vega around the corner of the garage. Like a fat Eastwood, Owen leaned against a post that held up The Store's awning, nodded at Eddie, and flicked a finger at the brim of a ten-gallon that wasn't there. Eddie grinned and dipped his head.

Ruth was there, too, up on her balcony with the French door open behind her, lording over the town in her blue hoodie and mug of coffee, her hair tamed by a bandana. With a cigarette pinched between knuckles, she waved and said, "Where ya headed, Eddie?" Her voice echoed off The Store.

"Just a walk," said Eddie. "Takin' in the town."

"Four at Frank's?"

"Yep."

"Rhea comin'?"

"Yep." Eddie flicked a two-fingered salute and crossed the highway where he shuffled down the sidewalk until the French door clacked shut. He looked back to make sure she'd gone inside then stopped at the Virgin Mary garbed in crackled blue. Flakes of lichen danced on her stone-frozen lips like a fire's ashes. Her bare feet were worn to concrete stumps that melted into the sign that read *Immaculate Conception Church*.

"Jesus Christ," Eddie said with a lazy exhale. "What the fuck am I doin'?" He shook his head. "Doing," he said, forcing the word from his mouth without the Midwestern laziness. Or was it defiance? A refusal to speak as taught to prove independence.

Remember.

Eddie shook his head and held the base of his skull where a cold, black pain wormed its way down his spine, splayed ribs, and burned lungs. Eddie gasped and dragged his nails over his T-shirt, biting skin.

Amos.

Rhea on the dock. Her hand. Amos's hand. Their touch. Her laugh. His lip twitched. "Amos." Eddie's hate was violence. Its hate was ancient.

Saul.

"Saul."

Now.

Eddie headed up the steps to the smoked glass doors etched with white crucifixes.

Go.

The handles were bent bars of brushed aluminum: flat, hard-edged, and cold. The hinges were silent. Inside, a woven

carpet of red framed in gold-covered fleshy asbestos tiles. Two
ropes, thick as a child's wrist, fed to the belfry through brass
gromets and the tin-tiled ceiling. The rope on the right smelled
of wet earth and was candy-striped red with blood. Paneled
doors, stained a thick yellow, swung on saloon hinges and
echoed like hammers as they swung shut. The musty, hymnal-
scented nave was lined with oak pews, and stained glass kalei-
doscoped the morning sun through incense smoke.

He sat in the second pew from the altar then slid onto the
bare wood kneeler. He lit up after a pull of vodka and set the
bottle on the pew in front of him. The glass's tap cut through
the quiet.

The dais where the altar rest was brass-tacked with gray
carpet. Behind the altar was a crenelated shrine that rose three
stories to the arched ceiling where a giant, white Jesus spread
his arms. On his chest was a flaming heart surrounded by
thorns. A spear pierced the heart's center, and blood gushed
from the wound, frozen in a failed art major's clumsy strokes.
From alcoves and pedestals, plaster saints grinned. Eddie
smiled back and took another slug of vodka.

"Startin' early," a voice graveled through the church.

Eddie took his eyes from a bearded statue of another white
guy this time holding a shepherd's crook and lamb. Saul stood
in an alcove behind the shrine and moved to the altar where a
Bible wider than his shoulders and thicker than a loaf of bread
rested. He scratched his throat cinched tight behind his clerical
collar.

Eddie shrugged and said, "Early? Time don't matter."

"Too true here."

"Your neck?"

"I'll get to that. First"—Saul knuckled his veined nose—
"I've got a few more questions."

Eddie shook his head. "Jesus Christ."

"You know he ain't got nothin' to do with this place." Lazy contempt soaked Saul's voice. The loose skin under his chin hardly moved, as though rigor had already begun. He sat in the pew in front of Eddie. "Least not what I've seen."

Eddie looked at Saul whose eyes bulged beyond ragged lids. "Who does? And what've you seen?"

"This is my house. Me first." He took a swig of vodka, tapped out a smoke, and lit up with a strong pull that blazed with a campfire crackle. "You murdered."

Eddie shrugged. He'd play the priest's game, give him control. It's what Josh needed, and it's what Saul needed. Hell, it's probably what everyone needed. "Yeah, I murdered. What of it?"

"Not only are you a murderer, you murdered Rhea's sister. Her mom. Her dad. Why?"

Eddie leaned back into the bench and said, "I already told you." The blood streaks on his palm deepened by the stained glass of a saint's red robes.

"No, no you didn't. You fed a line 'bout her old man," said Saul.

There it was again. Eddie clenched his fist. "Old Man, who—"

"Son, not yet. A line 'bout her dad."

Eddie shook his head and breathed, yet a seed of anger festered under his chest. "He used. Abused. Rhea told me everything."

"Word's loaded, son. Like your anger."

"*Abused?*" Eddie waved for the bottle.

"No, *everythin'*," said Saul as he passed the bottle to Eddie. "There ain't no such thing. All've got secrets. Rhea's got hers."

"And you know this because you're, what? A priest? Some

servant of your god? Divinity?" Eddie swept his hand that held the smoke. "Because you have this house?"

Saul shook his head and took a drag. "Listen to the sob stories comin' from behind screens like I have and you'll know no honesty."

"*No*'s a loaded word."

Saul laughed. "Let's just say, I ain't met a soul that ain't kept secrets. You got yours. You're here. Why?"

Eddie drank. "My car—"

"No shit, son. Why, really?"

"I can't. It's stupid."

No. Amos.

Eddie shook his head. The voice was strong, and his mouth moved with the steadiness of a doctor's scalpel when he said, "Amos." Eddie held his jaw. "He took Rhea."

"Did he now?" Saul looked over Eddie's shoulder.

Eddie turned too. There, on a balcony, an organ and raised platform remained empty.

Saul said, "Bothers you, eh?"

Amos on the dock. Rhea next to him. The sun cast their shadows long. "He held her. Touched her." Amos's shadow melted into Rhea. "On the dock. They're in Amos's boat now. They'll be in the cove, laughing, talking—loving."

Saul took a drag and cackled out the smoke. "Son, you're dumb. Ain't no way Amos is gonna horn in on your girl. Besides, she don't know what you done, right? But she'll blab enough. And then he'll figure somethin's off. Amos's got his ways."

Eddie reached down and clenched the bottle's neck. Dumb. He'd show Saul dumb. His hands shook with rage, and long ashes sagged and fell to the pew.

Saul said, "She's tasty, tempting."

Eddie dropped the bottle and reached for Saul. "You old fuck. I'll kill you!"

Saul stood and held out his hands. A grin cracked his cheeks. His milky eyes flared like he'd just made a soul-damning deal. "Whoa, now. You got a hot trigger. Look at me, you think I got any interest? What I mean is, this town'd love her. She ain't done nothin'. Least nothin' I know of." He took a drag from his smoke. "She done anything?"

"Nothin' I didn't get her into."

Saul paused then raised his eyes. "Kill anyone?"

"Rhea? Never."

"You took her to that park, Hans-oh—"

"Anzo-Borego."

"That's the one. She came back. Her family was dead."

"That's right," said Eddie.

"She thinks she left and her family died. That's selfish. In her eyes, that is, guilty. Those are the best ones. Innocents got tasty souls. This place'd love her."

Eddie took a drag from his smoke, tossed the butt on the tiled floor, and stamped it out under the kneeler. He'd see this through. "Okay, why?" He took a swig.

"Pain," Saul said as though that answered all.

"Pain." Eddie shook his head. "She dealt, muled. Those drugs killed, maybe."

"Ain't much worse than something that can't be proved, but what's known to be so. You feel anythin'?"

"For?"

Saul shook his head. His lips sagged. Pity dripped from each word. "This place don't want you."

"What?" A surge of envy pillared inside Eddie.

"This place takes a certain sort. I'm sorry, son, but you ain't it. And here I thought you were special." Saul slid that last word out like an axe on a grindstone and looked up. The stained glass watercolored his face. "That's all right. Maybe Rhea can—"

Eddie's chest ached. "I want this place."

Saul laughed through his nose and shrugged. "This place don't want you."

"This is bullshit." Eddie held the back of his neck and shivered. "Places don't want." He held his eyes on the base of the pew where it was bolted into the tile floor. There, years of wax had layered into an amber case that suspended dust and dirt.

"You, like others before," Saul said, "know more than what you're lettin' on. There's somethin' in that head of yours you won't let out."

"I'd—"

"Don't bullshit me, son."

Eddie looked at Saul. "You're an ass."

"You aren't? But you miss my point. Rhea's a person. You're . . . Well, if you don't feel nothin', you're already lost. This place don't need the lost. It needs the one who needs findin', and it don't let the findin' ever happen. It only gives a chance then snatches it up, rips it away. Unless . . ." Saul took the bottle and swigged vodka. The bottle sloshed, half-full.

"Unless what?"

"You lost yourself," Saul said as he stabbed a bent finger at Eddie. "I can help you get yourself back." He held that same finger up. "You just need to do one thing."

"That is?"

"Take my life."

"What?"

"Take my life." He pointed at his chest where it pressed into the fabric of his black clerical shirt. "Son, I've been here longer than most. This church's been mine since it opened."

"That's impossible. This place is—"

"You don't know. But you will." Saul thumbed over his

shoulder at the shrine filled with plaster saints and a gold crucifix only the rich could afford, all canopied by the giant Jesus and said, "He, well, they won't take my soul. I've tried." He unbuttoned his clerical collar behind his neck and yanked it free. It was soaked with blood. His neck was hatched and bruised. Under his ears, the white skin was burned free and piled up like a child's piss-soaked sheets. Slick muscle and tendons quivered. "I can't leave. I've tried. Many times." His eyes twitched with memories hidden to Eddie. "But it has always been for myself. If I die for you, for your sins, by your hand, maybe I can leave, and you'll become what this town wants."

The blood on the bell's rope. Saul's neck. Eddie shook his head. There were no words. Yesterday, he was on the road with Rhea. He'd expected to spend another night in the Vega, curled up with her, sure that she'd be there the next morning, with him, not knowing what he'd done. Now, with Amos and Saul, everything was uncertain. Beyond that, this old bastard was telling him—

Trust.

"No," Eddie said. He took the bottle from Saul and downed the last quarter then whipped it at the altar like a German grenade where it shattered, splintering the Last Supper embossing, marring its white paint and gold leaf. "You're a fool. And this. This church. Your stories. Are all shit. I don't need"—he held his palms above his head as if wrenching the shadow from his skull—"this."

Saul's lips quivered purple, loose, and wet. "Then leave. Try. Run. Run away and see. If the Saint wants you, you won't get much past the town sign. If it don't give a shit, well, then you're worthless." He took a drag from his cigarette that had burned nearly to ash and stood next to a stoup of holy water. Saul's cheeks sunk into black ruts and sinew. "Then go back to

Rhea." He stabbed his cigarette into the water, killing the hot cherry. "See how your dear Rhea is doing, murderer."

Eddie turned and left. His boots hit the tiles hard like wood posts driven into wet sand. Outside, beyond the frosted glass doors, birds flew as the sun drizzled through budding branches. At the highway, he looked south toward the road that led to Amos's office then north to what he knew—the sign that greeted him—and walked on.

CHAPTER TWELVE

RHEA AND AMOS curled east then south along the shore where cabins rested. "Rhea," said Amos just over the boat's motor. Rhea turned. He'd tucked his cattleman hat beneath his bench. His hair was combed into rough furrows like flames in the morning sun. "Rhea," he said softer as he eased on the motor.

He must've seen something in that moment, something hidden to Rhea because of who she was. She couldn't tell, but there was something there. Some lost moment that may have been one of the answers she may have been looking for.

"Hold on. I'm gonna goose it."

Rhea nodded and held onto the rails. Amos hit the gas, and the bow rose out of the water. The wind like cold fingers cut through her hair and clothes.

Amos brought the boat through a channel to a shallow cove where the water was unsullied by wind. Amos cut the engine. Waves like harp strings thrummed across the shallow waters as the boat drifted. Rhea peered over the edge. The lake was clear to the bottom where leafy stalks slow danced with fish.

"If only ole Al had a boat," said Amos.

His voice, usually lazy and slurred, had taken on confidence, a clarity, as though the lake had washed away whatever held him back on land. Rhea looked at Amos who was also looking over the edge at the fish below.

"He lost his son," said Rhea. She didn't know why, but it seemed right. There were times where that sense of rightness shouldn't be ignored, and maybe this was one of those moments.

Amos's head tilted down just a bit more, and he closed his eyes.

"Amos?"

"Yeah." He paused.

"I'm sorry. I didn't—"

"No, it's all right. There's just . . . His son was just playing."

"Playing?"

"Inside the grain bin. He must've broke through a top crust and got buried. It goes quick, I'm told. Kid couldn't scream. Al came along and turned on the auger. The grain came out bloody."

"I'm so sorry. I don't know why I brought it up."

"It's okay, Rhea. There's just some things." Amos turned toward the Manor. "That's why Al's here, why he won't—can't —leave."

"Eddie's thinking about staying."

"And this place'll keep you."

"I know what you mean."

"No, not yet you don't. I usually let others figure that out on their own. It's best that way."

"You're like talking to a crossword puzzle."

"I'm sorry, Rhea." He shook his head, still looking at the Manor. "I've gotten my nose in too many things over the years, and I've learned to stay out. At least until the time's right. Best, that way, I suppose."

Rhea shook her head. "Well, I've never had someone like that."

Amos laughed and turned toward Rhea. He had a smile that bordered more on a smirk. "Like what? Someone too lazy to give a damn?"

Rhea smiled. "No, someone who let me be me. Someone who let me choose, who trusted me."

"Rhea, this ain't trust. This is me knowing you need to do your own thing, that that's the only way you'll solve whatever it is that's eating you."

"Nothing's eating me, Amos."

Amos shook his head, slowly, like he was sawing the air with determination. "No, you've got something. Everyone does. You just need to know what that is and rid yourself of it. No, that's wrong. Not rid." He ran his calloused palm over his beard and mouth. "Well, let's just say you need to recogni—to reckon."

Rhea nodded, *reckon*. "Eddie," she said.

"Don't be so sure he's the answer."

"Could you talk to him?"

"He don't want me, Rhea. He's gonna take another route, and neither you nor me got any say in that. In fact, it might be best to just leave him be for a bit."

"I don't think I can do that. Not yet."

"Well, like everything, that's up to you." Amos shrugged then his eyes became vibrant. The sick had been washed away as if he'd pulled himself from a cave filled with fear. He turned toward Saint Andrew where the steeple peeked above the trees. "Look, there's somethin' you oughta know."

Rhea looked up at Amos. "Which selfish am I dealing with?

You need something or are you taking?" Rhea smiled. "Or could you be telling it to me straight?"

"The last bit, as best I can without gettin' in trouble. But part of me is startin' to not give a damn."

"Trouble?"

Amos sighed. "I hope you never learn its meanin' here. That's why I can't tell you just yet. And what you oughta know might keep you from that trouble. People gettin' stuck here is personal. And whatever it is, goes deep. Some got a lot of hate or anger. Some been lost and lonely. But most get stuck here out of guilt."

"Guilt?"

A light wind picked up and shook the boat on small waves.

"Yeah."

"Then just forget."

"Can you?"

Could she? Could she forget her family? Her guilt? She shook her head. It was never that easy. "No."

"There's your answer. You know more than you give credit. Now you just need to find the power to overcome whatever you think you done. My guess, the way you been thinkin' just now, it's guilt."

Think she'd done? What had Rhea done? Her dad. Her mom. Her sister. Who knew how many others. She didn't deserve a life free of guilt. Did anyone? She had never let her sister be free. Or she had never let herself be free of her sister. Even dead, Rhea needed her. Her dad could rot. Her mom? Rhea wasn't so sure. Had she done those things that led to her death? She hadn't before. Or had she? Had others died because of her? She always told herself, *no*. But liars lie.

God. Was she the liar? She had lied all that time running drugs. She was just as bad as her mom. Her dad was worse, but she had bits of him in her too. But because of her, her sister was dead. There was no letting go of that. That'd be wrong. No one should let go of that.

"What's your guilt?" she asked.

"Now ain't that a question."

"I'm sorry."

"Nah, don't be. More should be direct. Save us all a lot of time. Let's just say, I'm here because of what I didn't do."

"Which was?"

"Somethin' I don't want to talk about. Know this though, Rhea: You're a good person."

"I don't know about that," Rhea said. "I've done things that—"

"That don't matter. Everyone's done things. But here's the part that might piss you off." Amos held her shoulder as if protecting a child from the dock's edge and the deep water. "I got a bad feelin' about Eddie. Somethin' ain't right."

Rhea shrugged off Amos's touch. Her forehead tensed. "I've known Eddie for a long—"

"I know. I called it. You're pissed. It's just . . . He's too much like Josh's dad. He ever hurt you?"

Rhea shook her head slowly. She was back in school: counselors shaking their heads, her mom crying, and Rhea just being Rhea. "No. We've fought, sure, but just arguing. No hitting."

"I ask, Rhea, 'cause I can't let another get hurt like that. And, Rhea, I know I said I wouldn't get mixed in things and point fingers like a man in charge, but can you do somethin' for me?"

"Me?" She let a smile touch her lips. "Yes."

"Leave."

The smile disappeared. "What?"

"I don't mean to get rid of you. Not in that way. If this place wasn't what it was, I'd never ask you this. But I need you to try.

Just walk outta here. And if you get past that sign, keep walkin' and never come back."

"Alone?"

Amos nodded. "It's best that way."

"Why?"

"Someone like you don't deserve to be stuck here. I can't let you go through that."

"Let me. Let me? Jesus, can't people just let me be?"

"I'm sorry. That came out wrong. Not let you. There's just too much pain here, Rhea. And for me to just sit back and see another go through what goes on here . . . Well, maybe this is my selfish, but I can't take seein' more people suffer."

"Suffer," Rhea said. The wind settled, and below minnows sprinted from larger fish. Rhea whispered, "If I can leave, what will I find?"

"A future that's yours and no other's."

"Amos, what is this place?"

"Hell, Rhea, I can't . . ." He shook his head and scratched his beard. "You fish?"

"What?"

"You been fishin'?"

Rhea crinkled her brow. "Nah, no."

"I'll tell Owen to give you a pole, bait, and a bucket. If you want."

"Sure?"

"Best time's in the morning and dusk. Best spot's here. Just drag your lure above the weeds. Let's trade spots." Amos patted the bench he sat on next to the motor.

"Me? Now?"

"Yep, I brought you back here 'cause it's safer. Water's clear, shallow. You'll be fine if you take a dive." He jabbed his thumb toward the water. "Besides, I'm feelin' generous with words."

Amos held the sides of the boat as he and Rhea stumbled toward opposite ends. Old trees, earth, and coffee was what Amos seemed to be made from. It was in his uniform, on his breath, in his eyes as he gave her an awkward nod when they met at the center of the boat. There was no hate, no violence in those eyes faded green like leaves struggling against what fall would force them to become. Rhea let the moment pass and sat on the bench in front of the motor.

"It's in neutral. Give the cord a tug. It's warmed up, should start easy," said Amos as he gave the motor a lazy wave as if dealing cards to an old friend. Rhea grabbed the cord and tugged. The motor coughed but didn't fire up. "Get into it. Don't be afraid. Yank it like you're elbowing an ass on the dance floor." Rhea leaned against the motor's blue casing and smacked the groper's stomach with her elbow. The motor kicked up and sputtered with plumes of blue smoke. "Good," said Amos. "Now, test the gas. When you're ready, shove off."

Amos sat backward in the boat, watching Rhea on the bench. She twisted the throttle a few times then geared into forward. The boat jumped, setting her off balance. "Ease into it," Amos said. "Pushin' right makes the boat go left. Opposite's true for the other way."

Rhea figure-eighted the cove and brought the bow to bear on the channel.

"All right," said Amos. "You know the west shore: cabins and swamp. North shore's got Al and the ballroom. East shore got the Manor and islands. Let's head there first then east to where I dropped a dock a few years back."

Rhea resisted giving the boat what-for. After plodding along a few hundred feet, Amos sat on the boat's floor and kicked his heels up on the rails.

"You're confident," Rhea said. "I won't tip this thing?"

Amos shrugged. "Head over to the Manor."

Rhea did as she was told and skirted the Manor's island. East of the island was another swamp or bog clotted with cattails and muddy mounds sprouting thin grass like baby hair. "That always been there?"

"Yes and no. Place flooded a while back. May not have been a swamp before my time or maybe it was." He shrugged. "Don't much care either way. The Manor's not a place I want to go."

Rhea slowed the boat until the motor popped and idled just enough to keep the boat moving. Exhaust passed the boat in slow tendrils. South of the Manor was a clearing where one tree stood with a thick trunk and sagging branches. Other trees huddled around it like priests at a black mass. "Anyone live there?" Rhea asked, and Amos shook his head. "Who owned it?"

"The Old Man. Don't know his name."

"Can it be, I don't know, rebuilt?"

"Who'd want to?"

"It looks like something from the South, deep South."

Amos looked up from his boots and said, "That ain't far from the truth. Near as I can tell, it was put up around the Civil War. Built on top of some fur trader's camp and a cave."

Rhea brought the boat around, just off the west shore by a dozen feet or so. The wind picked up, and she throttled up but kept a slow pace.

The Manor slumped over the rocky shore yet was lordly at this distance, crowned with steep dormers that framed thin windows hiding the attic beyond. The balcony sagged between thick fluted columns that still showed flakes of once-white paint. French doors led into the ground and second stories. Floor-to-ceiling windows remained intact. Not a single shard of glass had been made by vandal's rocks. Burrowed in the stacked granite foundation, squat windows had yellowed and muddied concealing the basement. Dormant vines laced over clapboard siding, and gray granite chimneys cut rough yet morticed with precision.

"A place like this would've been home to the homeless where I lived," Rhea said with wide eyes.

"Most stay away, Rhea. Keep that in mind. Head up around the bend. Keep to the Manor's shore."

Rhea steered the boat as Amos said. The water between the Manor and the island of the white tree was deep and black.

"This place is so . . ." Rhea said.

"Old," Amos said without a hint of question.

"Well, yes." She felt a bit foolish like a tourist gaping at tall buildings. "Amos, how long have you been here?"

"A long time." His voice was muffled, distant. Amos pointed out a few houses hidden on the south shores. "Richardson the butcher, Klapke the widow, and Mrs. Carroll the teacher." He pointed north at a short, wood dock just outside the clearing he cut near his office. "Pull up here."

She cut the motor, and Amos grabbed the dock, stepped out, and lashed the boat. He gave Rhea a hand up. A wood dining chair stood at the end of the dock. Its dark finish was flaked, and its seat had cracked. Amos shrugged and tapped his boot on the dock. "Good fishin' here too. Not much, but it works."

He pointed up the wooded hill. "This path leads to a fork after a couple switchbacks. Right leads to my office. Left runs behind Josh's garage and The Store. Get you to Frank's quick. Both ways take ten or fifteen minutes." He pointed at a path no wider than a pair of feet that ran along the shore. "This leads to the Manor." He turned toward Rhea. "You need me for anything, go the other way."

Rhea nodded. "Can I give you a ride back to your truck?"

"Nah. You head off to work. I forgot the boat's gas can at my office. I'll walk."

Rhea looked up the hill and along the path that faded into the trees. "Amos?"

"Yeah?"

"Walk with me?"

Amos smiled and tucked his hands in his pockets. "Sure."

"Amos?" She looked sidelong at Amos and twisted her lip like she'd just drunk sour milk. "Josh?"

"Don't worry 'bout him." He looked through the branches toward the sky where thin clouds hung. "Eddie? He might. They tangled already. Eddie needs to watch his mouth."

"No, I know, I guess. But what happened to his dad? Josh's?"

"Let's just say that's one of those times I stepped in a bit too much. Maybe at the wrong time. I paid for it bad."

"What happened? Didi said something was off."

"Some people got it comin'. Josh's dad was one of those people. I just wish I'd done something sooner, wrong time and all. That boy's had it hard. His mom more so. Too many times Josh's dad left Frank's stumbling drunk. I should've done something then. Too many times I shoulda done something." Amos stopped where the path forked, lit a smoke, and scrubbed his beard. "When I saw that boy's face that morning —all cut up and bruised—and his dad's body with fists swollen by the beatin', I didn't much care how that screwdriver ended up in his head."

"Didi told me."

"Did she tell you his mom was shook up somethin' bad? That her nightgown and face were spattered with blood like someone had turned on a hose? How 'bout that it was Josh's prints on the screwdriver? She didn't, did she? She tell you how his body was still twitchin' when I got there? Then twitchin' and chokin' in my truck? And did she tell you how he stopped twitchin' just on the other side of the town's welcome sign?"

Rhea took a step back from Amos. "No. I shouldn't have asked."

Amos looked at Rhea and took another drag from his smoke. "Ruth said to me once. She said, 'It's my story to tell.' We all got 'em. This one's mine, at least one of 'em. I just told you because it's partly mine to tell. The rest of it's Josh's. You ain't got nothin' to do with what I just said other than me wanting you to hear."

Rhea nodded. "She told me as much. Still, I'm sorry." She turned toward the left fork, slipped on loose stones, and clenched her T-shirt as if she was pulling pain from her chest. "My family." She looked at Amos's badge. "I miss them."

Why would she say that? There were other questions, other paths that led to what she needed. She shook her head. The sign. "Amos, you said Josh's dad died just past the sign. Why move the body?"

"A part of me hoped you'd ask. The other part? Well, the other part ain't so sure."

"Why?"

"Like I said before, I paid for things in the past. I'll pay for this. And I got a feeling this'll cost more than most of what I've done just because I got a feelin' about you . . . and Eddie."

"Amos, you don't—"

"It's all right, Rhea." He held his forehead as if an ache throbbed. "I moved Josh's dad past the sign because dyin' here means you stay."

Rhea let out a breathy laugh. Was that it? "Well, of course." She waved her hand toward the church and cemetery.

"No, not that way. I wish it was. Near as I can tell, Saul's been here over a hundred fifty years. Died back then swingin' from the church bell rope."

"That's stupid. You expect me to—"

"No, no I don't. You don't know me. I don't know you. You don't know this place. Which is why I need you to try leavin'. If you can, keep walkin'. And all this will just be some fucked up dream about a crazy cop and a hippy bartender with a few dickheads sprinkled in for good measure."

The corner of her lip twitched into a quick smile that faded as quickly as it came when Amos's eyes reddened, and he cleared them with thumb and forefinger. "All right," Rhea said. "Say I believe you. Are you—"

"Dead?" He shook his head. "Not yet, but this place got me. I just try makin' sure those who don't deserve it don't."

"Ruth?"

"Nope."

"Josh?"

Amos turned away, looked down at his boots, and nodded. His voice cracked when he said, "I'll set the gas can in the boat and stop at Frank's. Shouldn't take long. Remember, I'm just up this path"—he nodded over his shoulder—"or down the road."

"That's it?"

"For now," he said and left.

She lost sight of his cattleman hat when he crested a hill. Only then did she turn toward Josh's garage, The Store, and Frank's. Her heart pulsed heavily in her arms and legs. "Frank's," she said. "I'm alone."

The forest grew dim. Lead filled her head. Rhea grabbed a young birch tree's trunk. Its bark was smooth and fleshy, cool yet broken into dry scabs. Lobes of bark flitted to the roots matted with gray leaves. Ruth's dead pretty boy and her baby —their baby. Josh's dad, his mom, Josh himself. Al and his son in the grain bin. Her parents twisted in the sheets and, a brown ant crawling from the scab near Rhea's thumb, her sister curled next to the drain.

She held her stomach sickened with grief. She needed Eddie. No, she wanted Eddie. She shook her head. He was back at the cabin, alone, still sleeping or just waking up. She wouldn't be there. He'd wonder where she was. She hadn't said goodbye. She just left. He'd know, though. He knew she needed to be at Frank's.

Where was Didi? Would she be there too? Rhea hadn't asked Amos about her and thought back to when she should have. It was a moment lost, a moment that'd never come again. Ruth, she'd know. But she was in Frank's. She had to go, but that jukebox, those hands on her body. That voice.

"Panic," she said. It was just a panic attack. That's all. Just like now. Eddie had been taken into the chief's station, the cops, just like in California. She'd nearly lost him, again. And then Amos said that shit about him and this town. Trust? Why not trust?

Eddie had been there for her when it mattered. Amos? Who was he? Then he pulled out this crazy story about the dead and this town. She breathed. The path hatched in shadows led to Ruth, and she followed it.

She could see Josh's garage and the back of The Store, but the path twisted back one last time before heading straight toward a grassy field where his truck was parked. The priest was there, Saul. He held Josh's upper arm; his mechanic's overalls bunched up in Saul's fist. Saul took his eyes from Josh and nodded toward Rhea.

Rhea stopped. "Dead," she whispered and clenched her fists at her sides.

Josh turned and yanked his arm away from Saul. Josh grinned at Rhea, but Saul moved close to Josh and held him by the shoulder. She could see Saul's purple lips lash out as he spoke into Josh's ear where that crucifix earring hung limp. Josh jerked his head from Saul, and he touched his jaw as if deciding on the right price for a used car. Rhea relaxed and folded her arms across her chest.

It was clear on his lips when Saul said, "Do it," followed by a string of other words.

Josh laughed through his nose and handed Saul something wrapped in a red rag. "Good times," Josh said. Saul nodded slowly. Rhea breathed and hurried past the gas pumps and on to Frank's where she hoped Ruth waited.

CHAPTER THIRTEEN

EDDIE LAUGHED. When they first arrived, Rhea had held his hand on this very road even though he'd been an ass, pissed her off with his idiot-show. She always came back, no matter what he did. Predictable. Being with her was like a car on cruise control—push her buttons and let life ride.

Now she was probably back there in her tiny T-shirt riding up just enough to show the lines of muscle next to her spine leading up her back to her thin bra strap. She'd be in her tight jeans, leaning across the bar on her toes picking up extra napkins a table of fishermen didn't need just to get a bump in her tip. He wanted her more in those moments as he pulled taps and slung cocktails. Those were the moments he had to share her with others. The only moments.

But Amos wanted to fuck it all up. He probably pumped something into her brain. No telling what it was. Amos was padded with sympathy, luring Rhea until she spilled everything.

Eddie shook his head. That bitch. Without him, she'd ruin

it all. He needed to hook back up with her before everything fell apart.

Then there was Saul and the blood on the rope, his neck. His stupid solution of sacrifice like he was Eddie's personal Jesus. He couldn't go back. Not yet. He'd do what that fool said just this once.

At the sign that welcomed him to Saint Andrew, he wasn't alone. An animal screamed like a blade ripping sheet metal cut through the clear day. There was metal on metal hammering and when the screaming stopped, two voices.

One high-pitched and thin, Cal, said, "Good shit, man."

The other, Owen, laughed like he was choking on food and said, "Yeah, good shit."

Eddie slowed and stepped onto the tar rather than kicking up gravel with his easy, heel-to-toe gait. Cal and Owen were behind the sign. A case of Blatz and an empty cage sat in the weeds. Owen clenched a ballpeen hammer and black nails. Cal ran his fingers through his blond hair, staining it red.

"Come on, man, let's get outta here," said Cal as he slapped Owen's sweaty back. He picked up the case of beer and cage. "Well, look who's here, Owen."

Owen turned. After laughing through his nose, his heavy shoulders heaved once, and he said, "Huh, look who's here."

"Where ya headed, Eddie?" asked Cal. "There ain't much out this way."

"What . . .?" Eddie said. Behind Owen, a fresh tabby had been nailed to the back of the sign. The other Eddie had seen when he first drove into Saint Andrew was gone. "Jesus Christ." Eddie shook his head, mouth hung open. "What the fuck?"

Cal nodded toward the cat and said, "Personal. Where ya headed?"

Eddie crossed to the opposite shoulder. Cal and Owen

stepped up from the ditch. Without stopping, Eddie said, "Out. Away."

"Really?" Cal twitched into a half-grin. "Yeah, I done that." He looked at and elbowed Owen. "You done that?"

"Yep, I done that." Owen nodded. His gullet folded below his chin. "You go ahead though. Ain't no other way."

Cal sat on the cage and pulled out two beers, cracked them open, and gave one to Owen who stuffed the hammer and nails into pockets before fisting the can. Cal guzzled his beer and cracked open a third.

Owen took a few gulps and pointed down the road. "Go on, now. We won't do nothin'. Promise." He crossed his heart.

Cal laughed and said, "Pinky promise," then slapped Owen's thigh. "Pop a squat, man." When Owen sat on the gravel, they hooked pinkies and tugged.

Eddie looked back just once at Cal and Owen downing beers then passed the sign. The highway was empty. Above, black birds, large and low, spiraled and dodged an angry sparrow.

What was he doing? There was no way he'd want to leave Saint Andrew. Not now, maybe not ever. Saint Andrew was his one chance for peace, to escape his family. To escape the moment he stripped Rhea's dad and slung his corpse on that bed. To escape the moment he wrapped his legs around her sister to stop her from kicking. The moment he stuffed the kitchen towel in her mouth and stabbed her with the needle as she snorted, her eyes wide and awful then dilated and sedate. Her body twitching in his lap as they sat together on the kitchen's linoleum floor molded with gold flowers frozen in time. Stroking her hair letting her know it'd be over soon.

He could escape that moment her heels hit the wood steps into the basement where he hid her next to the drain, so he could finish off the mom when she came home from her morning jog, tired and shaky from the run.

"Hey, Eddie," Rhea's mom said. She took long gulps of water from her coffee mug. Her eyes were closed against the sun that glinted off sweat and fine hairs covering her throat. He stabbed and plunged. With the syringe still stuck in her neck, she said, "What the fuck," and fell to one knee then her perfect face.

In Saint Andrew, he could escape the moment he undressed her too, her body tempting yet dead. He wrapped them together on that bed, twisted in the sheets, naked and cold. Those were the last needles he used to this day. He'd stayed strong. Something to be proud of. He nodded and smiled.

Eddie turned again, and Cal said, "Go on, man," and waved his hand. "Don't worry, you'll be back. It's different for all of us."

"Different," Eddie said and kept walking. Different for all of them? What the hell did that mean? Saul had said he'd tried leaving who-knows-how-many times. What was so tough about it?

Eddie kept walking. The sun glinted off wet stones frozen in the tarred road. A slip of wind cut through his SISTERS T-shirt, and his bruises ached just a bit more. He stood at the top of a hill where the road twisted into a canopy of trees split by a barn's roof. Beyond that, a green tractor dumped an old bale onto a hay rack pulled by a pickup.

"What the fuck?" Cal said behind him, but his voice was distant, almost a whisper or like he spoke through a thick window.

Eddie turned again. He'd gone farther than he'd thought. The sign was small. Cal and Owen were hardly shadows. Both were standing. Owen shook his head. Cal hollered through his cupped hands, "Get outta here, ya stupid fuck. The town don't want you. Leave!"

Didn't want him? Fuck that. The town wanted him. It had to.

The sign's paint faded and peeled. One of the three lights that stabbed out below the fishing family like crooked fingers fell. Cal and Owen sat and turned into black spots like grease on water. Behind him, a thin voice yelled out above the tractor's growl. Then the sign grew spare, lean, like the veins of the leaf he'd left in the bar. His bar.

It wasn't possible. The town didn't want him.

"No," Eddie said.

Again, like so many times before, he was just some castoff. Some accident to be forgotten. Not this time.

"Fuck that."

What the fuck did the Saint know? What the fuck did any of them know?

"Saul."

That crazy fucker. He was a lonely piece of shit that sat in his church and did what? Did anyone see his mass, or was he just some sorry son of a bitch who imagined a god who didn't give a fuck about him?

"Sorry as shit," Eddie said to no one. "Josh, that fuckin' birth defect playin' tough, cryin' about his fucked-up family. Ruth, that know-it-all, holier-than-thou fuckin' potato sack that lumped about the town like everyone's fuckin' mom. And Amos, that pompous prick in that uniform too tight to fit his ego."

How the fuck did that shithead expect to keep Eddie here? He couldn't. Eddie could leave. He sure as fuck could leave. He was standing at the edge. Just another step and he'd show Amos he was fucking wrong. But Eddie wanted to see it on Amos's face.

Eddie had the power. He had the will. He knew it. It wasn't because the town didn't want him. It was because the town couldn't control him. Or maybe it needed him.

"Fuck, yeah," he said. "It needs me because they ain't shit."

This time he'd show everyone how much they needed him. He'd show that fucking town the real Eddie. The Eddie with purpose. The Eddie of use. The Eddie that got shit done.

"That's right," he said to the birds, tar, and wind. He thumbed his chest. "I'm the one. I got everythin' under control. And I'll show them shits this town's mine. Frank's, the Manor, the whole fuckin' lake is mine."

From Saint Andrew, the church bell shivered with an off-pitch strike as if it was startled awake. And Eddie's boots met tar as if they'd done it for a hundred years, nice and easy, one after the other. And the bell tolled less loud with each following strike while the sign before him groaned back into what it once was: pulled the paint back, tugged up the light, and slapped that smile back on the dad like he knew Eddie'd come back to save them. Save them all. Cal and Owen stood there too, no longer the shadows they had become. They were whole again and shook their heads like Eddie was a fuckin' god.

Cal handed him a beer.

"Saul," Eddie said as he downed the beer and chucked the can in the ditch.

"Do what you gotta do, man," said Cal.

Owen took a swig of beer, ran his finger across his lip, and shrugged. "I ain't stoppin' no one."

———

At the crucifix-etched doors, the bell rang another tone, somber yet true. Beyond the doors, a shadow rose to the ceiling where it stopped with a thump like someone dropping a basket filled with wet linens. Eddie held the door's cold handle. The bell rang again. The shadow fell then rose. There was a thump, and the bell rang. Eddie opened the door.

Next to a leaning ladder, Saul hung limp, noosed by the bell's rope. His body rose, and his head smacked the ceiling where blood starred next to the brass gromet. His feet touched the carpet, and his body rose. The bell rang less and less with each rise, thud, and fall until there was no thud. Eddie entered. The door swung shut behind him. Saul opened his vein-ripped eyes.

When he saw Eddie, his purple lips twitched into a strait-laced grin, and he spat out flecks of blood as he wheezed a single word, "Cut." From his hand a red rag stained black with grease fell to the floor and unfolded to reveal a leather sheath, stitched with white.

Eddie picked up the blade, it was the only weapon he still carried. A weapon he'd hidden under the Vega's spare tire. He looked up at Saul who still grinned. Josh'd found it, found the blade. But why? They'd fucked with his shit. Josh'd learn his place.

The knife's black walnut haft was carved with a hard edge and oiled to a sheen. Out of the sheath, the blade was thick and profiled like a hawk's bill. The inside curve of the blade shaved skin from Eddie's thumb even though rust pocked its face. He stuck the sheath inside his boot yet held the blade.

"Cut," Saul said again.

Eddie succumbed to the unnatural thing before him—Saul, that thing that should be dead but spoke through blood and pain. No, not succumbed. Eddie embraced it.

After one last toll, the rope's frayed end hovered inches above the floor. Eddie climbed the ladder and cut. His head swiveled with the slow motion of the blade through the rope.

In a way, he denied what he saw, denied what he was doing. Yet, it was there before him. Every rope cord split like delicious tendons until the last thread snapped.

Saul's body dropped limp on the rug with a rotten melon thump. Before Eddie reached the bottom of the ladder, Saul had already stood. His arms hung at his sides, and his head lolled like an overly loved ragdoll.

Saul hocked blood on the carpet, dug his pack of Camels from his shirt pocket, and lit up, all with his head still resting lazily on his shoulder. He offered Eddie the pack. Shaking, Eddie took it and tucked his knife back in his boot. His eyes never left Saul. Smoke slithered out the corner of the priest's mouth.

"I need you," Saul said. "See why?"

"I don't...I...This can't—"

"Stop it. Stutterin' and shit. This ain't no place for bein' a pussy."

Eddie's blade burned next to his shin. In his hand, it would've swept through Saul's sagging neck, but there was no point. The man was dead or should be. Eddie closed his eyes, breathed, and said, "Yes." Eddie could be this man's savior, this man's god. If he gave a shit.

Saul nodded. "You try leavin'?"

Eddie said, "Yes."

"Could you?"

"Yes."

"Then I was right, you are worthless. The Saint don't want you."

"No, that ain't right."

Saul's neck cracked and righted itself just a bit as he raised his eyebrows. "*Ain't?*" He smiled. "What ain't right?"

"I learned somethin' 'bout myself, 'bout my place here."

"Huh, ain't that *somethin'*. Tell me."

"This place is afraid. This place needs me. This place can't control me. I coulda left. This town ain't got no power over me." Jesus, what the hell was he saying? "This town has no power over me. It'll be mine."

"That so." Saul rubbed his neck and pursed his lips before he said, "Well, maybe you are special. Maybe there is a plan."

"Plan?"

Eddie took a step back, but something was there: a wicked hand, thin and frail yet powerful. It bore down on him like a thousand years of hate and want coupled with insecurity and doubt that birthed rage no cage could house. The church's narthex swelled as if drawing breath then moaned.

"The Old Man's near," Saul said as he scanned the room and Eddie. "But he can't get you. Special, like I said. That's good. That means I can save you, son." He smiled and patted Eddie's shoulder.

"Old Man?" Eddie was tired of everyone's shit. Tired of bending words. Tired of having only half the Saint. "Tell me now. Who's the Old Man?"

"You seen somethin' right?"

Eddie nodded.

"Seen a shadow? Tells you things?"

"Yeah," Eddie said.

"The Old Man. Been here longer than, well, longer than most. But let me tell you this. He ain't been here longer than me. He ain't shit. Not like you." Saul's neck cracked and bent back upright as he pulled Eddie to the altar. The giant Jesus looked down with sympathy Eddie didn't want nor need.

"Here," said Saul as he swept the Bible and gold candelabras from the altar. "Sacrifice here. I'll do it willingly. By your will and hand, I can save you. Then you'll be pure. Your sins gone. This town loves the pure, the innocent. And it'll need you like you want. Then I can finally be free of this place." On his back, Saul splayed on the altar.

Eddie slid his hawkbill blade from its leather sheath. The pocks of rust remained. In the marred surface of the blade, his face was reflected, twisted like a car crash victim hacked together by a street doc's stitches. Bruised and black with hate and rage. In that blade, he was truth. He was power. He was control. He was death. He was something not even Saint Andrew could control.

Saul asked, "You see somethin', son?"

Or *was* it Saul? Was it the Saul who lay on the altar or the Saul of the past? His neck was thin and ragged, ripped and bruised by the hemp he'd hanged himself with. Yet the voice he'd heard was clear, strong, as though it was a force conjured by the church itself. Eddie brought the blade to Saul's neck. It touched wet sinew where a vein pulsed with urgency, maybe need.

"Son, what did you see?" This time the voice was closer yet still calm, subdued by sympathy and need—a need to help.

Eddie turned. Amos was there, standing in the aisle in this uniform, sleeves rolled up as though he was ready for an alley fight. He had a gas can in his fist that he set on the floor with a hollow spang of metal on stone. He held his hands before him like a negotiator at a heist gone bad.

"You don't know," said Amos as if pleading. "You don't."

"Dammit, Amos, it ain't your time. It's my time. Mine." Saul slipped off the altar and shuffled next to Eddie, stabbing his own breast with his thumb.

"No, Saul. You don't have a time. You have here." Amos pointed at the tile. "And-and you'll never get that. Never understand. No one wants you, Saul." Amos's eyes twitched under his cattleman, and his lips sagged.

"Fuck you, Amos," Saul said and faced Eddie. Saul held

Eddie's shoulders and massaged. "Eddie, he don't give a shit about you. There ain't nothin' there. You can help me. We'll be free. From ourselves. From guilt. And you'll own this place."

"What'd you see, son?" asked Amos. "In that blade."

Eddie looked back into his blade. "Ruin."

"That's not . . ."

Amos spoke more, but Eddie was fixed on the blade where he was a god. Where he was what all needed. And Amos was worthless, no better than that stitched car-crash failure he'd seen before. No better than anything he'd done before, killed before: Rhea's greedy dad, Rhea's tempting mom, Rhea's sister fighting until the end. And Rhea who needed him—more than she knew.

Amos would take her. It'd happen. He saw Rhea on the dock and Amos touching her. He saw her on the boat in the cove, laughing, happy. He saw her on the side of the road on their way into Saint Andrew. He saw her through the flames of the fire they'd built in Anza-Borrego as snakes rattled and insects hummed with the stars smeared above. He saw her as he stood and walked to the Vega, her yelling his name, him leaving her with satisfaction, knowing he had her, that she was his. Not Amos's. She'd never be Amos's.

Eddie clenched the dagger and brought it up. Saul released Eddie and exposed his neck, but Eddie walked down the aisle toward Amos and said, "You're right."

Amos nodded and said, "You made—"

There was a pop and spatter of hot blood that fanned across Eddie's face, soaked his *Sisters* T-shirt, poured over Amos's collar and badge, and spattered on the stone floor in a slick rain of red. That prick just had to go and ruin Eddie's favorite shirt, one last *fuck you* as he twitched and groaned before he thumped to his knees then twisted on his back. Eddie wiped the blade on his jeans and sheathed it as that silly ass tried to live just a bit longer by sucking air through his throat that fluttered like wet paper.

Good, said the Old Man.

Eddie's head throbbed, and his body seized. The church heaved. Plaster walls groaned. Dust drizzled from the ceiling. At the edge of Eddie's vision, the hunched horror—no, the Old Man—stood with a cane that clacked tile. His bony hand pushed Eddie to a knee. Cold breath touched his ear.

Mine, the Old Man whispered.

"No," Eddie said as he collapsed in Amos's blood like a puppet clipped from its strings. Pain split Eddie's neck and spine as the Old Man spread Eddie's arms and legs then forced himself inside, as Eddie yelled, "Stop, please, stop!" like so many Eddie had murdered before. But the Old Man did not care, did not stop until Eddie surged with a seething pitch of contempt and hate. And when the Old Man filled him to his satisfaction, Eddie stood, lit a Marb from the soft pack he pulled from his pocket, and walked down the aisle.

"Eddie!" Saul yelled. "Eddie, you can't leave. Take me. Save yourself. Save me. Special! You were special. No." Saul's rasping voice echoed into sobs.

Eddie trailed footprints of blood into the narthex. The doors clapped shut low and loud.

Saul said through the door, his voice like a blade on stone, "The damned can be saved, Eddie. Saved! Special!"

"You got one thing right," Eddie said as he walked into the sun's light.

CHAPTER FOURTEEN

RHEA ENTERED FRANK'S.

Ruth was behind the bar twisting a rag in shot glasses. She looked up and smiled. "Hey, Rhea," she said through the cigarette that jumped as she spoke.

"Hello, Ruth." The jukebox glowed in the corner. The cord was plugged into the wall. Loretta Lynn backed by a choir mourned all the world's forgotten people. Their long, sullen notes hung like the heavy regret of a lonely drunk, yet the bar was clean and ready for more. Ruth had already cleared the tables and mopped up. Heat billowed from the kitchen, prepped and ready.

"You're just in time," Ruth said with a smirk as she set another shot glass in line with a dozen others. She tucked the rag into her back pocket and placed each shot glass under the bar with uneven rhythm.

Rhea sat on her stool and said, "Sorry, long night. Odd. Would it be all right if I had some breakfast?"

"Sure, hon', what ya want?"

Rhea shrugged, and Ruth smiled. In minutes she had a

plate of eggs, bacon, and toast and a mug of coffee in front of Rhea, who ate wordlessly until half the plate was gone.

Rhea looked up. "Amos. Can I trust him?"

Ruth, who was on her knees stocking the fridges with cans of beer, looked up at Rhea over the edge of the bar. "Yeah, more than the rest."

"Why's he here?"

"Well, like most, he done somethin' that kept 'im." She lined up the last cans on the wire shelves, closed the returnable carton, and stood with the empty box.

"Like what?"

Ruth stacked the box atop several others in the storage closet. "Can't tell. It ain't my place, and I don't fully know. He don't talk much."

Rhea nodded. "He showed me around the lake. Talked a lot."

"Did he now?" Ruth dusted her hands and took her station at the taps.

"Yeah, this morning. He lent me—us—his boat. He's getting gas. Should be here around lunch. Ruth, I think Eddie wants to stay."

Ruth shook her head with pained ease and took the rag from her pocket.

"You okay?"

"Yeah, go on, hon', uh sorry, Rhea."

"It's okay, Ruth. I don't mind it coming from you as much as the others. They use it like I need them. You use it like, well, like how you took that boy that night. There was something there more than what you let on, just like when you call me hon'." Rhea reached out, hoping to comfort Ruth, who twisted the bar rag in tight fists. "Eddie said the bar was packed last night. He said, well, he thought maybe you'd like to share this bar with us."

"That so?"

"Yeah, he loves this place. He wants to stay."

"That what you want?"

"I-I don't know. I thought maybe I did. I guess it's peaceful? When Amos and I were on his boat in the cove, old Al on the dock, the way he talked about everyone. But something's off."

"What's that?" Ruth brought Rhea's empty plate into the kitchen.

Rhea looked back at the jukebox that had switched to Cash graveling on, stuck in prison. "Well, Amos said . . . This is stupid."

Ruth shook her head and mixed a bloody Mary. "Just go ahead and say it."

"He said I should leave. He said that if I can walk past the sign, I should keep going."

Ruth slid Rhea the finished cocktail on a napkin and poured a chaser. She mixed one for herself and drowned her throat with half the glass then tossed down the beer shot.

Rhea laughed and said, "Dixie-cup-Kool-aid."

Ruth shrugged and topped off her beer. "Sometimes ya need a drink."

Rhea followed suit and tipped her drink back followed by beer. "Amos said that if he told me this, he'd pay bad. Especially with what he told me next."

"Which was?" Ruth finished her drink and beer.

Rhea smiled and focused on her folded hands on the bar. "He said people were dead here. Like Saul's been dead a hundred fifty years. And Josh."

"Rhea, I can't—"

"No, let me finish. He said some are alive. You, him, maybe others, I guess. I didn't ask about Didi. I hate I didn't." She looked at Ruth. "Is Amos all right?"

"He's all right." Ruth turned toward the lake.

"No, you're not listening. Is he right in the head?"

"His brain's fine."

"Why can't you . . .?" Rhea bunched her fists and pounded the bar, just once, just enough to make the next word stick. "Ruth."

Ruth nodded like some fucked up high school shrink wannabe who had all the answers, still looking out the window where the morning light barely touched her pitted cheeks. She swigged beer and sucked her top lip clean and said, "If I tell you . . . I can't. I can't go through that again."

Rhea inhaled through her nose and tensed her lips. "God dammit, Ruth. What aren't you telling me? I can't stand it. Amos, you, no one gives things straight. At least not that I can tell." Rhea clenched her fists.

Ruth shook her head and took a single step toward Rhea. "Hon', you wouldn't—"

"Wouldn't understand? Maybe you are like the rest, like everyone."

"Hon'—"

"No," Rhea pointed at Ruth, stabbing the air. "Don't call me that. Not anymore." She stood, and the stool nearly tipped. She backed toward the door.

Ruth took a second step forward. "I just can't. It's how this all works."

"What works?" A growl grew deep in her throat. "Didi knows."

"Rhea." Ruth moved to the end of the bar and offered a single hand. "Didi isn't what you think."

Josh walked in and said, "Ladies. Hate ta interrupt." Ash fell from his cigarette as he stroked his stubble-stained jaw.

"What?" Ruth said to Josh as Rhea turned and stumbled back from the door.

"Nothin'," said Josh. "Just need ta have a word with Red, here."

"Josh, she's not—"

"Yes, she is. This town wants her bad." He pointed at Ruth with a greased finger. "The Old Man says so. And I got a job to do."

Rhea looked at Ruth. "He wants to talk. Let him."

Ruth looked from Rhea to Josh, squinted, shook her head, then pulled out her pack of smokes and lit up.

"Thought as much," he said as he grinned at Ruth. "You ain't meddlin'."

Ruth took a drag, closed her eyes, and exhaled through her nose. Her lips were bent low in lines that quivered like thin webs in the wind. There was anger there. Or something locked up. Good. Rhea wanted whatever it was to come out, and maybe Josh was the one who could force it free. She'd listen to Josh. Afterall, it was Ruth who'd said he needed care. He wasn't much different than Eddie. Rhea knew what Josh wanted and would use that. She turned from Ruth and smiled at Josh.

"Let's talk," she said with a hand on her hip. "Got a smoke?"

Josh smiled. "Yep, I got you." He pulled a smoke from his pack of Camels and held it out as his eyes slid up Rhea's body.

Rhea stooped and tongued the cigarette into her mouth. Josh lit it with his dad's lighter. It felt good. Both the smoke and tempting Josh. There was danger in both. "Come on," she said nodding toward the back of the bar.

Josh took the seat next to Rhea at a high-top and corralled her with his legs. She took a drag, smiled at Josh, and nodded while she blew the smoke out the corner of her mouth.

Josh leaned in closer. The crucifix hanging from his ear danced. Knots of hair bent like black iron over his unblinking eyes. His breath smelled like hot metal quenched in cold water when he said, "Saul said something just a bit ago."

"The priest," said Rhea.

"That's him."

"Outside your garage."

"Yeah," he smiled and took a drag from his smoke. "That's right. He told me somethin' 'bout Eddie. Somethin' bad."

"I know a lot, Josh."

"Not all of it. You and him, you runnin' from drugs and family."

Rhea shrugged. "Old news."

"Yeah, I figured. But . . ." He leaned back in his chair and tapped the ashes of his smoke into a black ashtray.

The jukebox spilled red, clapped down another record, and Rogers plucked his guitar and sang the music man's song better than he let on. Like her cigarette, Rogers's voice was the comfort of a familiar chair. The front door opened, and the boy Rhea had seen driving the pickup on her way to the cabin walked in. Behind him, two hard men followed. Their eyes had the same squint as they nodded to Ruth who nodded back and took their order. Josh waited for Rhea to say something, but she kept her eyes on the boy. She wasn't going to give Josh the interest he wanted.

Josh leaned forward. "That's how you play," he said.

Rhea looked at Josh. "Play?"

"Give a hint then back out." He stood and leaned in close. His breath grazed her jaw and snaked through her hair. "I know that game." He left her for the bar.

Rhea's stomach grew thick. She'd lost something in those moments before. Josh was smarter than she gave credit, and she was out of practice.

He leaned on the bar and spoke to Ruth. Ruth poured a tumbler of whiskey. Josh nodded toward Rhea, and Ruth

poured vodka and orange juice over rocks smeared with grena-
dine. Ruth pointed at Josh with her hard-knuckled finger but
said nothing, which must've been sort of enough because he
laughed, picked up the drinks, and brought them back to Rhea.
Ruth looked at Rhea then disappeared into the kitchen. Josh
slid the vodka drink in front of Rhea. He sat on his stool and
took a pull of whiskey.

"I been told," Josh said, "you lost your family."

She stopped before the glass touched her lips. "Who?"

"Don't matter."

"Saul?"

He shrugged. "What does matter is that Eddie did it."

"Meaning?" Rhea searched Josh's eyes. They were blue,
dull, and dry. They didn't move, didn't give a hint.

"Meaning . . ." He twitched a grin. "Meaning I been told
Eddie took a role in that day you found 'em."

Rhea stood. Her stomach churned.

"Found your mom in bed. Your dad too. The basement.
Well, the basement was—"

"How could you—"

"The basement," Josh said. As though delivering bad news
to a child, his voice softened and rose in pitch. "Well, the basement had Little Red, your sister."

Rhea shook her head, closed her eyes. She saw her sister on
the floor, never-changing.

"I can," said Josh. "And I do. I know."

She opened her eyes and swayed as though afloat in a black
sea. "Know what?" she asked as Josh and the jukebox became
haloed in that black sea.

"That weren't no drug." Josh smiled. His voice and the
music from the jukebox dulled as though a pane of glass separated them. "Nah, that ain't right. Your dad took the drugs
easy. Figures. Most men just ain't got the will."

"Stop," Rhea said.

"Your mom put up a fight. Eddie got a thing for her. Can't blame him. From what I hear, if she looks, *looked* anythin' like you, well." He smiled and shook his head. "Your sister, she struggled on that floor, in the kitchen, but Eddie did it real kind and held her to the end. Wrapped his legs 'round her to stop her from hurtin' herself, from screamin'." He elbowed up on the table. "Eddie had somethin' for Little Red. Love, I'd say. But that basement's cold, I bet. Dark too. You know, I never caught her name."

Rhea held her head. "Clara," she whispered. "I can't, Josh." Her eyes were wet with tears that spattered into messy stars on the wood floor. Her chest seized. Each breath came hard. She tried erasing the image by dragging her hand over her eyes and chin. But it was as useless as hiding under sheets. When she opened her eyes, Josh lurched toward her. She could smell him, thick with grease and liquor, smoke and welded steel.

He pulled back and sucked at his teeth with thick, jackhammer smacks. "Clara. Rhea and Clara. Must've been lonely. Maybe he'd fuck her corpse—thought about it, just for a moment, but that was crossin' the line for him. So, he dragged her into that basement by the feet—not her arms like he'd said. Her head popped on every step in thick, wet smacks like a willow switch smackin' a fat ass. Too bad. A sister who ain't no more, 'cause of Eddie." He looked at the ceiling and furrowed his forehead as if pained by his words. "The same Eddie who left you in that desert."

Misery and disgust clenched her stomach and tugged her face into an ugly mess. Not Eddie. Yet, it could be. It must be. Eddie, with her sister wanting, lusting, alone—the pool-side princess. Somehow Josh knew. The priest? How? No, they knew her family died. The rest were lies. Had to be lies.

She stood and with anger dug up from the horror of her

sister alone next to the drain, said, "Get away," and pushed Josh with her body and will. Josh stumbled and caught himself on the table. She shook her head, palmed away tears, but Josh and the jukebox never left her sight. "No, Eddie didn't. He couldn't."

Josh laughed limply as though Rhea's shove was a joke's perfect delivery. "You ain't got no sense, kid." He took a step toward her then a second, grabbed her arms and tightened. His fingers rolled over her muscles that popped on tendons. "You shoulda come to my home. I told you. Safe there. Safer than your murderin' hus—"

Rhea turned her head as he leaned in.

His lips were at her ear. "—boyfriend."

He let go and pushed her away. Rhea hit a table. A stool skidded but didn't fall. She held both arms, heaved ragged breaths, palmed tears from her face. Josh went back to the table where he sucked down whiskey. "Better run, Red," he said. "Old Man loves this place. Frank's lets us all in."

"Rhea," Ruth said from the kitchen.

Rhea dropped her head and pushed through three mud-caked men at the door. She ran past The Store and Josh's garage. Both were empty. Still holding her arms where bruises had already begun to shine yellow, she slowed at the trail that led to the boat.

A light breeze touched the dry grass at her feet. There, new grass and clover curled through the dead. The path twisted into the woods and hid behind hillocks. Birds, the same she'd seen flitting on swamp reeds near the cabin, perched on branches and called out with their metallic warble.

She needed the boat. Needed the seclusion, the peace, the loneliness with the waves touching distant shores.

She came to the fork leading to Amos. He stood there before, on those rocks, with his head down when she asked about Josh. She hadn't given him much, asked the right questions, said the right things: another moment missed. Maybe he was the one she needed. She looked up the path where he'd crested the hill. There was an ease, maybe a willingness to leave her. Maybe he didn't want her? Maybe he wanted Eddie? Maybe, like Josh, he knew more and, like a cop, wanted to . . . No, that wasn't him. He'd held her on the dock. There was no hate, no *want* to stop her and Eddie. He was the one person who really reached out to her.

No, that wasn't true either. She looked back up the trail toward Josh's garage barely shadowed by the sun that'd soon crest and fall. Behind that garage was Ruth. And Josh. Why. It wasn't a question. It was a reason—reasoning. There was always a why behind every choice she'd made.

Most of her choices had been wrong. No, not wrong. Empty. Done without cause, done on the cusp of emotion like the tip of a wave about to crash down only to scatter in the waters lost as a memory of the fading and old. Like Al casting his line every day and drawing the same fish. And washed out like the paint on the Manor. Like how she suffered at Anza-Borrego where the fire licked the desert-dusted air, and Eddie picked at a string on his ripped jeans while looking at her through those flames.

He was close to dead then. Or at least that's what he wanted—a closeness to death, an image of death. But he'd changed since. Or had he? He just left her at the Vega, not only in the desert, but outside Saint Andrew. It was always her in tow, her who needed, her who held his hand. He tempted. He pushed. Then came back just when it meant most. When she was on her Wensley Avenue balcony staring at the terracotta tiles, he pushed open those French doors.

He knew. How did he know? Things like that don't just happen. Can't happen. She should have been on those tiles, bleeding out, the junkies inside snorting her blow while the *Sisters* beat on about ribbons and razor wire. He should have stood over her in a coffin. But he hadn't. He was there, slick and certain.

"Wanna get the fuck outta here?" Rhea repeated his slick line and shook her head.

Why'd she say yeah? He stood in those doors just like he hid behind those flames. In those flames, he changed. His face washed in fire. She'd said, *I need my sister.* He said, *You don't need nothing but me.* Need nothing? Don't? He was right.

"Rhea." Didi's voice burned through Rhea's frantic thoughts.

Rhea didn't jump. She knew someone would come. They always did. She looked up from where she stood. She'd somehow left the path's fork, left Amos's memory, and had made her way to the dock where, next to the fading dining chair, Didi stood in a white gown stained with mud and flecked with sand. Tiny specks of red dusted her buttoned collar. She was soaked, and her hair and gown clung to her as it had in the cabin.

"Sorry," Didi said. "I fell gettin' this." She held a rope. "I saw you and Amos. Saw you on the lake. I figured I'd wait for you."

"What? Wait for me?" said Rhea.

"I've got time enough." Didi's Alabama lilt came on strong as she tilted her head and smiled. "You got somethin'. There's somethin' goin' on. In your head." The boat listed lightly under her weight. "Come on. Let's talk."

It wasn't what Rhea wanted. She needed to be alone, to be herself, not put on a show for another, not enter another combat of words where she'd pry every bit from Didi. Didi was different, though, wasn't she? She'd been open with Rhea. There were answers that were given, or, in the very least, stories of the town that helped Rhea understand not only the place but herself. She opened to Didi that night. Was it last night? So soon. Yet, Ruth. She'd turned Ruth away, and she didn't want to turn Didi away and miss another moment.

"No," Rhea said. "I need . . . I need time."

"Oh," Didi said.

"To myself."

"Then would you mind?" Didi looked down at her dress and the boat. "Mind taking me home? We don't need talkin'."

Didi bunched up her face and wiped water from her eyes. Rhea couldn't leave Didi on the shore, soaked and dirty as she was. Afterall, she'd come to be with Rhea, one of the few who did. "Sure. Where?"

"Around by the Manor." Didi wafted her hand. A crooked branch's shadow swayed over her face as the boat moved with waves. "It's not far, on the way to your cabin."

Rhea stepped in the boat and sidled next to the motor, started it with a quick tug, and backed the boat away from the dock. Didi sat at the front as Amos had. She lounged with her fingers in the water and the other clutching the boat's rope. Rhea picked up speed, and the chill wind combed her hair. Didi's hair stuck to her shoulders, and a thin line of water from her dress fed down the keel of the boat to Rhea's feet. In the shadows of the birch that bent over the lake, Didi glowed white then sallow as they pulled into the open water. Rhea squinted against the sun, yet Didi grew sedate as if she and the boat were carved from the same stone.

The lake was choppy and tossed the boat that lurched between waves, so Rhea kept close to the shore. If she lost the boat under the waves, they'd at least be able to swim ashore. She passed the butcher's and Richardson's and slowed near the Manor.

"Around here?" asked Rhea.

Didi smiled and said, "Yeah, south just a bit."

Rhea curled the boat around the shore north of the Manor. It loomed, breathed, and burgeoned as if in a fevered speech before a crowd whose voices rose from the waves. Rhea pulled the boat away, cringed from the Manor into deeper waters, toward the white tree. Didi lolled her head onto her shoulder and gazed at the Manor.

"Beautiful," Didi said. "Here." She pointed at the southwest tip of the island.

The boat scraped against sunken granite slabs then against the pebbled beach. Didi stood and slipped out of the boat. Her dress dragged over the rail and slapped into the shore. She looked at the Manor then Rhea. Didi swayed with the waves.

Rhea said, "Where are you—"

"You said it was beautiful," Didi said as she dipped and grabbed the boat's rails.

"No." Rhea winced.

"Yes, you did." Didi's stoic inflection was betrayed by lips pressed to a thin line. "Let me show you." As waves heaved the boat, she strained and pulled it further on the rocky shore. "Rhea, I can't be alone. I can't go home."

"No. Didi."

Josh's voice intruded. *Better run, Red.* Rhea shook her head. Her sister stared at her next to the drain. Tears fell from Rhea's cheeks. Her parents' purpled bodies knotted together. She strangled the motor's throttle and jammed it into reverse, grinding the gears. Water surged and frothed behind the boat that yanked from Didi's grasp and ground against granite. "Didi!" Rhea shook her head.

Didi's face was ugly misery like a cinched rag, and she dipped her head. Her red hair hung like wet knives, and her shoulders heaved. When she looked up, her jaw was thrust forward, and her white teeth were bared when she yelled,

"Fine!" She lurched into the water and pointed at her chest and Rhea. "Remember, Rhea, I needed you." Her dress coiled past dead trees as she hobbled toward the Manor.

"I'm sorry, Didi," Rhea said above the motor and waves. "Eddie..."

Didi was a lonely wisp of white at the corner of the Manor that yawned above. "I'll be here, for you, Rhea." At her feet, young flowers, yellow and vibrant, shivered.

Rhea eased off the throttle and let the boat drift before crunching it into gear and heading toward the cove. In the open waters, a confused wind kicked up waves not nearly as bad as those Rhea'd seen on Coronado, but bad enough for the Johnboat to take on a few gallons of water slowing her pace. The cove was another story. The water was sullen and lazy as though repressing the lake's rage. Rhea cut the engine and dropped the round, red anchor mounted at the bow; its rope zipped through the greased pully. Taking a note from Amos and Didi, Rhea sprawled at the bow. Her fingers touched the water, staving off her hangover.

Her tongue was thick and mouth dry from the smoke she'd sucked down at Frank's. It'd been weeks since she'd lit up. She just had to take Josh's cigarette. She controlled the situation— or so she thought—as though she could force him to do and say the things she needed. She shook her head, and the sisal rope pricked her skin. She was stupid. She trusted herself, trusted Josh to be the dumbass Eddie thought he was.

Then there was Ruth. Rhea left Ruth standing at the bar, chose to not trust her, to go alone, be her own person, her own self. Yet, Rhea would just find herself back with all those who told her what to do. How long would she go on this way? How long would she rely on everyone but herself?

Even Ruth was someone she'd lean on, eventually. She almost did, in the cabin when her foot touched Ruth's thigh.

Rhea wanted to keep it there, her foot, her toes warm under that woman's weight, have that contact with a person whom she should have trusted, should have touched not only with her body but with what she needed to share—her story.

That would have been faith, would have been opening herself to another, making the choice, on her own, to let someone in like she had never done with anyone, not even Eddie. Yet, every time she went on her own, she fucked something up.

Hell, if Eddie hadn't come when he did, she'd be on those terracotta tiles or in a coffin. That'd be better than where she was now. Or would it?

What was wrong with this place? Nothing.

The people? Josh, why'd he say what he did? He knew things, knew too much, knew what he shouldn't.

Had Eddie given that to him? To Josh? Eddie hated him. Josh beat him bloody. He wouldn't spill to Josh.

The waves picked up through the cove, and the boat swung away from the inlet. The cloud-licked sun spiraled until the boat pointed into the wind and waves, yet the anchor held. To the west, towering clouds bulged like white fists touched by gray. She'd never seen clouds like that above the Imperial Valley where those that came in from the ocean were torn into hazy wisps. The clouds here were more like the sandstorms that charged from the north and consumed her Wensley Avenue house for a few brief and terrifying moments as the windowpanes shook and clattered.

Yet those storms touched the ground—were grounded—as they made their way to Mexico and into the gulf or some other town to be dusted brown and red. Somehow that made those storms real, manageable, as though contact with the ground made the dust storms into something closer, familiar, less alien.

Anza-Borrego rarely had the storms Rhea had seen. And when Eddie and she spent their last night there, it was calm, and the stars were clear and brilliant, set in dense patches that melted into clouds like burrs sticking to the black sky. She wanted night now. The sun burned, and she knew she'd pay later when her skin peeled like wet vellum.

Her sister didn't have it as bad. And, in those moments as Rhea lay on her bed with a fan blowing on her nearly naked body, her sister would spread cool aloe with her pudgy hands.

Rhea closed her eyes against the sun, and her sister spoke, "It's okay. We won't go back. Back to the pool. I'm sorry."

Rhea cried. Cried for what she didn't let her sister do. Cried for the moments she held back her sister's happiness. Cried for the moments she hated her sister for taking what she wanted, whatever that was in those moments that lacked reason, lacked caring for the only one who knew Rhea. The only one Rhea wanted and did let in—at least in that way that no one truly sees another's truth. Later, her sister's hands would mimic her body's sleek lines but never go beyond the first hints of adulthood that ended in that basement. First hints of adult-hood that were taken by—

"Rhea," Eddie said as he sat on a dry stump next to the fire in Anza-Borrego. "Your dad's bad. You can't stay. You stay, I'm gone."

Rhea sat next to the fire flickering in the desert breeze. "No, Eddie. My sister. I can't leave. We can take her."

"That won't work. Your mom. She won't let her go. She don't know."

"Don't know?"

"Nah, she don't know what he done," Eddie said.

"No, he . . . Why are you talking like—"

"What he done to you. And you ain't got no clue, do ya?"

Your sister's gettin' old enough, her dad had said as he

knuckled his nose and snorted then clenched Rhea's forearms, smacked her ribs. After, her sister spread the aloe on sunburn and bruises.

"No, Eddie. We'll take both," Rhea said with the frailty of a rotted tree limb against heavy wind.

"That ain't happenin', Red," said Eddie through the fire. The cactus behind him twitched with shadows and flame.

"No. That's not it. That's not how it went." Then the fire and Anza-Borrego were gone, and she was back on the boat shuddering with sobs that bent ribs. "My dad didn't . . . Eddie, Jesus, what'd you do?" She stopped the dead memories, pulled the anchor, stumbled to the motor, and fired it up. She peeled out of the cove. Waves crested the bow in white plumes, so she kept to the shore. But it was there that reeds and weeds bound the propellers. The boat slowed, coughed. She forced the throttle, and the engine howled and stalled.

She pulled on the motor, hoping she could hinge the propellers above the water, but it was stuck. Waves leaped over the sides, submerging the keel and forcing the boat back into the reeds. She tugged and yanked, yet the motor just thudded against the boat. Falling over the motor, she gasped as tears of futility and frustration flowed.

When she opened her eyes, the tilt lock was there near the motor's hinge. She yanked the pin and heaved the weed-wrapped propeller above the water as the boat filled. Tiny leaves and slime coated her skin as she freed the three rusty blades, dumped the motor back into the water, set the locking pin, and fired up the engine. She pushed, urged, the boat twenty yards, but it lunged into the waves and took on more water. She cranked the gas, and the engine whined, but the water's weight was too much. It belched blue smoke and died.

"No. No. No!" It was useless. She screamed at the sky, but even her voice was washed away by the wind. The boat filled nearly to the rail, and oars floated away from the walls. A gust pulled them from Rhea, but she clung onto both and pulled them close. With the oars tight to her chest, she bobbed as waves smacked her shoulders. She kicked, but her shoes made every thrust a nightmare of escape from a horror that froze her limbs. Her sweats, thick and heavy, slid to her ankles where they knotted with her shoes.

Then she was pulled under. Not just by her clothes but by dozens of tiny hands and thin fingers that clawed her calves. She screamed. It was a choked scream made liquid by the green water. Gouts of air fled her throat and rose like a sad clown's clutch of lost balloons.

Through the churning water, the sun's murky streaks of yellow framed by her arms and the oars she still held. She sucked in and coughed out water. Her hoodie billowed, a twisted mess. It couldn't end this way. She couldn't give in to whatever held her legs. She elbowed up on the paddles, kicking frantically for a longer life.

Her shoes fell. Her sweats slid. And the fingers clung desperately to her legs yet slid into blacker waters. She retched with stomach-twisting seizures. Water, warmed by her lungs, spilled over her tongue and into the lake where it belonged. Her muscles burned, yet she couldn't stop. The waves grew in height closer to shore, struck and washed over her head, pushing her faster until her feet touched the silt shores that reeked of rotted fish. She toed the lake bottom, crawled, then crab-crawled away from the waves heaving for air, hoping that thing or things didn't follow.

She was free. She was safe. She rested against a tree and vomited more of what the lake had given her. Lake water ran from her mouth, down her chest, and soaked the leaf-matted soil where hard-carapaced bugs, sickly and gray, dug.

She still shook, and the coughing would not stop. She

clenched her hoodie over her chest, inhaling and exhaling with rib-stretching gasps, calming her muscles. She pulled her legs close and rested her head on her knees as her shoulders heaved, grew limp, heaved, grew limp. Her chin quivered, and her lips bunched into a sneer, one she hated since a sunny day on an elementary playground holding skinned knees. Tears pushed, but she pushed back against the sorrow, the grief, the fear.

She opened her eyes toward the yawning trees where clouds clotted the blue sky but had yet to conceal the sun. She sunk her palms into the lake-soaked mud. Amos's boat struggled to stay above water then was pulled under. Wet and freezing, she needed shelter. She was just a mile short of the cabin, and it was when she scanned the distant shore that a light in the Manor's attic throbbed like the dull ache in her head. And, on the end of the cabins' dock, a man, a white stalk of blanched skin and black hair, stood naked with what looked like a liquor bottle. It could be Josh, or maybe Eddie. It was hard to tell, and both options were bad.

If it was Josh, he was waiting for her. Rhea tensed, not just from the cold that filled her body but from what Josh may want from her. Her belly sickened. If it was Josh, with his sneer, with the crucifix that dangled from his lobe, what would she do? What could she do?

She shook her head and streaked mud across her face when she tugged wet hair from her cheeks. Algae clung to her legs where gooseflesh had pricked up. She brushed at the algae but ended up just trading it for mud. She looked back toward the dock.

If it was Eddie, what was he doing? Yet, if it was him, at least it'd be someone she knew, someone she could reason with, talk down, share moments of the past to ground whatever it was he was feeling, or, in the very least, bring down from whatever ledge on which he balanced.

Rhea didn't want either of them. Eddie had become an unknown just like Josh. What or who would Eddie be? If it was him. Whomever it was slipped behind the trees toward the cabins after taking a swig from the bottle.

Rhea stood and heaved in another calming breath. She tugged at her black hoodie that hung low but not low enough to cover much of her mud-pocked legs. She curled her toes, and the silt slid between them in thick globs. The lake could wash her body, but whatever might be there was too much, so she pushed herself up, resigned to go through the woods toward the cabin.

CHAPTER FIFTEEN

THREADS OF SMOKE lingered at Eddie's mouth, and a lake breeze washed over the birch- and pine-wooded hill. Amos's blood speckled his face, and he smiled like a grim Howdy Doody. It felt good to kill. The Old Man inside him swelled black and evil. Eddie wanted a drink, but Rhea was probably in Frank's, so he crossed the highway and entered The Store. The bells above the door rang.

Owen was back behind the counter. His goggles magnified the lure he was tying. He looked up with jellyfish eyes and said, "Eddie," and went back to his lure.

"Liquor," said Eddie.

Owen swirled his finger over his own face. "You got somethin'."

Eddie smeared the blood across his face and wiped it on his bloody jeans. "Liquor."

Owen nodded. "Got a stash in back. Amos don't know, least not that I know."

"Don't matter no more."

"Meanin'?"

Eddie shrugged. "Scotch."

"Amos's?" Owen pointed at bloody chevrons staining the tiled floor.

Eddie nodded. It didn't matter much if Owen knew. He didn't do shit anyway. "Scotch, Owen."

The stool creaked with relief when Owen stood. He slid open a back door that smacked shut behind him on heavy springs. There was a shuffling of boxes and clinking of glass before he came out with a bottle of Johnnie Walker. Owen set the bottle on the glass counter next to the register and said, "Twenty." Eddie flicked him enough bills from last night's tips to cover, plus a couple more, and left The Store to ringing bells.

Eddie uncapped the scotch and took a few swigs and leaned against a pump. He pocketed the cap with Saul's coins. He pulled them out and rolled them in his palm. Their burnished silver glinted. One was his and one was Rhea's. He'd lost track which was which. There wasn't anything special about the two coins: a fat-necked Lady Liberty on one side above the year 1921 and a spread eagle holding a bunch of shit in its talons with the typical God-fearing slogan above its long-necked head. Any god should do if any at all, but someone needed *that* God.

Eddie shook his head. He hated it all. Yet, there was something missing. His leaf. It was still in the bar, between the napkins. He turned. He wanted it. Rhea could be there, still should be there.

The door rang behind him and stinking Owen leaned against a thick pole holding up the roof. "You know, Eddie," said Owen, "Ruth's been lookin' for ya."

Eddie looked back at Owen. "And?"

"You came in lookin' for booze."

"Your point?"

"You don't wanna go into Frank's lookin' like ya do, but Ruth ain't there. And, well, she—"

"Where'd she go?" Eddie looked at Frank's.

"Amos's."

"Why?"

"Said somethin' 'bout Rhea runnin' off, maybe needin' you . . . or Amos. Course, she'll find Amos dead."

Typical. Rhea left work early, couldn't handle it. Didn't want to deal with everyone—anyone—but him. She still needed him, wanted him. "She won't find 'im."

"How's that?"

"He's with Saul."

"Saul dead too?"

"Not yet."

"Well, like I said, Rhea's gone."

Eddie took a swig. She was probably back at the lake. Back in the cabin, lounging on the couch, sucking down vodka like a prim priss, waiting for Eddie. Like her sister, prancing beside that pool, flaunting but never giving. She'd fuck this up somehow. Ruth'd wind up finding Amos all because Rhea couldn't keep her shit together.

Now, like a child's nightmarish fear, the voice boiled inside Eddie's mind and body and blackened both with new hate. *Selfish.*

Right. Selfish. A deep pit of anger filled his belly and bound his chest. He'd taken Amos. Eddie smiled. She'd never have him, have Amos, and Amos'd never have her, have her to distract her from him, from Eddie. She didn't need what Amos'd give her—and take. Typical, like her father, wanting and lusting, taking, abusing. The same, weak Rhea.

Weak.

Weak. Worthless.

Worthless.

Ungrateful.

Ungrateful.

"Mine," Eddie said.

"What?" asked Owen.

Yours.

"Ours," said Eddie. He crossed the highway to where Ruth liked to lord over the bar, over the town, on the balcony. It wasn't hers to have. It was his.

Yours.

"No, ours," Eddie said. "And we'll have it." He hobbled up the uneven steps as though one leg was dead. Frank's was dark and locked. He clenched his fists, and a growl at the back of his throat fed off that pit of anger.

Key.

Right, the key. Ruth, so trusting. He had it. That old bitch had given it to him so long ago. How long?

Ages.

Ages. Longer than he'd known, longer than he could grasp. Time had become more than just days. He wanted more, wanted it all. He *needed* more. He didn't have what he needed. Rhea knew, though. Knew Ruth. Knew Amos. Eddie only had that damned priest who gave little. He'd have it.

Yes.

Rhea'd give it to him. He needed to get back to the cabin, force what he needed from her.

She'll leave.

The Old Man was right. Either that, or she'd pitch herself off the balcony.

The Manor.

Right, the Manor. There were balconies there too, nice and high. She'd love that, stepping out onto that balcony or maybe one of those windows high in the roof where she could see all of Saint Andrew before her and that dock where she and Amos bonded.

More than that.

Fucking loved.

Of course.

She'd cry for all she'd lost, probably remember her family and wish she'd taken a face of terracotta down in California. Rhea knew something, more than he did, and he needed it if he was going to get her to stay.

Eddie unlocked the door. Frank's gaped before him. The bar throbbed with need. The walls groaned and creaked as though vermin clawed within. It was hungry. Not for liquor or food. For them. For Eddie. And he'd give when the time was right. He locked the door and looked in the mirror. *Whadda ya see?* Saul had said. Blood streaked Eddie's face like doomed meteors. The mirror's flaked silver aged him to a scaled leper. His bloody *Sisters* shirt stuck to him.

I see my face, he'd said. That wasn't true. That wasn't him, not his face. What was in the mirror, now, was him, what he wanted: a miserable wretch holding hands with death. Saul was wrong. There was a need for more, but he did have himself and knew where he was. He'd have more. All he wanted.

He pulled the stack of napkins from under the bar and peeled them open like an old book. He held the leaf by the stem and blew on the ragged remains. Brown flakes of the leaf's flesh spread on the bar like a tiny mob fleeing a flood. "Sorry, Frank," he said to the walls that heaved.

He held the leaf against the light of the jukebox. Only the veins remained. Amos's blood stained the stem. It wasn't what he wanted, but it had happened; the leaf was tainted by that man's blood. The jukebox flared ochre, and Jorgenson grated out vocals to electric drums that pushed the rhythm and moaning synth lines as he—those—believed in forces that pulled down those called to sacrifice, those who followed. He wouldn't sacrifice. Eddie'd be the one the Saint followed, what the Saint wanted, what Saint Andrew wanted.

They'd come. He'd serve. He'd want, yet they'd want more, want him. Him and him alone. Frank's, his and his alone. He'd take. It'd be his. All he wanted. This town was his like nothing he'd had before.

"Mine," he said to the walls. "You're mine."

Ours, said the voice.

A radiator hissed. "Mine." Eddie clenched his leaf's stem. Its veins quivered, thrummed with his rage and the loudening music. The Old Man dug deep. Pain flared across his body. Then his palms split as though sliced by a surgeon's scalpel and blood dripped off his elbows.

Ours.

Eddie leaned against the bar and said through his teeth, "Ours."

Go.

Muscle and sinew tugged in short tendrils, and his palms closed. The pain fled. Eddie sighed. The Old Man was right. It was time. He was still bloody, still wet with Amos's death. He needed the cabin—for now. Frank's and the Manor would come later.

The door rattled. Through the smoked window, he could see Ruth's cauliflower sprout of hair. God, he hated her. Little fuckin' busybody gettin' her shit in everyone else's. He shook his head and closed his eyes as he strangled the bottle in his fist and took a swig. The liquor slid down his throat, hot and harsh.

Leave, Eddie. The Old Man convulsed, forced him to move.

Through the kitchen, Eddie twitched and limped to the Old Man's whim. He slowed the screen door from smacking and made his way past the dumpster and chipped granite stained with his own blood. Keys clattered as Ruth locked up inside Frank's.

CHAPTER SIXTEEN

Blood from Eddie's hands dripped off the leaf and bottle and spattered the gravel-dusted tar. Slump-shouldered, he stared across the street at a Hawaiian-shirted hulk of a man, fried crisp by the sun, pumped gas into his rusty RV. A yellow, sun-paled VW Beetle, its engine sputtering like a tightly bound spring, tugged an aluminum boat past Josh's garage where the pops and spatters of his welding would stop only for a quick curse like drum solo rimshots. The RVer stuffed himself into his vehicle and chugged past bloody Eddie who crossed the highway and kept as far from Josh's garage as he could.

Josh stopped welding, and he shouldered against the garage door's frame with a saloon-shitkicker pose. He flicked up his welder's mask, thumbed his nose, and yelled, "Rhea knows."

Eddie sighed. That ass just had to talk. Eddie gave in. "Knows what?"

"What you told Saul."

"What's that?"

"You know."

"Yeah. And you?"

Josh stuck a thumb in a pocket and nodded. "Yep."

Eddie laughed and shook his head. "Told you?"

"Yep."

"And you . . ." Eddie swung his arm as if bringing Rhea in on the conversation.

"Told Rhea, like Saul wanted."

"She believed you? I doubt it. She wouldn't. It's me."

"Yeah," Josh said. "It's you. She will though. Believe, that is."

"Suppose she will." Eddie brought the bottle to his lips.

"Ain't nothin' you can do 'bout it." Josh pushed himself by the shoulder and stood tall. "'Cause you ain't shit."

"Fuck's that mean?"

"You don't say nothin' different, do ya?" Josh took a couple steps toward Eddie then pointed at Frank's. "You're like that damn jukebox, playin' tunes like it means somethin', like it's helpin' or fuckin' with you or some shit."

"Fuck you goin' on 'bout?"

"Just like I said. You ain't shit. Let me tell you somethin', Eddie. This place will take you. But there's better shit than you."

"Not followin' you."

"This's what Ruth talks 'bout. Stories and shit. Look, my dad ain't here, but I am." He shook his head and looked at the cloud-streaked sky. He scratched his throat where his Adam's apple bulged and bobbed as though his insides tugged the next words from his mouth. "My mom, she's here too. I didn't kill my dad. My mom did. Yeah, I hit the wrong breaker, and my dad got a good spark, but that didn't do him in. My mom and that screwdriver did him in, right through the ear."

He stroked his chin as though he had a beard, focusing on a memory lost in the shades of blue stone scattered across the driveway. "Shit, my mom. That'd been the first time she'd done somethin', straddling my dad in her sweaty nightgown, still holdin' the screwdriver stuck in my dad's head like a joystick." He looked back at Eddie and pointed with a black greased finger. "You think you're special 'cause Saul said? You ain't shit. Rhea, she gives a shit. In her, there's pain: what this place wants. The only reason this place really wants you, or will take you, is Rhea" Eddie shifted. The gravel crunched under his feet. "Yeah, that's right. You want to stay, but she ain't sure. Now that she knows what you done, she ain't gonna stay."

"Rhea'll stay," Eddie said, yet the words came out like sludge. "She needs me."

"Damn, you dumb. You got it wrong. If Cal got it right with what happened down the road, you need her."

"Meanin'?"

Josh shook his head. "You still don't get that neither. That road. You might figure it out, but it don't do no good me tellin' you. Let's just say, Rhea don't need shit." He lifted a finger and wagged it like he had more inside him than most knew, smarter than most thought. Maybe that was true. "Bet if she tried leavin' right now, this place would stop her. She's good, better than most. Tasty. Sweet and tasty. You're a murderin' ass. Rotten fruit. That's easy."

"He killed again," Owen said as he leaned against the back corner of The Store. His T-shirt hung limp at his sides.

"Did he now?"

"Yep," Owen said. "Told me just a bit ago."

Eddie held his head low. He'd crossed the road and stood at the end of the shop's driveway. The granite chips at his feet glittered with quartz in the afternoon sun. Their edges were sharp. He'd trusted Owen. Told him what he'd done. Eddie crouched and picked up one of the stones. Now, Owen was here at the right time—the wrong time—lounging at the corner of The Store.

"Who, Owen?"

"Amos. Course, I guessed wrong. Figured it'd be Saul." Owen snapped his fingers flippantly.

Eddie raised his head and looked toward The Store and said, "That's right, Owen. I told ya that."

Owen pursed his lips, and the thistles he hadn't shaved swayed on his gullet like stiff reeds in waves.

"Where at?" Josh asked.

"Dunno." Owen twitched his head to the side either by will or some strange tick that had risen to the surface.

"Where at, Eddie?" Josh now closer, tilted his head to the side.

"The church," said Eddie. "Saul was there. Didn't do shit."

Josh's shoulders jumped with a couple nose-snorted laughs. "That explains why you look the way you do. Yep, you're well on your way, ain't ya?"

"Where'd she go?" Eddie asked as he clenched the rock that bit the insides of his fingers.

"What? Oh." Josh shook his head and rubbed his forehead. "I just 'bout forgot. Rhea, she came from the trees before, which means she got a boat, probably from Amos."

Eddie glanced at the path leading to the lake.

"That ain't gonna do you no good, dumbass. If she went that way, the boat's gone." Josh went back in the shop.

Eddie followed. Grease, iron, and sweat soaked the air. Josh's office was lined with filing cabinets, walls plastered with centerfolds, and a black wall clock that read close to noon. The first week of June was struck with a line and a smudged note in blue pen and block letters: PARTY KEG. Next to those block letters were Eddie's keys, a mug stained with old coffee, and a heavy wrench polished by years of use.

"Jesus, Eddie," Josh said. "You got some stones comin' in here like this. What you want?"

"This place," Eddie said. Josh had been the first to come out and say something honest, something about himself, and Eddie couldn't let that go. "I don't get it."

"No, you don't. Want somethin'?"

Eddie turned toward the shop's rear where square cages of welded flatiron hunkered in shadows on blackened concrete. Each cage was no more than three feet on each side. Their doors padlocked. Bolted to the top was a brushed brass crucifix. He looked at Josh and said, "What the fu—"

Josh said, "Business is good."

Eddie shook his head. He didn't know what to say. Josh was the ass who'd taken him to his Vega then stabbed his back by spilling everything to Rhea. Josh could suffer, but it was Saul who'd done it.

Josh leaned back. His chair squeaked. Behind Cal, Owen stood. Josh said, "You know what? I'm done. I ain't tellin' you shit. Unless you wanna get your ass hung in a sling again, you better move on and fuck up whatever you gonna do 'bout Rhea." Josh pulled a pack of smokes from his desk drawer and lit up with a clack of the Marine Zippo.

Eddie clenched his jaw and said, "You done?"

Josh looked past Eddie at the cages and smiled. "No, one last bit. Know your place, Eddie. We all got 'em. This here shop's mine. Ruth's got Frank's, mostly. Amos got his dock. Saul's got his church. Owen, The Store. Cal, well"—Eddie looked over his shoulder at Cal shaking his head—"as Ruth says, that's his to say. You? Well, you ain't got no place, which is a dangerous thing in this town."

"I got Frank's key."

"That place ain't yours. And she ain't givin' it to you, not for nothin'."

It'd be his. He knew it would. It was just a matter of time, and this ass in front of him knew nothing. Nothing he needed. Cal sucked his teeth. Owen had his hands in his pockets.

"We'll see," said Eddie.

"No, we won't. You're worthless, and this place knows it. It ain't given you shit. It'll take."

Eddie took a step toward Josh, but Cal grabbed Eddie's shoulder. Cal had changed. That stupid weasel was gone. His eyes watered, softened, and he said, "Don't, Eddie. You don't know nothin' yet. Just move on. We all gotta sometime."

Eddie spat on Josh's calendar. He'd let Josh go, for now. Eddie had taken Josh's punches before. His belly churned, and his body ached. Josh smiled and said, "That's right, back the fuck up. And, Eddie, if Rhea stays, you bet she gonna be mine when the time comes."

Do it.

Eddie opened his mouth, but there was nothing to say. A flood of hate and rage opened a door inside where he saw himself take that wrench and lunge. Josh fell backward, and he did one of those stupid, cartoon balancing acts, windmilling his arms before his chair and head hit the concrete floor. When the wrench caved Josh's skull, Eddie's wrist sparked with pain. It wasn't the best tool for the job, but it'd do in a pinch. And it was a good pinch. One of Josh's eyes popped like a weasel from its box, and his lips did that fucked up sneer like he'd done in the truck when he saw Rhea. Josh sighed and wet his pants. Eddie smiled with his eyes and slid the wrench from Josh's steaming skull.

He turned toward Cal and Owen, who backed off, holding up their hands, calm, almost indifferent. They probably hated Josh just as much. The wrench clattered on the floor.

CHAPTER SEVENTEEN

Eddie made his way to the cabin where the trees nestled along the swamp showed early green. Birds no longer swayed on the reeds. A wind picked up from the west. The lake was restless. Whitecaps rose near the middle and spread to the shores, and a distant boat motor gargled. At the cabin, all was as he left it, yet he was alone. He scrubbed his bloody boots then stoked the boiler, stripped, and burned his clothes. Naked, he stood at the end of the dock. He held the leaf and bottle of scotch. He was a grim silhouette against the distant Manor lit yellow in the mid-afternoon sun. Wind and waves churned at the dock. His skin prickled, yet the liquor deadened his body and mind to the cold. The Manor loomed, and it was there that a sullen light flickered behind a corner window.

Go, said the Old Man.

Eddie shook his head. "Not yet."

The Old Man didn't push back, accepted what he'd said. As he should. The Old Man wouldn't control him forever. Couldn't control him forever. And the Old Man, again, failed to reply, failed to force himself onto Eddie as though the Old Man had burrowed deep within and receded into that festering seed of pitch.

After taking a swig, Eddie showered in the stall Rhea must have cleaned. With a twist of a creaking knob, the hot water pelted his head and freed the blood from his face and body in twitching rivulets that spiraled down the rusty drain. As the last of the shampoo drained foamy and blue down the drain, waves pummeled the shore. Pinecones and twigs pelted the corrugated metal roof.

"Eddie?"

He'd have stumbled back, but he kept focus and control, and his heart slowed when he saw it was Rhea. She'd come in silently. He shut off the shower and grabbed the towel off a rusted screw, dried off, and wrapped the towel around his waist. He held the tips of his fingers against his eye lids, one of which was still tender, shook his head, and looked at Rhea. Her hoodie was soaked. Her legs and feet were bare and muddied, covered in leaves and algae. Her hair draped over her shoulders in straight lines of red. With her head held low, she hid her face in the fading sun's shadow. Her arms were folded across her chest, and she shivered.

Eddie looked at the shower floor where water, no longer tinted with blood, gurgled down the drain that fed the lake. "Get off early?"

Rhea clenched fists and walked away.

"What?" he asked. Liquor numbed his face, slurred words. The porch screen door smacked behind her.

He dried himself as dead leaves skittered around his feet toward the lake and tucked the towel around his waist. Inside, Rhea sat at the table where the map was still spread on the gold-flecked table. The potbelly stove had dimmed but still put out heat. She tapped her finger near the middle of Minnesota where Eddie had scrawled in the lake and town.

"Eddie, you didn't tell me."

It was a statement, yet it was a question in that annoying expectancy of a reply, a passive order for answers that he never wanted to give in to, never wanted to succumb to. Why didn't she just ask the question? Why was it always a game? Why'd she always hide the truth? Hide what she wanted?

He wouldn't give her the answer right away. He wanted to let that moment of power he had last, so he opened the stove's door and tossed in a log from the metal basket. Still hunkered next to the stove, he looked up at Rhea and said, "Tell you what?"

"Where this town is—was. Here. Right here." She jabbed the map with a nail speckled with the last of the polish she hadn't chewed free.

At her feet a puddle of water formed. Her legs were taut with gooseflesh, and her hoodie covered only the parts Eddie didn't want. His heart thumped his ribs, and he felt warm and hardened. He wanted her. He'd take her.

Take her.

Bend her over the table.

Yes.

She'd scream.

Pain.

She'd scream at first not wanting, but she'd know it's what she needed.

Slut.

But she bit down with the merest of clicks of teeth, crossed her legs, and pulled the hoodie over her knees.

Harlot. Tease.

Her lips tensed and pulled into thin lines.

He shook his head. Of course. She'd tempt. Then take. She knew what he saw.

Whore.

She did it on purpose. Let him see on purpose.

Yes.

The Old Man was right. He, Eddie, was right. She distracted Eddie, confused him with that give-and-take of hers she was so good at. He dug his nails into his palms.

Yours.

Right, she was his, and he'd take what was his, what had been his, and always would be his.

She wants it.

That's how she worked. She flaunted then kept, like her sister.

Sister.

Outside, clouds blotted the sun. Eddie thumped his fist against his temple like some padded-cell inmate knocking the crazy shit from his brain or back in order. No, he'd keep her. Keep her with him. In his town. In Saint Andrew.

Yes.

"Eddie," Rhea said. She tapped the map.

"It ain't there. Just scribbles." He turned toward the lake as he stood to hide his early erection.

"Ain't there," Rhea said. "You don't know where we are."

It was judgement. She'd slammed the gavel. He was wrong. She was right.

"Eddie, this place. I can't..."

He dug his nails deeper. The pain melted her voice that was always the same. Never changing. Just like what she wanted. No matter where they were it was what *she* wanted and knew was right.

We need to leave, Eddie, she'd say at every town they'd settled in. *We need to go, now.*

Fuck that, he'd say. *Fuck that and fuck you. We need a place to stay, and we've found one here.*

Eddie, if we stay, they'll find us, and I can't go through that.

Those people, at the house. We left them there. At my house. That house that's still mine. *The cops would've come eventually. They might be after you, but I doubt it. Your dad. Your mom. They'll cover for you, pay off who they need, but I've got no one, and they'll find me. Oh Christ, Eddie. What did I do to those people? I did exactly what my dad did to my mom, to my sister.*

You don't know that, Eddie said, and he was right because he was the one who'd done it. He'd always have that. No matter what she thought, he'd be innocent to her, and she'd be wrong. He wasn't innocent. He was their end, yet he was the one who saved Rhea. The one who controlled her. And he loved it.

He ended the past in his mind and said, "What do you want me to say?" The lake was marbled black and green without the sun. He could hear her leaning back in the chair.

"Want you to say?" She probably had her arms crossed. "How about something?" She dug her eyes into the back of his head. "You've said nothing since we got here, to this town. I want words. Your words. I want something that isn't hidden in slick lines. Like-like in Anza-Borrego. Like on that balcony. Like in the back of the Vega."

"The fuck you talkin' 'bout?"

"There it is."

"What?"

"That voice. That isn't you. Where are you, Eddie?"

"Jesus, Rhea. What the fuck does that mean?" Eddie turned toward Rhea. He'd lost his hard-on. Her voice took it from him. "Who got ta you?"

"Got *ta* me? Fuck you." She stood, and the chair skidded across the tile floor into the kitchen. "You don't know. You know nothing. Don't know me." She shook her head and held her lids closed with the tips of her fingers.

Eddie searched the walls as anger churned in his chest, tightened like it fought against deep water. Know her? The fuck's that mean? He knew her. She was Rhea, that stupid fuckin' girl standing on the balcony. That stupid fuckin' girl taking her dad's shit. That stupid fuckin' girl who took and handed out drugs. Nah, she needed something. He smiled. She needed something good. And he knew. Girl, that's what she was. A girl. And girls need—"Rhea, I love you."

"What the fuck," she said, hands limp at her sides.

He couldn't follow. It was a statement made simple yet out of some place he had no right being. No, some foreign part of her he had never been, never seen, never known. Her psychobabble had gotten him off track. He was done talking, at least until he could figure out what the fuck she was going on about.

"You say that now? Like that'll solve some *thing*?" Her lips moved as though in private conversation that led her to say, "I don't think you do. I'm sure you don't. Not that I give a fuck anymore. To you, I'm still on that balcony, weak and lonely." Her face sunk with resignation. Or was it hate and defiance?

He reached out to her, and she backed away.

"Stay the fuck away, Eddie."

He obeyed. He had no other choice. She pointed at him, stabbed the air. And like a limp leaf waved him away—Where was his leaf?—yet there was power in that gesture that dismissed him. "This isn't you showing up at the right time on some fucking balcony. Where were you back then? Were you out there on the street, looking, watching? Checking to see what I'd do after."

She was right. God dammit, she was right. How? And there were no tears in her eyes. Why? Rhea had changed. There was a will Eddie hadn't seen before. Something had changed. Something had happened. He needed to know. And he needed to end it. Pound it down to nothing. He step-slid toward her on the dead leg. The Old Man was still there.

"My god, Eddie, what . . .?" She pointed at his leg and backed into the kitchen's fridge.

He smiled at that. He was still in control because she feared. Yeah, she feared, and that too felt good. There was control. He controlled. Controlled her. Controlled himself. And controlled what was within.

Good.

That's right, even the Old Man knew who had control, and he'd use it.

Use me.

He tensed. The Old Man wanted her throat. He bit down and sucked in through his nose, exhaled through his mouth then said, "Josh," as if that'd be enough or answer whatever the fuck it was she was stuttering about.

"Eddie, where were you when—"

He shook his head and said, "Rhea."

"No, Eddie," she said again, yet her throat closed and made it a whisper.

God, he hated her.

Yes, weak.

Why did she always have to be there when he wanted her least?

Prying.

She was supposed to be working, tempting the customers with her ass and pouting lips, not in the kitchen stabbing that fucking map with her finger covered in chipped polish like some sloppy street slut.

"Eddie, did you kill them?"

God damn it. He was glad Josh was dead. Saul would be next. But that wouldn't be enough. She'd push. He couldn't argue, couldn't let the rage take over.

Murder. Kill. The Old Man filled him with ancient hate.

Eddie swallowed, shook his head. Never. He'd never kill her. Not unless it got real bad. Then she'd know.

The Old Man understood and said, *Soon*.

Give in. Give in like she was right, then take it away. Give her hope, clarity, and rip it from her. "You're right, Rhea. You're always right." He hated those words.

She stumbled back. "You killed my—"

His back cracked and his body strained.

Pain.

He shook his head. "I didn't kill your family. I don't know who told you that, but it's not me. They twisted my words. Yeah, I told Saul about your family. I had to tell someone."

"Who—"

"No, Rhea. Please." She'd love that, *please*. Now, bunch that face up like pain hides inside and stutter like she does. "I need to . . . We've been . . . No, *I've* been on the road for years now." Fucking brilliant shit there. Now, self-hate then guilt dashed with truth. "Running from home like some stupid kid. And I did that to you. I took you from your house. From your family." Fuckin'A right he did. "You could still have that home, but I came and took that from you because that's what I thought you needed, and I'm sorry." Jesus, what a bunch of bullshit.

"Eddie, I—"

Eddie held out his halting hand, looked at the floor, and shook his head. "I need to tell you. When I talked to Saul, I needed to tell someone who'd listen, who wouldn't judge. Now, I don't know why or how Josh found out, but that ass would say anything to get to you. You know that, right?"

She looked toward the lake, and Eddie let her feel whatever it was she needed. She closed her eyes before he continued.

"I gotta tell you. In the truck, when we were heading out to the Vega, you were a sweet piece, he said. Remember the pumps?" He reached for her too early. He knew it would be, and she cringed. Perfect. "He wants you, Rhea. I-I told Josh what he needed to hear after I found out his dad was dead. He needed to know I was weak, and that was my days with my dad. Doing what I did. Doing what I made you do. And, well, I'm sorry about that too." He dug into his mind and pulled lines he'd heard often enough, lines from bullshit scripts written for those who wanted to believe, and she wanted to believe. "And it's something I've never told you. And I should have." His delivery was good. He softened his voice with just enough timidity as the wind outside settled. He'd have smiled, but that would have ruined the moment, ruined the mood, ruined what he was hoping she'd say and do.

"Eddie, why now?"

"Because, Rhea. We've been in this town for what feels longer than long, and we've been apart, and you're leaving me, so I need to tell you these things because I'm going to stay."

"Eddie, I'm not—"

"No, you are. And you know that. But I gave you those drugs, told you where to drop 'em." He paused just long enough for her to open her mouth. "But I didn't love you then. I loved you when I saw you with your sister. When I saw you leaning against that vending machine, watching your sister prance in front of those prisses. And I needed you then. Wanted you then."

"Eddie, I can't be here right now. My god. I need . . . I don't know."

She walked past him, and he let his knuckles graze her hand. She stopped at the door and looked at her legs then back at Eddie. His scene wasn't perfect. She wasn't crying like so many would have been, should have been, in those scenes up on the screen. But she needed something from him, which *was* perfect.

Eddie looked at her legs. "If you have to go, take your bag."

He turned and picked up her duffel, zipped it shut, and held it out for Rhea to take, but he didn't move from the kitchen. She'd have to take it from him. It was a hand-out that'd break her just enough. And she took it by the strap, close to the zipper, so they didn't touch.

Were there tears? Maybe. Just at the corners next to her freckled nose that she'd salute the sky with when she thought she had the one-up on him. She looked at Eddie's chest then his eyes as if searching for truth in what he'd said. She held the edge of the table. She fought back those tears. In those tears was Rhea, the lonely girl who felt worthless, the lonely girl who needed him. Needed Eddie. He smiled.

He'd get his perfect scene, soon, but not yet. Control was time. Control was pause. Control was giving what the controlled had given up. So instead of confrontation and more psychobabble bullshit, he avoided, feinted to the bedroom where his leaf sat on the bed next to Saul's coins.

"Where are you going?"

It was that squeal again, that prissy whine like when they first pulled into Saint Andrew. He ignored her. It was what she needed. He dug from his duffel his third and last set of clothes and dressed: the same black boots, shredded blue jeans, and a white button-up shirt with a stiff collar. It's what he wore when he wanted tips, yet everything was wrinkled to sharp edges and smelled of fat-fried doughnuts and burned coffee, so he sprayed it down with a couple shots of truck-stop cologne.

"Eddie." Rhea was at the door.

He held up a single finger and said, "Go, Rhea." She wouldn't go. Not if he told her. Typical bullshit she'd pull just to dig in deeper. In the bathroom, he brushed his teeth with a load of paste. He didn't want to look at her. He didn't want her to look at him. He needed to avoid those prying eyes that'd figure something out, get what she needed. He stabbed his teeth with the toothbrush. Spat in the sink. Turned on the tap. The water sputtered brown then clear.

Rhea's memory flickered inside him as though a reel projector tossed her image on a limp sheet. All the timeless possibilities of what they'd done, what he'd done and could do while a song of screams sizzled out the projector's weak speaker. Those screams were hers joined with her sister and mother who lurched from the background and framed her in family while he hid in his black room, felt their bodies go limp. Other's pain was his worth.

What he hated was that now there was no return. No going back to those slick lies. There was too much blood. Too much truth. And more to come. But he couldn't lose her. He needed her. For the first time, he knew he needed her. And in that need, maybe he should let her go.

No, he couldn't. She didn't say it, but she wanted to stay. She just didn't know it yet just like all the other times. Josh said the town wouldn't let her leave. What a bunch of bullshit. It let *him* leave. How could it want her and not him? It made no sense. This place and the thing inside him had needs, and he needed to find out what they were, what they wanted, what they needed. If he could find that out, he could keep Rhea.

I'll show you.

Show him what?

Keep her forever.

Forever?

Forever.

"Mine and only mine?"

Yes.

"Eddie, you didn't answer me. Did you kill them?"

Fuck her. Prying bitch.

He spat again and looked in the medicine cabinet's mirror. His face was twisted, contorted not just with rage, but with what was within. Eddie's back cracked, and he hunched close to the mirror. Minty foam drained from a wicked grimace. His eyes glinted like silverfish flicking through blue-gray water. He wiped the paste from his lips. The grimace was gone, replaced by an open-mouthed, toothy grin. He wanted to wipe that from his face too, but his limp body would not obey. He looked down. No, not limp, epileptic, shredded to sinew. He step-slid closer on that dead limb and clenched the porcelain sink against not only of his own weight but what was within.

It, *he*, was strong. In the mirror, the silver peeled away like feathers. The demon, the Old Man, the hunched horror was there, staring back at him. The same shadow with its paper-torn edges fluttering as though suspended in a black pool. No, not a pool, a black room with no edges.

"Rhea," Eddie said, yet it wasn't his voice. The words slid out like a knife honed on a whetstone. "You're not here to find yourself."

Eddie—the Eddie inside—was pulled from the controls of his mind, shoved into that room decorated with rage and murder. It was a room he knew but had only visited of his own free will and a desire to set Rhea free. So long ago in that room, he saw himself wrap his legs around Rhea's sister. Smother her mother's mouth as he stabbed the needle. From that dark room, he saw himself twist the surgical tube around her dad's arm who bounced his knee with excitement and need. He saw himself flick the vein, prep the syringe, and pump the shit deep inside that loser. It was a comfortable room, a room that separated him. Yet, now, the room closed in, held him. No longer could he leave that room. He was trapped, and the Old Man moved him.

"You'll never find what you need. What you want," said Eddie's knife-honed voice.

"What?" Rhea said. Her soft feet padded on the tile floor into the carpeted bedroom.

In the bathroom, Eddie turned—or, rather, Eddie's body turned, and Eddie witnessed from that black room.

Eddie's body lunged and grabbed her throat. She squeaked. The Old Man loved it. Yet, it wasn't just the Old Man's love. Not fully. Eddie felt that love when he slit that shithead cop's throat. Bashed that shit-eating grin off Josh. It was a shared love, and Rhea's throat was soft, tempting. Tendons popped and her esophagus bent.

A piece of Eddie receded, cringed from the Old Man who cackled with something more than love. And he envied the Old Man, too, who was doing things he'd done before but in a way that terrified him.

Rhea. Rhea was his. His to keep. To have her dead—*No,* he said within. He wanted her living and with him. As Rhea's face reddened, a tear pooled then slid down her cheek as though it didn't want to leave, as though it looked back and longed for where it had come, longed for home. A home. Its home. Her home.

What was inside him churned. His stomach rolled. "You know," slid the words from his mouth, "she told you. He told you. They told you."

"Eddie," his name was barely a gurgle from Rhea's mouth. "I—"

The Old Man twisted and threw her on the bed still clutching her throat and planted his leg between her bare legs. Yet, it wasn't her the Old Man wanted. He wanted hurt. He wanted misery. Pain. Her mouth flapped like a fish's sticky lips gaping on the shore. She was ugly, and the Old Man grinned.

"No one wants you."

He smacked her ribs.

"Only me."

Another smack.

Rhea gulped and twitched her knee, but it wasn't enough. She delivered no pain, so she reined his hair and with the other hand dug in a yellow-chipped thumb into his left eye.

Within, Eddie said, *No, not like this.* The black room constricted, held, suffocated. He'd stop it. *No,* he said again, yet the black room remained, and the Old Man seethed like a furnace next to him. It wanted control. It wanted Eddie.

"I need you," the Old Man said. "I want you."

No, Eddie said again through the teeth of his mind. *Never like this.* Hot with rage as red as all the blood he'd spilled, he turned toward the Old Man in that dark room and surged forward. Grabbed the thing's throat—or tried. Yet all was immaterial like clouds ripped by an angry wind.

Eddie's eye popped slick down his cheeks. Her thumb, inside his skull, wriggled then was yanked free as the Old Man howled and held Eddie's face torched with pain. She gasped long and hard with a baritone grating of her raw throat. She rolled from the bed and slid something from the floor and padded out the cabin, gasping. The Old Man reeled, hobbled.

Stop, Eddie said. "Stop," he said again, but this time the words met the world beyond the room, beyond his body. He opened his last eye, and the mirror's silver skin pulled back upon itself and sealed that black room. Sealed the Old Man within where he suckled on Eddie's pain, drank it down to a dull ache.

Eddie inhaled smoke and must, liquor and rot. He waited. A log in the stove hissed. Branches broke. Then he pulled open his other eyelid, sealed shut by jelly tears that clung slick to his fingers. The eye itself sagged. Blood haloed his iris now white and ripped with veins, it twitched like it wanted what it no longer could do. Had it been someone else's eye, he would have let loose the liquor in his stomach. But it was his. And it would always be his: a grim slideshow memory of Rhea thrown on that bed. Rhea screaming. Rhea struggling. Rhea's face twisting like a plowed field as she dug her thumb into where his eye would never be again. A part of him permanently lost to that fucking bitch.

Eddie turned on the faucet, held the water in his palms, and washed away his thoughts and the wounds of the Old Man who took his body and Rhea. The Old Man whom he'd keep until he needed him most. He erased what he could and bandaged what he needed. Blood swirled down the sink like an omen of his own, personal hell. He turned. Water wet his curls and dripped from his chin.

In the pit of his stomach, no, upon his back, just below his shoulders, he felt the weight of responsibility, felt the weight of control, or power. And he'd embrace it. He'd wipe his bullshit past and gain worth through that town. Through Saint Andrew. Through the Saint. Eddie pulled a beer from the fridge, picked up his leaf, and sat at the table. The map was still there, stained and wet with rings from a half dozen bottles. He cracked open the beer and spun the leaf between his fingers.

Eddie nodded, answering a question that was not asked. Through the screens, the Manor was before him, sick with age, breathing with timeless misery. Eddie nodded again, he wanted it, and soon it'd be his. Eddie's lid slid over the muck of what remained of his eye. The Old Man had done that to him. Now it was his turn. He'd keep him there until he needed the Old Man most. When he started his own new scene where he was in control.

CHAPTER EIGHTEEN

Rhea shook and shivered as she stumbled from the cabin. Thankfully, she had the sense to pick up her duffel before getting the hell out of the cabin. Eddie yelled something, but it was muffled like she'd just gotten off a long flight. All else blazed bright, even the smells: the lake, budding leaves, the shower's mildew, a breeze that promised spring, the damp earth under her feet. She hated it all. She needed to leave. Now. There was no other choice. She couldn't give a damn about anyone there—well, most anyone.

Cold and muddy and, to top it off, her thumb was slick with Eddie's eye. She could feel it under her nail, across her knuckle. It was harder than she thought it'd be—not thumbing his eye, but the eye itself. At first, it resisted, like plastic-wrapped cartilage. When her nail scored that plastic, it spat something sticky and warm, and his eye rolled aside like a polite doorman and the pad of her thumb slid along slick bone. When Eddie yanked away, there was a slight pop like a fat tongue clicked on a mouth's roof.

She exhaled. Her mouth fluttered like an over-inflated

balloon giving up the ghost. Near the showers, she leaned against a tree. Her heart pounded. Her chest heaved. Her knees folded. Then her stomach took over, and whatever Ruth had fed her came up and splatted on the tree's roots.

Through tears not of misery but from the strain of vomiting, she said, "I'm sorry." Those words, rasped by the bruised memory of Eddie's hands, weren't to herself or Eddie. She said it to the tree, that'd been there for who knows how long, as if her vomit would kill it, make it sick, sick with everything she'd drunk, eaten, and seen. From her vomit, it'd twist into an evil or sad tree lost among all the others that ridiculed it for seeing and knowing things the others didn't. Its bark peppered her palm, and she said, "I'm sorry," again and again until—

"Sorry for what?"

It was Didi. Rhea's shoulders slumped. No one could just leave her the fuck alone here. Didi stood next to the boiler that flickered sullenly as though it was breathing through steady hunger pains. Her arms were folded across her chest, and she curled her toes in the moss carpet that somehow resisted the boiler's heat.

"Sorry for what, Rhea?"

Rhea shook her head. "It doesn't matter."

"Everything matters, Rhea."

"Not anymore." She looked at the cabin. Eddie sat at the table sucking liquor while spinning a leaf between his fingers. The fire in the potbelly stove glowered orange.

"What happened, I saw it." Each word ended with her Alabama in full force: long and smooth, lacking the throaty Midwest that hocked out words like thick spit.

"Saw what?"

"I couldn't stay away. I saw Eddie on the dock and knew you'd need me."

"I don't need—"

"You don't look it."

Couldn't she finish a God damned sentence? Did everyone have to cut her off? Did everyone have to squelch her voice to nothing with what they thought she was going to say?

"And I don't think you believe that," Didi said.

Jesus Christ. Believe that?

"I heard somethin', Rhea."

Oh, god, there it was. Some shit she was supposed to give a shit about. Didn't Didi see? Had she eyes? The mud? The blood? Christ, Eddie's eye stunk. It was a sick scent like hamburger left out overnight. She stood, looked Didi straight like few others ever did, and just said, "What."

"Eddie killed—"

"My family. He said he didn't." She wanted to be angry. She wanted to hate Didi just like she hated Eddie. She wanted to yell out everything that was locked inside. All the years wasted. All the sick moments with Eddie in the backseat of that shitty car. All the hours prancing though pancake shacks like she gave a fuck about those she served just for a few coins tossed on the table for her to scrape up like secondhand donations. "Didi," she said. "Watch Eddie."

She dug out an old towel. She was weary, and it was that weariness and the muck from the lake that brought her down, brought her to lose the will to move and speak, give a shit about the danger that was just steps away.

Didi nodded, picked up the broken broomstick, and opened the boiler door. Before tossing a log in, she said, "Rhea?"

The weight of the clouds dragged down the late afternoon sun and Rhea's anger. "Yes?" She leaned against the cold metal of the shack, and a gust of air cut through her damp hoodie.

"Look, please," Didi said as she pointed at the fire that flickered on her white face.

Rhea kneeled near Didi. Inside the boiler was the outline of clothes charred to ash with a few hems breathing red and gold. Rhea took the stick from Didi and poked at the remains which fell to ash among the logs turned to coal. She looked up at Didi and opened her mouth as if to speak, but no words came out.

"I don't know," Didi said. "Clothes. Eddie's?"

"Why?"

Didi shrugged. "Same reason as any. Gettin' rid of 'em."

Rhea looked back toward the cabin. "I need to talk to Ruth, maybe Amos."

"What about me?"

"Not now, Didi. I'm going to Ruth."

"I can take you there."

"How?"

"The canoes." Didi looked at the sky. "It's calmed. If we keep to the shore, we'll be safe."

"No, I've had enough of the lake. Keep watch while I wash up?"

Didi nodded.

Rhea stripped and hung her hoodie on the rusty screw and made short work of showering. Didi handed Rhea fresh clothes from her duffel. Rhea pulled on her last pair of Girbaud's and a white T-shirt leaving her soaked hoodie behind. On a tree's roots, Didi had tossed Rhea's babydoll gown. Rhea wouldn't need it, not again, not ever.

Dragging her brush through tangles, Rhea said, "Didi, will you walk with me?"

"Sorry, Rhea," Didi said. "I'm not one for going into town." She pointed toward the boathouse. "I'll take a canoe. Meet me at Amos's dock when you're done?"

"Maybe." Rhea squeezed Didi's thin shoulders and said, "Stay away from Eddie. He's changed," and left her behind. When she looked back, Didi was gone. On the way in, tiny pins of cold rain pricked Rhea's cheeks. She slung her duffel over her shoulder and picked up her pace, flipflops smacking her heels.

Ruth had lived through so much, knew so many in town, knew the town itself. If anyone had answers, it'd be her. Hopefully. Rhea would be honest with Ruth. She wasn't a cop. Rhea would tell her everything. And in that honesty would be answers, would come the answers Rhea needed.

How could she have trusted Eddie this long? Not just trusting, *blindly* trusting him, moving from town to town without a thought that he might not be the Eddie she thought she knew. It was her fault. She fell for those slick words and soft hands.

She shook her head and sheltered under a tree. Dry grass licked her calves through jeans. The rain was fresh, unlike the lake that thrummed with waves killed by the swamp. He was a criminal, Eddie. She should never have trusted him.

Of course, she, too, was a criminal, but she'd done those things just to . . . No, if she was going to be honest with Ruth, she needed to be honest with herself. She did those things because she wanted to. Because she hated the people she gave those drugs to—*may* have given those drugs to. People like her dad.

Certainly, she hated all those she left behind in her house: worthless, abusive people not only to themselves but those they should have loved. What had happened to them? How long did they linger in that house haunted by her dead family? Were they dead too? Had some of them nodded off with their noses dusted never to open their eyes again? Did the rest stumble over the bodies and back to their double-wides—if they were lucky—or their slumlord's chopped up, second floor efficiencies above some gun-toting freak's liquor store?

Jesus, that place was a shithole.

She should have left sooner, before-before that pool, before the drugs, before Eddie. She was glad she left it behind, but those people. How could she? But she knew. She knew why she did those things. It was the end. The end of that life and hers. All of that would have been lost and forgotten. She'd have been another headline on the second page, her photo shredded and pissed on by some kid's puppy.

What was the point?

No. She opened her eyes. Rain spattered gravel. A toad loped into the swamp where blackbirds again bounced on reeds.

"No," she said to no one. She shook her head. Not to no one. To herself.

"Move." Her body resisted. Or, rather, something inside her willed her to give up, to give in.

"Move," she said again, and she took her first step, then another, and another until she emerged from the suffocating road and cabins sunk in shadow. To her left was a route she had not traveled. Out there, somewhere, were the others who lived in that town or lived on its edges, teased by the life and family it promised. Within, were Ruth, Amos, Saul, Josh, Cal, Owen, even Didi. And there were others.

She had wanted to join them. She thought there was a love. A love she'd never had or had with only one person before. A love that wasn't with any *one* person. It was just there. Hidden in the reeds. Hidden within Frank's. Hidden beyond the shores. Hidden, yet there like a mystery hunkered in a cave, afraid yet hoping for release.

"Afraid. Release," she said. Yes, there was terror or fear. While they were intimate, knew each other unlike any town she'd slummed in, there was a hidden distrust or caution. Something that held them back from being who they really were. And maybe she—Rhea—was like them or something like them who had yet to find their own truth.

And like that love, that terror or fear was hidden behind

kind faces. Kind faces that lied. Kind faces that judged. Kind faces that spun secrets of hate, sin, and distrust. Why did she need Eddie? Amos? Or Ruth? Why did she need anyone? She couldn't become what this place was. What this place had become—the old clinging to the past yet suffering in time.

The rain picked up, and the crackling tires of a heavy pickup pulled up behind her. A young boy said, "Give you a lift?" Rhea turned. It was that same tired boy. There was another round bale in the pickup's bed—or the same one? In the cab, the boy scooted over and opened the passenger door with a metal squawk. "Come on, get in. It ain't far, but it'll rain good soon."

Rhea looked at the dark clouds that hung low. Her feet ached. Her legs were sore. The thought of being wet again, soaked through the clothes with the smell of the lake was enough to make her step up into the cab.

CHAPTER NINETEEN

THE KID WAS YOUNG: ten, maybe younger. It was tough to tell. Rhea'd already taken on an adult perspective of age. The young looked younger, and the old looked less old. She thought it was a bit early for that, but it was what it was. The boy had blond hair dashed with the brown of dirty beach sand. His eyes were muddy gray, and a few freckles sprinkled his nose like red pepper flakes. Wrapped around the steering wheel, his hands still hadn't lost all that baby plumpness. The cab itself was doused with dust and hay mixed with gas fumes curdling from a tankard set on the seat.

"I seen you, before," the boy said without putting the truck into gear. "You were walkin' with Ruth, right here." He pointed at the side of the road. The wipers groaned against the windshield.

"Yeah, that's right," Rhea said. "I was lucky you came by."

The child coughed and held his chest. The wipers skidded and groaned again. "Luck ain't got nothin' ta do with it, lady." He flicked the wipers off. The rain popped against the glass and ran like fat tears.

"Meaning?" Rhea asked.

"I drive this road. You walk this road. I chose to be here just like you." He scooted to the edge of the bench seat that was already shoved as far forward as it could, so much so that Rhea's knees nudged the glovebox's metal cover.

"You're good." Rhea smiled. It was an honest smile.

"Wrong again."

She tilted her head, so her wet locks fell across her legs. She rung them out on the truck's floor that was already damp and muddy. "How so?"

"I didn't do what my dad said." The kid had his eyes on the hood. He dipped his toe toward the pedals like he was testing a pool's temp, pushed the clutch, and swung the steering column's stick into first. He stabbed at the gas with his other toe, and the truck jerked forward.

"That's normal," Rhea said.

"How's that?"

"You're, what, ten?"

"Just about."

"And you drive?"

The boy shrugged. "It's the way it is here. When it's needed, it gets done."

"The way. Boys your age don't do what their daddy says. Not always."

The boy shook his head. "Father don't say that."

"Saul?" asked Rhea. The boy nodded. "Don't listen to . . ." She stopped. The kid was young. It wasn't her place to tell him one way or another about Saul or what he believed. "Why aren't you in school?"

The rain fell freely, so he flipped on the wipers. They gave a single groan then slid smoothly across the glass. "Dad says I don't need it. Farming's what I do, and farmers don't need talkin' and numbers."

"That doesn't—"

"Off, a bit, right? Tractors get grain to cover a field. Seems like numbers to me. But, some day, he says, he'll teach me."

"That's okay with you?"

His bottom lip pushed up like he'd just taken a bad pull of chew, and he shrugged. "Do what I'm told." His knuckles whitened around the wheel. "I miss the others."

"Others?"

"The kids. School. Mrs.—the teacher."

"Where do you live?" There was an honesty to this kid that Rhea hadn't had with others. A directness that she hadn't had, really, ever.

"Up the road, just a bit."

Rhea looked over her shoulder where the checkered silos stood smeared with clouds and rain. "Old Al's farm?"

The kid coughed, wiped spittle from his lips, and rubbed his eyes. "That's right."

"What's your name?" She'd have asked earlier, but the kid didn't seem too interested in names.

"Luke. Luke Jones."

"Then, your dad must be Al Jones's other son?"

Luke looked at Rhea. His face was bunched up and his lip twisted like she'd just said something stupid. "Nah, lady. Al's my dad."

"But I thought. So Al Jones Jr.? You're too young for Al to be your dad."

"Only one Al. Not followin'. Too young?"

"Al Jones. On the dock. Fishes." Rhea cocked a corner of her mouth into a smile partially out of how the boy looked, but more so because the smile put up a wall against what she already knew but didn't want to admit.

"I'm gonna—" Luke coughed. "I'm gonna show you somethin'. Somethin' that'll help. Somethin' others are too afraid to show."

"What?"

"Like Amos always says, I'll pay for it. But I don't care 'bout that."

Luke eased the truck up to the lake's public access. He ground the gears into neutral and coasted onto the chips of blue granite until he was a few dozen feet from the water's edge where lazy waves lapped the shore. Luke pointed at the dock as he clutched noon on the steering wheel. Al had kicked up on his cooler and leaned back in his aluminum folding chair. The plaid straps sagged under his weight and years of use, maybe abuse.

Luke coughed again. "He's always fishin'. Fishin' and drinkin'. He ain't never home." His voice grated through a desert-dry throat. "He'll never teach me."

Rhea turned toward the child, toward Luke. Her stomach was empty. Her chest tight. "But you're . . ." She breathed out her mouth and held her stomach that cramped with hunger and fear. Her legs weakened, and the dull pain of old liquor filled her head like neon spotlights zeroing in on where it'd hurt most.

Luke's eyes bulged at the edges, red and packed with tears. He gagged and wretched. His shoulders heaved and bowed toward the front of the truck. He brought a fist to his mouth and coughed again like a mule taking a hard boot to the gut. Away from his mouth, his palm was slick with bloody saliva that soaked two kernels of hard corn. He looked up at Rhea. Tears streaked his face made thick by a white powder that had dusted his face and highlighted the red of his eyes. In his mouth, more corn, bright yellow, slurred his speech. "I gotta— I can't get—" Rhea reached toward him, but Luke shouldered the door open, rolled out of the truck and heaved.

Outside, the redwing blackbirds screeched *murder* made metallic in their throats as they bobbed on reeds. Rhea covered her ears. Luke heaved again and said, "Hurts," garbled by orange vomit laced with blood and riddled with kernels. He grabbed the door's armrest and pulled himself up. Through coughs, he reached out to Al and said, "Dad-dy," but it was broken in two by his wretches. Luke stumbled then crawled toward the dock. Rain spattered the windshield and pelted the rock. It was a clean rain that washed the scent of moldering hay from the truck's cab yet watercolor-smeared what Rhea saw until the blades wiped the image clear. Ole Al sat and chugged another beer.

Rhea opened the passenger door and screamed Al's name, who set down his bottle and clutched his pole. Rhea ran to Luke, who was still crawling toward the dock. She fell at his side, grabbed him around the chest, and turned him over in her lap. Corn filled his mouth, and his eyes were packed with the white dust. He looked up at her, unable to blink, eyes crackled with red veins like an aged vase. His body twitched and seized. A bone in his leg popped, and blood soaked his jeans. His back arched. Rhea jumped and would have screamed, but the whole scene fogged into a sliver of time, a moment torn from all else. There was only Luke's tiny face placid and his oval mouth that gaped for air. Only his eyes knew death was close. Rhea held his tiny hand. Luke hissed his last breath and grew limp. She wiped strands of the boy's hair from his forehead and held him close. His half-shuttered eyes gained an emptiness only afforded to the dead. The same eyes as her sister. Her tears met the boys and ran down his muddied cheeks.

Rhea raised her head and looked toward the lake, the Manor, and the end of the dock where Al still sat. She set Luke's head down on the hard granite chips, just out of reach of the lake's water. She stumbled toward Al and said his name

with weak uncertainty like a child stepping into a dark basement looking for mommy, but Al did not turn. The dock
creaked like a hollow chest under her feet. She was behind
him, yet he did not move. His hands roped with veins that
strangled swollen knuckles were wrapped around the cork-
covered haft of the fishing pole. Next to his feet, a spaghetti
pile of nightcrawlers squirmed in a plastic bucket. His beer
bubbled, and rain smacked the dock. Rhea reached out and
held his shoulder that was all bone under thin skin and soft
muscle.

Al turned. Under his seed-cap, tears or rain wet his red lids
and cheeks that hung from his bones like layers of fleshy yarn.
The crooks of his lips were crusted white, and his chin
twitched as he chewed on his own gums. He turned back
toward the lake, picked up his beer, took a swig, and wiped his
chin. Rhea released him.

Ruth, she needed Ruth. Or Amos. Anyone. Her knuckles
scraped stone when she picked up Luke. His body was small,
light, ribs barely hid under his shirt. Wisps of hair curled with
the breeze from his head that hung limp over her arm, and
corn dust drank his tears. Rhea's own tears wet her cheeks
when she set him in the truck's cab, buckled in a parody of
safety. But he was hers now, for a short time, and she wanted
him safe.

The truck whined as she pulled from the lake. There was a
wet pop, perhaps a stone punched down by the truck's balloon
tires. Then another pop, this time closer, louder, and Luke
twitched. She slowed the truck. He didn't move, just slid from
the seat only as far as the seatbelt would allow. Rain fell
harder, pelted the metal roof. She shook her head and pulled
onto the road. Luke sighed, and those tiny ribs rose like the
timelapse of a seedling breaking through soil. Rhea slammed

the brakes, shoved the truck into park, and jumped out. She held the door open, holding herself up at the same time.

Luke's arms moved, grabbed the seat, reached for the wheel. He sat up. Opened his eyes. Wiped the corn from his mouth. And looked at Rhea through those dust-packed eyes. "Did you see?" he asked.

"See?" Her question was a throaty whisper as images and sound slapped her mind like surfed TV channels: scene after scene, voice after voice, and all of them making little sense together. Rhea knuckled her nose and wiped away tears. Her flipflops were soft under her feet yet wet with rain as she crept back into the truck and closed the door. "I saw you," she said. Her voice shook, not only from the cold but from what she had seen. Had she seen it? Had it happened? These things didn't happen, couldn't happen. And yet, there Luke was. The boy who hadn't changed from the moment she first saw him driving down the gravel road. The boy who had died. A strand of rain-soaked hair dangled across her nose and lips when she said, "You're . . . You're alive."

"Yeah," Luke said with a skewed lip and huff of air.

Rhea shook her head. This was the child who'd died in her arms as he looked up at her with those packed eyes. Al still fished, either didn't care, hadn't heard, didn't love, or was too drunk. Her voice was little more than a rasp. "No, this can't—I saw you. There was corn. Your leg."

He nodded. "Hurts a bit, but all better." He kinked the rearview mirror toward himself and spit corn from his mouth. "No," he said to the mirror. He shook his head and said, "No," again. His chin bunched into tiny dimples, and his lips thinned to a taught, pink line as he said, "No," one last time and looked at Rhea. "I'm tired, Rhea. Tired of it all. Tired of seeing the same thing every day. Tired of seeing some come in and leave, and some come in and get stuck like the rest of us. Those who leave, forget. Those who stay, remember. Forever."

"Amos. He said . . ." It was just too much for her to say, to accept. Dead for over a hundred years? Saul? Instead, she asked, "What happened back there?" She nodded toward the lake where the rain blurred the dock.

"The town told me not to, but I don't listen."

"The . . . town?"

He nodded. "My dad over there? He's not dead. I am. He'll die soon enough though. He just sits there fishin' all day. All night. When he dies, he'll be stuck here forever. There ain't no changin' that."

"Then you're the little boy who—who Ruth said—in the corn bin."

"I died. I died in the corn bin. I was stupid. I didn't listen. Then I died. Now I'm stuck here. Forever. Why? I don't know. I guess this place, this town just likes pain, likes suffering. Feeds off it or somethin'. It's a bad place. You talked to Amos?"

Rhea nodded.

"Ruth?"

Rhea shrugged.

"Then they probably told you about the Dakota who never came here, stayed away. Well, other people came and stayed, and now we're all here, I suppose, because of them. But it'd happen sometime no matter what."

"Why are you—"

"Rhea, do you hear voices?"

Rhea drew back from the question as though Luke had feigned a punch. "What?"

"Since you've been here, have you heard voices?"

"Yes, in the bar."

"The Old Man," Luke said. He blinked and brought his eyes

to hers. "He talks to me—hard, sometimes. I don't want him. He wants me. Always has."

Her mouth dried. "He has."

"Don't listen. Try not listenin'. Push back 'cause what he wants ain't good. Do you still hear them?"

"No."

"That could be good. What about that man you were with?"

"Eddie?"

He shrugged. "I guess."

"I don't know."

"He changed?"

Rhea cocooned her thumb with her fingers and swallowed past bruises. "Yes. Or was always that way."

"Talk to himself?"

Walking to the cabin, on the shore, maybe other times too. She nodded.

"Be careful, then. Those who listen can't be trusted. Come on. You drive. Like I said, it ain't far, but this rain'll get stronger."

Rhea pulled the truck up to the highway where Frank's stared at The Store.

"Where to?" Luke asked.

"Have you ever tried leaving?"

Luke nodded. "Yeah, it's never good. Besides, the dead can't leave. Sometimes the living can, I guess. Have you tried?"

"No."

"Then leave. Try. If you can, keep going."

"Amos said that."

"He's right. He's good, but he can't leave. Told me so when he found out I was dead."

Taking a left would bring her back to where she'd already been: down that straight road now melted in rain where Eddie left her in the Vega. The other way through town would plunge her down that hill past the school and who knows where, and that's the path she took.

When she reached the edge of town, Luke said, "Stop here by the sign. I can't go any further. I know it's raining, but it's best if you don't take my truck. I tried that before, going as fast as I could like I'd punch my way out." He shook his head. "It hurt bad."

She was already soaked, so she draped her jean jacket over her head and stepped onto the road. Held up by split logs, the back of the sign was sprinkled with useless graffiti and the word STAY in a brush's black swipes spanning the entire sign. She looked at Luke, nodded, and he closed the truck door. The first few steps were easy, but when she reached the sign, she paused.

Nothing stopped her. It was a choice, a choice not to go further in that moment. Then she took the next step and another until the weight and silliness of what she was doing overcame her.

She looked back. Behind the wheel, Luke kept the wipers running and shooed her down the road. Anchored in the ditch, the sign's face was a brush-stroked snapshot of another time, a time where perfection was a rolled-up-sleeves, muscled dad tossing a football above a leaping dog to an eager son. In the foreground, like a footnote stressing their place, the mom and daughter in plaid dresses and white aprons sat on a checked cloth. A granite stiff smile was chiseled into their faces as they set out lunch and a perfect bundt cake. Scrolled across the clouds was *Welcome to Saint Andrew!*

CHAPTER TWENTY

BEYOND THE SIGN, Rhea lost herself in the time she'd been in Saint Andrew. It was a time that felt longer. Had it been two days? Was it only two days she'd been here? What had she done yesterday? Had she only slept the one night? Had one night with Eddie? Her stomach turned with the thought of him inside her as she drunkenly hung over the bed that squeaked like a sick animal. God, why? None of it made sense. Was that the limit of her time here? None of it held weight as if her body floated in Lake Andrew. The cold water surrounded her and calmed, tempted her deeper, warmed by the sun above as her body listed like a boat abandoned through disease and time.

She was back at the Vega. Then the school. Then Frank's. Then the cabin. Then the boat and the Manor. Now here. There was nothing. Nothing had happened. Yet everything had changed. She'd seen so much yet knew so little about the town. About Saint Andrew. About the Saint who called her, said her name without speaking, so spoke for it.

"Rhea," she said.

In her mind, she had returned to the lake, floated there, her body framed by the dark water. That voice she did not hear was no longer a voice of power or a voice of dominance. It was a voice that offered. A voice from the past, or a voice that felt as though it belonged to the past.

She wanted that voice, wanted to know that voice, but she didn't know who it was. It wasn't what she heard in Frank's, and she wanted more. Wanted it all. Wanted purpose, and maybe in that voice was purpose. What she had needed since she had left her Wensley Avenue house, burdened with the white stucco that sagged and cracked, stained by the sandstorms that she feared so much. Stained by the time she had been there. Stained by what she had done. Stained by the death of her family.

That house was her. That house was what she had become: an abandoned building filled with death, abuse, and doubt, pummeled from the outside by time unmoving. She hadn't moved. Not within. Sure, she'd been on the road for years now, but she hadn't changed, and it was time for change.

What had happened to her family? Was it Eddie? She needed to find out. Was it her dad? Had her family really done those things? Her sister spoke to her. "No, Rhea. I would never. Not to you. Not to mom. Not ever." Yet it wasn't her sister. It was what her mind had made her sister into after all these years.

The water surrounded her, held her. Wanted her to stay. And she wanted to stay. This place had the answers she needed.

"Rhea," said the Saint through her. "Stay."

She left that lake, wrenched her body from its grasp, and awoke in the truck. Water spattered the bench seat's woven fabric and onto the floor at her feet. Her hair curled around her face like red ribbons. The lake's dead scent filled the cab.

"You can't leave," Luke said through lips without hope.

It seemed wrong, but she turned toward Luke and said, "You're dead." She knew yet hadn't said those words. Hadn't accepted. But saying it aloud was a release she needed, a reckoning with the truth of what she'd seen and what or who was next to her.

He'd changed. Not only in his eyes but in the way he sat at the wheel: straight and stiff like if he curled over the burdens he carried would never allow him to return to what he once was. A child, but he wasn't that child any longer. He was something new. Something old. Something held in that moment, in that town, frozen in time, static before Rhea. Unyielding to her words. In that place that wanted everyone. Did it want everyone?

Did it want Al? Al knew nothing. He was there, still at the end of the dock. In pain. Pain for what he had done to his son. But was he really? Really in pain? No, it was Luke who was in pain. Luke who suffered. And like he had said, the town needed suffering.

The voice through her said nothing. It had left. It was no longer there. No longer held the weight it had before. She wasn't sure how she knew. But she wanted no more answers from it. Ruth would be there. Luke stirred and toed the clutch. He shoved the truck into gear and swung toward town. Rhea let him take her, willed him to take her, and he did. There was no danger, no evil in the child she'd come to know in those few short moments. Those moments that lasted longer than any she'd felt before, longer than the total time she'd been in Saint Andrew.

Luke pulled the pickup into the parking lot between the church and Frank's. She held his shoulder, wetting his flannel shirt. "Luke," she said. He turned toward her. "You're dead, Luke, and I'm sorry."

"I know," said Luke. His voice was old and angry. Tears welled.

"Please, wait for me?"

Luke nodded, popped the truck into park. The engine sputtered and jumped when he turned the key.

"Food?" Rhea asked.

Luke shook his head. "Not hungry."

Rhea nodded and stepped outside. It hadn't stopped raining, yet the air was heavy. The gravel had been oiled, which leached its scent, killed nearby grass, and beaded water. A dog barked and another replied. A dust-brown sedan packed with kids pulled next to the pumps, and Owen chugged in gas to the tune of a few bills and nod of his head. He looked up at Rhea and leaned against one of the posts that held up the porch roof safe from the rain. She waved at Owen, but he just scratched his gullet.

Grass crunched under her flipflops yet grew soft and green near Frank's. The rain softened to mist that curled and lapped with the lightest wind. Rhea stepped onto the sidewalk and to Frank's front door. It was dark inside and was locked. "Ruth," she said through the door hoping she'd be mopping or cleaning up some mess Eddie hadn't bothered to clear, but there was no reply. Smudged in the window was Owen's reflection, his eyes still on her.

She wound around to the back. The screen door's rusty spring crooned. She knocked and called out Ruth's name to no response. Granite crunched behind her.

"Ruth ain't here," said Owen.

CHAPTER TWENTY-ONE

UNDER THE GAUZE Eddie packed into his missing eye, the bleeding had stopped, and the pain faded. Like his hands before, the Old Man did Eddie a solid. He downed the last of the spit-beer at the bottom of the bottle and switched to scotch. He had a strong buzz going. His cheeks twinged with hints of liquor laziness.

"Just right," he said as he massaged his jaw.

He didn't want to get blitzed, so he watered the scotch down with a can of soda from the fridge. Scotch gave him the edge he needed to temper doubt. And he didn't doubt what he was doing was the right thing. She'd come back. She always did. She'd talk to whomever it was she needed at that moment, realize they weren't Eddie, and come back to him.

"Predictable."

He set the leaf down on the table, lathered up, and shaved away the afternoon stubble while swigging his scotch. In the mirror, the black room appeared again, the dark room he was so fond of years ago when it was a safe place. Now, however, the Old Man lived there and yet had retreated at his touch.

There must have been power in that touch, a power that Eddie didn't know he had. Who was he kidding? He'd always had that power, just like when the Saint couldn't stop him from leaving.

Nothing controlled him. He was Eddie. He smiled and laughed through his nose as though he'd just dismissed a small child. He picked up his hawkbill blade, stuffed it into his boot, and sat next to the potbelly where he could see the shower hut that snaked steam through branches silhouetted black in the stormy afternoon.

Rhea stepped from the shower and ran the towel across her back, over her thighs, then tousled her hair with her ass saluting him. He pushed down where he grew hard. She stayed. Hadn't left. What was she doing? His eye ached. She must still trust him. After all that, she trusted him. How stupid she was. That could have been his last chance to be with Rhea, but that was far from truth. He'd have another. Like he said, she'd always come back.

She reached into the shower and slipped on her babydoll and covered it with her black hoodie. She pulled the hood over her head, turned, and tiptoed to the cabin.

"Already? Jesus, she has no fuckin' clue what to do with herself."

That babydoll meant one thing. She passed the window and smiled under the shroud of her hood. The screen door smacked, and she walked in. Her hoodie was still soaked with lake water, but that didn't matter. She was there, and she needed him. He knew she did.

She took his hand and said, "Eddie, I'm sorry. I believe you, Eddie. I always believe you. I just needed time alone. It's my fault."

He stood when she tugged his hand. She held him close. She slid her thigh between his legs and lifted on her toes. "Not here, though," she said through wet lips and lake-green eyes. She combed her fingers through his hair. The hoodie was cold against his shaved cheek. Even her breath was cold when her lips touched his lobe. Eddie's heart swelled. His head swam. And his limbs became liquid.

"I need ta show ya somethin'," she said. There it was again, that little bit of the South that had somehow made it into this Midwest town. Did she want to stay too? This town was hard to resist.

He wrapped his arms around her and pulled her toward the bedroom, but she held him back as if they'd marched to the front of a smiling congregation. "What?"

"No, follow me. There's a place that's perfect for us, perfect for what we can become. A place where we'll be safe. The Old Man told me. The Saint . . . told me."

"They talk? To you?" She never told him. And what the fuck, the Saint? Why?

"They do, and they want us."

"Us?" Was Josh right?

"Yes, Eddie. They want you more, of course. They want your power. Because you're special. I didn't realize how special you are until out there, in the showers. They told me. You're what I need. You're what I've always needed, and I'm sorry. It's all my fault for what happened, to your . . ." She touched just below his missing eye. "I pushed too hard before. Come. I want this town. But I want you most. Here. With me. Forever."

She leashed him into the rain, pulled not by force but by what he wanted, and he wanted her. It may have been the only reason he stayed with her all these years. Did he really need anything else from her? What good had she done for him? He was the one who saved her from her dad.

That bastard.

Her mom and sister would have just dragged her down.

Good riddance.

So he let her lead him to a canoe she tugged from the boathouse. She didn't ask for help, so he stood and waited. There was a confidence in her, something that hadn't been there before. Or, rather, something that had only come up in the cabin. Rhea had changed, and he wasn't sure if he liked it. It confused him. He wasn't in control—not total control. Or maybe he was. Afterall, he was letting her lead him, and he still had fear on his side.

The lake cradled the canoe. She tempted him with her nakedness under the babydoll, looked up, and smiled. "Com'on, Eddie. Get in."

At the front of the canoe, he took an oar. She pushed off.

"Just row," she said as she steered the boat east through calm waters. He turned, but before he could see her, she said, "No, look ahead, Eddie. Soon."

She wanted control, even now. He'd give it to her, just this once. In a way, it was fun, exciting even, giving her the perception of control. Just once and only once. The Manor was dark, but the window he'd seen from the dock still breathed light.

"The Manor?" Eddie said.

"You'll see. Stop paddling."

He did, and she ran the boat ashore between jagged rocks. The Manor loomed over Eddie. Rain wept over its roof and down its walls.

"Get out. Pull the boat in."

It was an order, plain and clear, free of those games she'd always played where she never gave the full story. Where she only spoke half-truths just to get his reaction, get him to give her something she knew he had but wanted to come out of his lips, to hear directly from him.

He got out and pulled the boat further ashore. Rhea stood and stepped out while he held the boat steady. She led him through newly bloomed flowers like yellow teacups held on a star of white petals. Above, the balcony sagged, and the porch remained abandoned with no access from the shore. Its French doors and windows were closed, and the panes were frosted with years of grime. Rhea led him to a side of the Manor facing the cattailed swamp separating it from the rest of Saint Andrew.

"Boat's the only way to get here? To the Manor?" Fear pinpricked Eddie's abdomen.

Rhea shrugged. "Sometimes the swamp."

"Rhea?"

She nodded but didn't stop until she reached the top of granite steps that led to the front door flanked by two black, coved pillars bearing a dormer. There were no handles, just a cast iron beveled plate with a single keyhole. Rhea pulled out a key no one this day and age had business carrying and twisted it in the lock with a whisper of oiled metal and pushed the door in.

"Come on," Rhea said. "It's everythin' you'd've loved before runnin'."

CHAPTER TWENTY-TWO

THE TEACUP FLOWERS shivered as the rain fell. Eddie wiped his eyes. Above, another dormer jutted from the steep roof. Its wall was swallowed by a stained-glass window. However, unlike the rest of the slender windows, this one was an obese circle nearly as wide as Eddie was tall. Most of the window was opaque cream except a blue X that pie-pieced the white.

Rhea's bare leg slid inside the Manor. She said, "Eddie," in a voice as clear as if she stood next to him, and the door closed but did not latch.

Eddie entered.

The Manor was cold as if it guarded itself from comfort. A gloom had settled on the interior. There were no light switches, only gas lamps that sprouted from a webbing of brass pipes mounted to the walls. However, the foyer was not weathered. A bucket and mop would have brought the dark-stained trim and paneling back to life. Rhea ignored three doors on the main floor and slinked up the right of two stair-cases lined by lathed spindles and thick rails that curled up to a balcony and another set of doors through which she disappeared.

Eddie's boots echoed in the foyer as he followed. On the balcony, he turned. The front door closed with a devil of dust. Above the foyer, a grand gasolier hung from a rosette of knotted ropes plastered to the ceiling. The ceiling creaked, and thin lines of plaster sprinkled down next to that rosette. There was another creak, and more plaster fell. A creak, more plaster fell, closer and closer to Eddie until it dusted his hair, and his eyes teared up.

"Eddie." Rhea laughed. Again, her voice was beside him, inside him, but the laugh wasn't hers.

Beyond the door, shards of plaster littered the hallway where it'd fallen from the walls. The hall extended to the left and right and simply ended at two, tall windows gridded by a dozen or more square panes and two doors. In front of him was a seating area with two fireplaces and French doors that led to the balcony beyond. The furniture in that room had all but crumbled and was covered in black mold.

"Rhea," Eddie said. His voice soaked into the walls. Rodents skittered as he neared the northwest room where a wedge of gold light flickered on the floor. He pushed the door open.

Beds lined the walls like mirror-on-mirror reflections, other than one where Rhea lay wrapped in a nest of stained sheets. Its mattress, pinstriped blue, sagged on an iron frame. Her back was toward the door, and she'd flung her hoodie over a moldering fireside chair. Next to that chair, a single log warmed the room in a metal fireplace while rain tapped the windowpanes like children's fingernails. Through the west window was the cabin and dock. Deeper in the room, a second window opened north beyond which Al still sat and fished.

Behind him was a pickup, and a redhead held a child near the water.

"Rhea?" Eddie asked.

On the bed, she curled the sheets over her thigh and shoulder. Eddie sat on the chair, took off his boots and pants, then unbuttoned his shirt. He crawled onto the mattress and pulled Rhea's soft body close to his.

She pressed against him and said his name. Except it wasn't his name, not the way Rhea always said it. The South was strong, and that last syllable left her mouth like a shawl falling from a moonlit lover's bare shoulders. "This place could be ours, Eddie."

"I know," he said as he buried his face in her hair and grew hard.

"Do you want it?"

"Yes, and I want you." Too easy. Again and again. She'd always be there. He slid his hand from her chest and down her stomach.

"No." Rhea grabbed his wrist.

Jesus Christ, more words. More talking. "Why?"

"Because I know," she said.

Another one of her fucking games played on scales measuring who gives a fuck more. "Know what?"

"I know you killed my sister."

The scales tipped. Fucking broke. Eddie took his hands off Rhea and shuffled away. "No. I told you—"

"You lie, Eddie. You've always lied."

"No, I haven't."

"Yes, you have. You always have." Rhea stood and looked out the west window where the gray light glowed through her babydoll. "And, I never saw it before. It seems so long ago. You, standing on that balcony, framed in those doors. There, at the perfect time in the perfect way."

"No, I—"

"Yes, Eddie. And I need to hear it from you. I need to hear the words."

He balled his fists. He needed to leave. Leave now. No, he needed what she'd say next. "What words, Rhea?"

"You lie."

This again. Too easy. He eased his body and exhaled the next words with just the slightest pubescent crackle to her name. "I never lied, Rhea. Never."

In the perfect parody of calm, she said, "True."

"Then are we? I never—"

"That's not what I said. You did. You killed, Eddie. You just never said. But if you want me to stay—because I'll stay—you need to tell me."

"You'll stay? No matter?" Too much. He'd tone down the hope in whatever came next.

"Yes. Because I know. And I want to stay. With you. But in the Manor, not there." She pointed toward their cabin.

"You want to stay here. In this place?"

"Yes."

"You've already spoken to—"

"Yes. We'll stay here. Together. I want you, Eddie. Saint Andrew wants you."

Eddie rested his forehead in his palm. His wet hair was cold between his fingers. Damn right the town wanted him, but she knew. Somehow, she knew. She must've not been honest at the cabin, not told the whole truth. Or *thought* she knew the truth. The game, her game of half-truths was how she brought him here when he wanted her, needed her. Just like he needed this place, with Rhea. Safe, away from what he had been, yet still was.

Had been.

Still was.

Guilty.

Guilt would keep her. Not her guilt. His guilt. He looked at Rhea. "Yes, you're right." He eased his body as if he'd unloaded years of secrets, years of lies.

She turned toward him. "Right about what, Eddie?"

He closed his eyes. That's right, close them. Deep in thought. Weigh what had to be said. Not knowing if they should be said. The script called for it, needed the words to nail it all home as she needed them too. "I killed them, Rhea. I killed your family. Your dad. Your mother. Your sister." He looked at her and shook his head. "But not the way you think. Those drugs. They came from me, but I had only one . . ." He looked at the fireplace and hoped its flame danced on his mime's frown. "I had only one mule."

"Thank you, Eddie."

She wanted it.

"I killed them," he said again. Those words were power. He loved their honesty. Of course he killed them. And he did it for her. There was no other reason. It was all for her. He'd known that from the very start. Everything he'd done was for her. Because she needed him.

Rhea dropped her head. "No, you didn't kill them. We did." There was no inflection in her voice. She wasn't the Rhea he'd known in the Vega outside Saint Andrew. There was no flippant gesture, no twisting out that childish squeal. There was no pushing him to say anything else. She was something completely new. She'd forfeited all his debts of the unforgivable.

"Rhea." He kneeled and reached toward her, but she didn't want it.

"No," Rhea said—this new Rhea who'd found or maybe lost something inside her. Her bare feet padded on the wet floor littered with vermin filth and star-dustings of plaster as she walked out the bedroom.

He'd gone too far. Pushed too far. "Rhea, I . . ."

She paused at the door and said, "I don't need you, Eddie. Not anymore."

"But Rhea." The log in the fireplace popped, and she left. There was no one. No one she needed more than him. She'd come back. She always did.

Through the window, he saw the cabin that he loved and where he loved—and hated. Through the other window, the girl and child were no longer there, but Al still had his hook in the water. Al knew what he needed, and it was simple. Just like this town was simple. Free of all the shit that cluttered Eddie's life. Shit that Rhea piled up. Shit he'd burn just like those clothes. He'd get rid of it all.

The fuck if she didn't need him. Who the hell was she to walk off like that?

Follow?

Stay?

Both options were shit because this was a new game. A game she hadn't played before. Sure she'd walked off other times, but never like this. Never so hopeless. So . . . broken. That wasn't true. That was a lie. There was another time when—

Weak.

"No," he said.

Useless.

"No." The word crawled out of his throat as a growl.

He took Rhea's hoodie along with his jeans and boots and chased her down the hallway. The balcony doors clattered. Wind, cleaned by the rain, rolled through the hallway. The doors were open, and the wind pushed them further.

On the balcony, framed by the gray lake, Rhea stepped atop the railing, a perfect dance that defied her strength. Before he could say her name, she fell. She did not scream. There was no last squeak as the breath was pushed out her lungs when she hit the ground. There was only a thud like a heavy timber dropped in mud and a wet-twig snap.

CHAPTER TWENTY-THREE

EDDIE STOPPED short of the balcony doors. He didn't want to see her. He'd remember her body on that rail, still living, still alive. Yet a part of him wanted what Rhea had done. Needed to see what he'd become if he did the same. His palms itched where they'd split. Would he die? Would he twitch and stand like Saul? Stumble to the lake like a broken toy? He closed the doors and latched the brass hook. On the decrepit couch, Eddie slumped, dumb with grief. Dumb with what no one should ever have to see. It was worse than holding her sister, holding her mother, feeding her father. This was Rhea's will, broken by a desire for the end. Pain rose in his chest, spread through his ribs, into his arms and legs, and across his face where tears burned.

Eddie's black room built its walls inside him. They were hard walls, and he entered because it was safe there. Because it was the place where he'd seen his own horrors, and it was there the Old Man waited, hunched in that impossible corner that could not exist.

Yes, it said with a throaty wheeze. *Come.*

Even in his black room, Eddie was tired, weak, unwilling to move. He wanted to stay there forever, forget about everything outside and focus within. Focus on . . . The vision of Rhea was still there, standing on that rail, strong, powerful. Singular in choice. Filled with will.

"No," Eddie said. "Changed."

That's right, Rhea'd changed.

"Drew me here. Dressed in that gown. Why? And that hoodie, always over her head, in the shadows. Was that even her? Her at the cabin? In that bed? On that rail?"

Inside, the Old Man stood. *Yes, her.*

"I don't . . . No."

The Old Man hobbled toward Eddie, grabbed his throat, and said, *No, listen.*

Eddie choked. His tongue swelled like a butchered steer. He scratched at his throat outside where no hand held him.

Listen. Her, with you. Damned.

Eddie shook his head.

Lost. Alone. Tortured . . . Used.

Damned? Rhea? Saul, what'd he say?

The damned can be saved, said the Old Man. The demon, the horror, the ancient evil bound Eddie with its will. *Saul has answers. Has a way.*

He wanted to say Rhea's name, cry out to her, plead for her to come back. But the Old Man strangled his will, erased it. Erased everything he was. Erased his will that fled in the tears that soaked the bent collar of his shirt.

The Old Man released Eddie's throat.

Eddie nodded. "Saul."

Eddie pulled out his smokes. Saul had said he could save him. Saul wanted it. He was ready, and he'd be at the church. Eddie slipped a cigarette between his lips. It'd been too long. He lit up, closed his eyes, and fountained smoke. If Saul could save Eddie. Eddie could save Rhea. He was special. He had power. He'd save her and be with her forever. Have control forever. He'd lost what was his, and he would have her back. "Saul."

Yes.

Eddie peered through his own eyes, and the Manor was there, yet the black room remained where he wanted it, where he knew he could retreat and be safe. So he tugged on his jeans and boots and headed out the front doors of the Manor where a boat was moored that had not been there before.

A white-gowned boy stood near. Fingers of black hair clung to his scalp. His feet were bare, and his face was a clean white only marred by two pits from which he leered at Eddie with dark eyes. The boy uncurled a bony finger and pointed at the boat.

Eddie shook his head.

That pinprick of fear he'd felt before multiplied, spread throughout and seized him in a moment where there was no clear choice. Or perhaps infinite choices that clotted reason. Eddie dug his feet into the black ground splattered with teacup flowers, but the Old Man wrenched Eddie and filled him like a corpse's baggy suit. It stumble-strutted Eddie's body over the flowers and toward the boat. No longer was he in command. No longer did he have control. The Old Man had taken what was left of him and thrown him to the curb inside Eddie's black room like the street sluts Eddie himself had used.

But they deserved it.

Eddie? He sure as fuck didn't.

He couldn't become them. It wasn't his place, his lot, yet the force of the demon was black and powerful. It bore down on him. Left him alone and cold. Eyes closed, shivering like some pathetic alley wasteoid raked clean of worth and purpose.

Eddie needed worth.

Eddie needed purpose.

What the fuck was he thinking? Worth? Purpose? He had both because he too was powerful.

Special and powerful, he whispered inside.

This town. This place. Needed. Wanted him.

And then the Manor spoke. "Eddie," it whispered, sad and needing. "Save me."

Behind him, the Manor's door groaned. Against the Old Man's will, he turned, and a white hand and red hair frosted with mud snaked behind the door's black wood.

No, Eddie said. Wanting her. Wanting everything she was and had become.

The Old Man spoke truth.

Damned, Eddie said. *Save her.*

If that was possible in this town of the impossible.

Powerful, he said.

He wouldn't become her.

Lost.

He wouldn't be the used, the abused.

Alone.

Abuse would not take him.

Tortured.

It would not be him.

Used.

Could not be him.

Powerful.

He'd control. He'd choose.

"Choice," he said to the twitching flowers, dark child, and hunched horror within, as if all had become clear, all had released him.

Eddie ended his pathetic shivering and flung himself across his dark room. He wrapped his shadow hands around the Old Man's throat and squeezed. Invisible sinew popped, and the horror strained. Eddie's body stopped short of the boat. Water filled his boots and released a hidden stench of rot and death. Eddie willed his body back, and it moved, dragged its heels through peat and into the ice follies.

The child stepped before Eddie. The Manor doors opened. Eddie ripped the Old Man from his body and flung him to the ground in a heap among the hanging heads of the daffodils. Eddie stood, and the Old Man was there, hunched and wicked with his slender cane.

For a moment, the Old Man did nothing, then the dark child said, "Go, Old Man," and the hunched horror limped inside the Manor. Its doors closed.

Eddie turned toward the swamp. No fear remained.

The child still stood at the stern of the flat-bottomed boat and smiled like the curl of a cracked whip. He bent into the boat and hoisted a pole that he stabbed in the shore. In a voice that had little to do with children and all to do with years of the old who suffered, he said, "Come, Eddie." The words were slippery metal. They were ice. They were knives, razors, needles.

Eddie sat at the front of the boat. With ease, the child maneuvered through the swamp to the opposite shore that led to the butcher and teacher and others who had made the Saint their home. All those whom Eddie had never met, yet knew well enough to call them a part of his life.

The child dug the boat into the opposite shore and said, "I'll be here, Eddie, waiting."

Eddie stepped onto the shore and gravel road that led east to the highway and north to the Immaculate Conception Church. Just off the road, Amos's station was lit up in the gray light of the storm. A shadow moved within. Eddie followed the driveway where leaves skittered across stones and new grass and weeds sprouted a line down the center. Amos's truck was there too. Its thick tires ballooned under its weight. Trees swayed and clacked their branches like hoodoo bones.

Eddie opened the screen door slowly, yet the spring still popped as the tension increased. He twisted the nob like he was cracking a safe and entered. Inside, the ceiling fan churned coils of smoke into a thin haze. A block of light splayed from the rippled glass of Amos's office door. Behind that glass, his desk lamp glowed.

Someone sucked on a cigarette and shuffled papers. Amos's desk chair squeaked. Eddie opened the door. Inside, Ruth sat in Amos's chair with her flipflopped feet kicked up. She held a yellow legal pad and a cigarette. She looked up and caught herself before she tipped the chair.

"Jesus Christ," she said.

"Not quite," Eddie said. "Ruth, what're you doing?"

"Lookin' for Amos."

"What's that?" He nodded at the pad.

"Something I should have known long ago, but no one bothered to tell me."

"And?"

"Eddie, Rhea's parents and sister are dead."

Eddie laughed. *Stupid broad.* "No shit. But you already knew that."

"Amos, here"—she tapped the top sheet of the legal pad where Amos had scratched notes—"says murder."

Eddie sat in the cushioned, steel chair in front of the desk. "And?" At his knee, Eddie bunched up his pant leg and exposed the knife stuck in his boot.

Ruth tossed the pad on the desk and wheeled away with a nudge of her toe. She sucked on her cigarette held between yellowed fingers and said, "He wrote you killed them. You did, didn't you?"

Eddie slid the knife from his boot as he stood. "Yeah, that's right. And I can't have you knowin'."

"Eddie, Amos knows."

"That don't matter. He's dead." He rounded the desk and stood above Ruth with the knife comfortably at his side.

"My god, Eddie." Ruth's voice cracked.

"Ruth." He mimed hopeless misery, held out his knifeless hand. "Rhea's dead too."

"That can't . . . How?" Shaking, she wiped an eye. Ash fell onto her hoodie's sleeve.

"She jumped."

"No." Tears welled in her swollen eyes.

He bent that same hand into a fist. "Josh got it too."

"Eddie, you have a choice. It ain't over. If you kill here—"

"That's right," he said as he stepped toward Ruth and swung the blade under her ribs like some ballroom flourish at the end of a routine. He smiled, satisfied with the judge's score, white-knuckle-held the chair arms, and looked into Ruth's eyes just a breadth away. "Now it's over."

Ruth gasped. Her arm holding the smoke went limp. The cigarette rolled onto the tile. She said, "Eddie, I'll—" but she coughed out those words, and blood spattered Eddie's shirt, chest, and face. She slumped and gurgled air like a punctured tire. From her hoodie, Eddie pulled her smokes and lighter and lit up. Ruth's cigarette sizzled in a ballooning puddle of blood.

"I'm glad you were here, Ruth," Eddie said. "Crazy, but I thought you might be Amos, but he's as dead as you. Guess I'll be takin' Frank's after all."

CHAPTER TWENTY-FOUR

HE LEFT the station and made his way to the unlocked church. In the narthex, the bloody rope was coiled on the floor. Through the double doors that led into the nave, Saul wept. It was a cry that began in his stomach and clawed from his throat as though guilt itself was tired of being housed in that pathetic man. Eddie pushed through the saloon-hinged doors and proceeded down the center aisle where Amos's body laid in a pool of blood already grown dark without Amos's heart and lungs to keep the brilliant red that spattered Eddie. Saul was kneeling on the shards of the whiskey bottle in front of the altar. He held his head in his rutted palms whispering a useless prayer. The doors behind Eddie swung shut and echoed like two great fists pounding the arched ceiling.

Saul stood. "Eddie?"

"I'm here, Saul."

"Why?"

"Rhea killed herself." Eddie's heels tapped the tiles.

"You knew."

"I did. She was weak."

"You can still save her."

"You know?"

"I do. You know what this place can do?"

"No, but I have seen enough." He dabbed his boot toe in Amos's blood and painted an arc across the tiles.

"Have you?" Saul turned. His face was wet with tears and marked with a miserable roadmap of veins. "For some, for the powerful, the special, death has no hold here. Come closer."

Eddie stopped at the dais's first step. "I've seen a shadow and child" Eddie receded to his black room. The Old Man wasn't there. "That shadow was inside me."

Saul nodded. His face was a sagging sack folding over his open collar. "Was?"

"Yes, I forced it from me. It's gone. In the Manor."

"That place, Eddie, is filled with lies. And that shadow, that horror . . ."

"What is it?"

Saul shook his head. "He was someone special. Least I thought he was. But he chooses. And, if he left you, maybe you were what I thought you were."

"I was strong."

Saul pursed his lips. "Rhea's dead," he said as he looked at the ceiling where the giant Christ hovered.

"Yes," Eddie said.

"How?"

"Jumped. From the balcony."

"The Manor," said Saul who looked through Eddie and the church walls. Eddie nodded. "You want to save her. Have her." Saul spoke without question. Every word that came from his mouth was fact, but Eddie still answered.

"This place loves misery, suffering. So too does the Old

Man. But I can take away your misery. I can take away your suffering. I can take away your sin."

"Saul, sin ain't got nothin' to do with me. I don't believe that shit."

"It don't matter what you believe, son. This place got its own rules, and I've got the answer. If you kill me, Eddie, you'll feed it. But if I die, for you, for your sins, you'll become what it wants, you'll be innocent. I'll save you from your sins. And in your innocence, you'll be powerful. Special. Like at the edge of town.

"Eddie, I can't lie. I need you. I've been here for over a hundred and fifty years, so many I should have lost count. But I'll always remember. Remember that moment where I lost everything. The moment I was hanged from that rope. The moment no one saved me. The bell had just rung four, and minutes later I was gone. But I came back, resurrected. I swung from that rope for days until my altar boy cut me down, just like you done. And my flock followed. But I'm done, now, Eddie. I want to pass that power onto you. The power of resurrection. I'll give you what I have, and you'll grow, surge. Overcome what this place is. And with that power, you'll raise Rhea up. Save her from the damnation she's in now. And if you save her, Eddie—oh, if you save her—she'll be yours just like women should be. You'll rule Saint Andrew, and she'll be here with you forever.

"That's what you want?"

"Yes."

"Then take my life," Saul said. "I'll die, for you, and be released from this place. Finally."

"Shouldn't I"—Eddie shrugged—"be forgiven? Like you do?"

Saul shook his head. "Pomp, son. Lies and control."

"And you. What will happen?"

"Don't know."

"Heaven?"

Saul laughed. "Hope not. Happy? Forever? Sickening. I ain't searchin' no more. I want nothing." Saul pushed himself up and laid on the altar. A grin cracked his face.

Eddie shook his head. "I don't get you."

"You don't need to. Come on, finish this." He unbuttoned his shirt. "Got that knife?"

Eddie pulled his hawkbill blade from his boot. He slid the knife from its sheath and turned it, catching glimpses of himself next to Amos's dried blood. Eddie looked into Saul's eyes. "You want this?"

"Like I said, it don't matter." Saul's throat quivered under Eddie's knife. The rope burns from that same day had scarred over. Saul snatched Eddie's wrist. "Do it good. I ain't comin' back."

Eddie nodded. From the black room, he saw himself pull the blade from Saul's rotted-apple throat and tree root fingers. In that rust-pocked blade, he was Eddie. He lowered the knife and slid it across Saul's neck. The blood was slow to come to the surface, but when it did, it ran like water cascading down rock onto the altar. Saul whimpered as Eddie sawed. The whimpering stopped when two bursts spattered and ran down Eddie's chest like thick wine. With a final crunch and pop, Saul's head fell to the floor.

Inside, Eddie looked on like a child pressed against a window displaying toys. Above Eddie, Jesus hadn't moved, hadn't changed. He just lay flat on that arched ceiling with his palms spread and that same smirk. Eddie wiped his blade on Saul's black slacks and stuck it back into his boot, now drenched in blood. There was no hiding what he'd done, and that was okay. It didn't matter. What mattered was that he had freed Saul, and Saul had died for him, saved him. His sins were gone, erased. He was free, and he'd find Rhea and save her too. Because that's what Eddie did or had come to do and be. He freed. He saved. Everything he did was for others.

"Right," he said. "I do this for others. Never for me."

CHAPTER TWENTY-FIVE

RHEA TWISTED and dug her back into the knob of Frank's backdoor.

Owen smiled. "Startle you?"

Rhea shook her head and pulled a curl from her eye. "I-I was looking for Ruth."

"I heard." He knocked the air.

"Seen her?" She looked from his fist to his face.

Owen took a couple steps toward Rhea. She cut the space between them with the screen door that broke his face into dots like he was behind the glass of a tube TV. Owen stopped. The dumpster was just to his right. Through his threadbare T-shirt that stuck to his body in the cold rain, he seeped a stench of honey and bait vats, overpowering the dumpster's old beer and ditched burgers. Rhea held a slender finger under her nose and pulled the door closer.

"I done somethin'?" Owen backed up and rested on the rusted dumpster. He toed at stones and wiped rain from the pits of his eyes.

Rhea relaxed and opened the door just enough to see Owen

beyond the door's frame. "No, I . . ." Was she being foolish? It was just Owen. He hadn't done anything that she'd heard. He hadn't even come up in conversations, really, except for Eddie's tirade after leaving The Store for the first time and finding Josh. Maybe it was just her. No. She closed her eyes, just long enough to see Luke in her arms, dead. She didn't fully know why, or even if she should, and yet there was a bit of her that felt it was the right thing to say. "Why are you here, Owen?" It was a question others had asked her. Now, it was her turn.

Owen looked up from the stone that held importance for him in that moment and said, "I like fishin'."

"That's it?"

He shrugged. "Guess so. Why're you here?"

It was her turn, again, but this time she'd give the half-truth like so many others. She jerked a thumb over her shoulder and said, "Vega."

"I thought you'd say as much, but you know that ain't true. Just like fishin'."

"What?" She stopped herself from shaking her head and looked at him from the corners of her eyes as though she'd caught him in a deep lie. "Meaning?"

"Meanin', you got problems."

"Doesn't everyone?"

"I ain't sayin' I don't or no one else don't, but you got problems here." He pointed at his chest. "And here." He presented Saint Andrew like it was a consolation prize for guessing the right price. "You especially got problems with them, you know."

"Who?" Rhea slid from behind the door and sat on the wood steps. She couldn't stand. She didn't want to stand even though sitting soaked her clothes further. She wanted to be inside Frank's where it was safe, safe with Ruth, safe behind the bar or carrying a tray where the worst that'd happen would be a smack on her ass which she'd deflect with an extra-hard cocktail spilled just enough to let the guy know another smack would mean her calling the muscle. "Who told you?"

"Saul. Well, Saul through Josh."

Rhea shook her head, fully this time because that's all she could do. "And Josh told you what?"

"Well, it weren't so much as Josh told me like we sat down for a beer, but he let it fly on Eddie walkin' to the cabin earlier."

"Owen, please, tell me."

"Josh said you'd know or knew, I forget which. Eddie said you wouldn't take it, wouldn't believe it. He said you trust too much."

"Trust what?"

"Trust Eddie. Trust what Eddie told Saul. What Saul told Josh to tell you. It's a bunch a shit I don't get much into." He shrugged. "It is what it is. Mostly, I put on a show for Josh to stay in the circle."

Rhea stood and approached Owen like an unblinking doll and held his hand slung limp off the dumpster. Owen jerked and stiffened. But for a glimpse of a moment, he held hers, so she held tighter. "Owen, what'd Eddie say he did?"

His mouth wouldn't obey. The fat under his chin jumped when he swallowed and finally forced out the words. "S-sorry. He, Eddie, killed your family."

She heard as much before. She knew it was coming or at least felt she did after hearing it, again. She held her head back and closed her eyes. Tears streaked her temples. They weren't tears of pain or suffering. They were peace, belonging. Something she had never had, never felt.

It wasn't a belonging of place. It was a belonging of *self*. The Imperial Valley, Anza-Borrego, the shores of San Diego, the mountains of Washington, Canadian bays and backwater towns, that diner in Montana where she sucked down the last

smoke she'd have until—until him, Josh. Until Ruth. Until
Amos. Until Eddie. She let them go. She let them all go. And a
release of power, of energy, of emotion began at the top of her
head and fled through her arms, her body, and her soles.

It was a peace she hadn't known before. A *something* that
she had never attained, never felt, never achieved. The fear, the
boat, the water, the cabin, Frank's, the town itself were no
longer betrayers. They were simply a part of her. And in that
moment, the skin covering her skull shivered like a bolt of
power feeding the sky, as if that power were sapped from her
body, consumed by a shared misery.

She looked into Owen's eyes. They were an earthy brown
glazed with fear or uncertainty or timidity. Rhea couldn't tell
which, but there was something in Owen she was seeing that
maybe no one here had ever seen. "Owen, did Eddie say he
didn't do it?"

"No," Owen said.

Rhea's stomach tensed. She clenched her T-shirt tight,
digging into her skin. She winced, but it was a good pain that
somehow took back that energy she'd lost to the sky. She
looked up at Owen who'd become soaked by the rain.

"Owen," she said. The next came with a thousand possibilities that drenched Rhea's mind with the future, and she chose
the most unlikely future yet most likely to end with a scream.
"We should go to The Store."

He nodded. They said nothing as she held his hand and
crossed to The Store.

Eddie had killed her family. Must have killed her family.
There was no other way. She looked up at Owen who let his
arm hang limp at his side. Rhea hadn't let go of his soft hand
that swallowed hers. There was something in her touch that
opened a piece of Owen, and she didn't want to lose it.

They reached the front door, and Owen pushed it open.

Bells rang. Bait vats hummed. A furnace somewhere clicked, and hot air pillowed into the aisles from ceiling vents. Rhea let Owen go, and he sat behind the glass counter. The stool creaked. He snapped his magnifying goggles around his head, grabbed a pair of tweezers, and tugged at feathers clenched by alligator clips.

She stopped and sidestepped when she saw bloody foot-prints. "Owen," she said and met his eyes.

He raised his goggles. "Yep."

Rhea closed the door. The prints on the floor were Eddie's boots. She knew it was the truth. Her body weakened. Raising her head was work, but she had harder things ahead, bad things like Luke said. And Owen had answers, answers others gave like gifts wrapped in packing tape. Maybe Owen would be different, so she ignored the blood and asked, "How long have you been here?"

"Don't remember."

"Why are you here?"

He set the tweezers down. "Even Ruth ain't never asked that, and you ask again."

"I'm sorry. I didn't mean to." She looked at the blood and picked at her nails.

He scratched the whisker-thistles sprouting from his neck. "No. It ain't nothin'."

Her shoulders relaxed. Owen wasn't angry. No one was in The Store. It wouldn't take much for him to take her. Nothing, he'd said. No, it was something. He knew that, but no one had ever bothered, but it was still his choice. "No, Owen. If you haven't told it, you don't need to say it. But, it's not worthless."

"Soundin' like Ruth."

Rhea raised her right shoulder and tilted her head, so her wet hair hung like a shredded curtain. "Could be worse." She smiled.

Owen's lips sagged. "There's worse."

Rhea stopped smiling and looked at Owen straight-on. "I-I'm sorry, I just."

He took the goggles off his head. "You always say sorry for what you done or ain't done? There's no need."

Rhea crossed her arms. She nodded. It was something expected of her, maybe of people, maybe of women.

Eddie had apologized to her once, at the cabin, but he needed something. Rhea had forced him to talk, so he used that as a tool—a tool against what he'd done and a tool against her. But on the highway into town, there was no sorry. And Owen was no longer just that man leering at her.

There were words in him that few heard or wanted to hear because he was Owen: a man who offended because he was fat, because he wasn't pretty, because he wasn't clean, because he was silent. She was guilty too. She'd laughed at him through Eddie's story, but she still laughed at him like others had.

"Sorry, Rhea," Owen said. "You do what you do because that's what you been taught. One way or another, you came to be who you are. That'll change. You'll change. Unless you stay here."

"Okay, so you stay here," Rhea said. "Have you changed?"

"There ain't much to me. Maybe there ain't even much left of me, so I gotta keep what I got. You asked why here. Lemme say, I done enough to keep me here. And I don't need leavin'. Maybe don't deserve it."

"You think you could leave?"

"I know I can't."

"You tried." She knew he must have, but she needed that doorway into what he knew.

"Yep. I tried. A lot. Trickin' this place don't work neither." He tapped his badge that read JOSH. "Stupid, probably. I wanted Josh's hell just for a change, but that ain't never gonna happin'."

"You watched Josh leave?"

"Try to leave but couldn't. Watched Eddie too. Man, when I saw Eddie come back—"

"Eddie tried leavin'?" Rhea tensed. "Leaving?"

"Yep."

"He couldn't?"

"He could. Chose not to. Still here, far as I know."

Eddie tried leaving? He wouldn't. He needed her too much. Or was that a lie too? "He chose to come back?"

Owen nodded.

He still needed her like that silly goth boy he once was and still was. Or he needed this place. Wanted it like he said before: the bar, the town. And Eddie was someone who'd take and keep taking.

But why would the town keep *her*? To tempt Eddie? To keep him here? Did he give it the suffering it needed? He'd killed and was a killer. The blood was on the floor—traces of other's suffering.

Or was it her suffering it wanted? Just like Luke, it kept her, wanted her, one who was just innocent enough. Someone who hadn't killed yet touched what killed others. Or had the town let Eddie go because it knew he'd return to what he wanted? Make him feel unwanted just so he'd return and finish what it wanted, what the Saint wanted: death and misery, black like iron on a grindstone, except the iron was each person's *self*.

God. She'd brought him here. Would he be the grindstone?

Rhea pointed at the floor. "These prints."

"His."

"How?"

"I don't know if that's somethin'—"

She stepped away from the door and up to the counter.

"Owen." Her throat was dry, her voice husky, what she'd expect in fifty years if she made it that far. Saying his name was enough.

"He killed." He pointed at the floor. "Here."

"Saint Andrew?"

"Yep."

Rhea stepped back. He knew. He knew Eddie killed, and he just came up to her behind Frank's then sat at that counter and picked up those tweezers. "Eddie?" Owen nodded and she said, "You didn't bother telling me."

He stood and set his fists on the glass. "It ain't mine ta tell, Rhea. That ain't how this place works. That ain't how we work in this place. I don't get myself into business that ain't mine, because that way is pain. I was dumb comin' up behind you and Frank's. Dumb talkin' to you now." He pointed a thick finger at her. "But you just gotta. Gotta be. Gotta be you." He waved her away and sat down as if he'd answered all her questions, released all he knew.

Ruth hadn't been in Frank's, unless she had been . . . Maybe Ruth's body was there on the hardwood floor. She was always in Frank's. "Owen, who'd Eddie kill? Please, not Ruth."

"I ain't sayin'. I'm tired. I'm done. I already feel pain comin' for me."

"Tell me where, then."

He sighed. "Dunno. He came into this store, less like you just done, more like the rest, expectin'. I asked, and he said. I didn't get the spot, where he done it. He said somethin' about Saul knowin' though."

"The church," Rhea said.

Owen sat and shrugged. "That bell ain't rung in a bit."

She looked up at the ceiling where a rusted vent churned out more hot air. Amos, it must've been Amos. Ruth was out looking for Eddie. Maybe it was Ruth. Her heart sagged. She backed into the door. Hope. Hatred. Anger. Relief. They all came to her. Someone was dead. Another person, dead. And she brought Eddie to them.

He wouldn't have made it this far if she wasn't with him. She should have left him long ago. She should have never stepped over those junkies and into the Vega. But she always needed Eddie—or thought she did. Rhea shook her head, closed her eyes, and held her forehead where the grief ached cold like an empty house that echoed memories, like Eddie's clothes flaring in the boiler. Clothes that heated the water she'd bathed in.

She was covered in him, filled with him. Filled with what he'd done not only in California, but here, in Saint Andrew to people they'd known for . . . Rhea fell back in time, fell back to when they walked down the shoulder to the steeple and the cross that gleamed silver. Back to the playground where children squealed, abused, and were abused. Back to Frank's where the lost called for her. She opened the door and stood framed by the light outside where the rain fell like wafting linen.

"Rhea," Owen said, "be yourself."

Rain-cooled air swelled past Rhea's legs, and The Store's furnace fired up. She looked over her shoulder and said, "Thank you, Owen."

He shrugged, popped on his goggles, and tweezered a line around his lure.

CHAPTER TWENTY-SIX

RHEA CROSSED to the church sidewalk where Eddie's bloody footprints led away from the church and faded south toward Amos's station like birthday party cray paper. Eddie had been here. He must have been here, moments ago. His nearness sickened her. But without her, he'd do worse.

She lowered to one knee next to Mary's statue where Eddie's bloody chevron footprints refused the rain. He wandered through this town like Rhea, but their paths never crossed, rarely crossed in this town: Saint Andrew. This was a town where the dead knew her, where the dead spoke.

It was an impossible thing. But it wasn't just her. It wasn't her being crazy, being a silly girl like so many had accused before. Josh, Luke, and the bar had shown her that. She knew there was more, more to Saint Andrew than what she'd ever seen before. Even now she resisted the truth. And yet she'd seen those things, seen those people, and experienced those voices.

Alone, there was always doubt. There was no one she could turn to who'd give her what she needed, the reassurance, the stories, the proof that she wasn't insane. There was no one who had shared those experiences or seen what she'd seen. Only the insane feel normal. Who else was there?

She looked at the steeple through trees and branches like boney hands reaching for something. Reaching for release? Comfort? Or the end? How many did that very thing before their death: bend their arms up with hope before it ended? Hope for someone. Hope for some *thing* to happen only to come to a simple end of nothing. Maybe there wasn't an end.

Luke died in her arms, and he came back. Luke was still in that truck, waiting for her. She shook her head. She'd forgotten, but he was still there with the engine running. The church doors were right there, just up a few granite steps muddled black and gray. She didn't want the blood, so she returned to the truck and tapped on the glass. Luke stared in the mirror as though something was in there talking to him or with him. He shook his head, scooted forward on the seat, and cranked the window open.

"Yep," he said and rested his forearm on the door's sill.

"Luke, I need to hear it one more time."

"Hear what?"

"I'm sorry."

"I know," said Luke.

She smiled, but it quickly faded. "Luke, you died. How?"

"In a grain bin."

"You died. You died in that grain bin?"

"Yes. It looked full, the bin. I needed to sweep the sides. I stepped into the bin and the grain fell, and I fell with it. There was a crust like thin ice that broke. My dad warned me, but I didn't listen. I jumped in and was buried. I sucked in corn, not air, and my dad took my leg with the auger but"—he picked at the steering wheel's flaked padding—"I was already dead."

"And you're here," Rhea said. "Why?"

Luke shrugged. "This place feeds." He tugged his shoulders up to his ears and tears welled.

"Luke," she said and held his forearm.

"It's okay, Rhea."

"No, that's not . . ." She squeezed his arm. "Luke, am I dead?"

He screwed up his face and shook his head. "No, but you're here with me. I showed you things."

"I don't—"

"This place won't let go. It wants you," Luke said as he returned Rhea's touch. "You don't deserve to be here which is why you're stuck."

"Why?"

"You ain't done nothin'."

Rhea shook her head like she was sawing through her years with Eddie, hoping to sever their bond. "That's not true, Luke. I've done enough, and I brought Eddie here." She looked to where the Vega stalled then past the church and Amos's station hidden in the trees. "I need to do something in the church. Wait for me?"

Luke nodded, and she cut across the grass to where Eddie's prints grew thick on the church steps. She entered and forced herself past the ladder and rope and through the paneled doors stained a creamy yellow less bright than what remained on her nails. She wouldn't look until she was ready. Lowering her head, she closed her eyes and exhaled deeply like she had after her last cigarette outside that dinner.

But that wasn't her last. Her last was with Josh when she thought she had control. She'd cracked. Still, she wanted one between her fingers, warm and soft, tip glowing red, smoke lifting in straight lines until it curled under some unseen force. Without raising her head, she pushed the doors open.

Burnt leaves, smothered candles, and old wood filled the heavy air, but there was something else. Something from that Montana greasy spoon. Something from its trash-clotted alley where a dog, pinned under a dumpster, leaked its insides from convenient holes while a litter of a half-dozen puppies licked its dead belly. Back then, the pancakes and bacon left Rhea's stomach. She tossed her last smoke into that spatter of vomit and went back to work after gargling cold coffee. But she wasn't there. She was in the Immaculate Conception Catholic Church, a name that still made little sense to her. There was no dumpster. There were no dogs.

She opened her eyes and saw Eddie's silent horror show, keeping whatever was in her stomach down. Amos lay there in a pool of blood bigger than she thought possible. Saul was on the altar. His blood on the carpeted dais. Above the bodies, serene Jesus was frozen in paint. It was enough. She left the church and leaned against the steps' rod iron rail. She was sick, yet there was nothing to purge, nothing to give her the relief of release from the site carved in her mind.

By his dock, Amos had said, *Dyin' here means you stay.* And now he was dead. Dead meant damnation. Alive meant there was hope. And Eddie ended hope.

Tires crackled on stone-strewn tar, and the bloody images dissolved. At the end of the sidewalk, Luke waited in the pickup, but he didn't look at her. Instead, for a moment, he stared at the rear-view mirror. His lips moved with silent words. He shook his head, punched the gas, and popped the clutch. The rear tires, bulging under the weight of the round-bale, dug into gravel down to bare tar. Dust and smoke trailed as the truck swerved. Rhea ran and stood in the exhaust and dust. Luke's name surged from her throat, but it was a useless token meant only for movies and parted lovers reunited in rain.

Luke's beach-sand hair peeked above the seat as he barreled down the highway past the town sign. The truck lunged, and the front wheels dug into the tar. It flipped and hung in the air for an impossible moment, flung the bale from the bed, and rolled onto the cab. The bale burst into a pile of thick sheets, and the truck spat a spark under the popped hood, engulfing all in rolling flames and cottony black smoke. From the passenger window, crushed as it was, twitched little Luke, or what was once Luke. Flames licked his body that had already turned black. He rolled from the cab. His arms were glued to his torso, so he pushed himself up by the shoulder, took two steps, and fell.

Rhea ran to him even though there was no hope, nothing she could do, and no one she could call. Even Amos was gone, but there was his station. She could call for help, wherever that may come from. But did it matter? Did anything matter here? Who were the dead? Luke said he was. Would he come back? Would he? Was this his pain? His suffering for what he'd done? And yet, he'd already come back once. Or was that something in her mad mind? Would Amos come back? Would Saul? Who else in this town was dead? Or damned? All of them? No, that couldn't be. There were people who tugged their boats and campers and slipped away as though this town was just a memory.

What about Ruth? Where was she? She was damned. There was no question. And Didi was at Amos's dock, waiting for her just like all the others who waited. Why did they want to help her? Help Rhea? Maybe Luke.

Poor Luke. She looked down the highway. The truck burned, and his corpse smoldered. She looked away. Her legs weakened. It was too much. And, maybe Luke was right. Maybe she hadn't done anything wrong.

But she knew the truth. She had done wrong, and there was no taking it back. And again, she brought Eddie here. Amos's station, like a father hovering over his sleeping children, peeked through the trees. She knew where she needed to go as though the wind whispered secrets that compelled.

CHAPTER TWENTY-SEVEN

THE STATION'S door was open, and the scent of death churned there too. It was Ruth. Somehow, she knew it was Ruth, and her body lost hope. No, not her body, her will.

"Go," she said, but it wasn't her voice. It was the other that returned and spoke through her.

"No," she said with her own voice to the trees. Each step would be the birth of terrible futures branching off into limitless possibilities, so she chose none of them.

"Yes, stay," the Saint said.

Another choice. Another missed moment. Inaction was a branch she had not seen.

"Look," said the Saint.

The station's floor creaked and wheels groaned. A hunched shadow, ripped at the edges, limped behind Amos's office chair on which Ruth's corpse sat. It stopped, framed in the doorway and pushed chair and all, down the steps. Ruth's body crashed on the leaf-matted driveway. The chair tangled her limp legs. Ruth's face was frozen white, and her jaw sagged against a stone. Rhea screamed, and the hunched horror, the Old Man, brought a finger to where its lips did not exist and hissed. From its robes, it tugged a slender cane and gaveled the floor.

Rhea turned and ran into the woods, looked over her shoulder, and stumbled. The Old Man stood over Ruth's body, dug his cane into the gravel, but did not follow. Rhea ran until the trees blotted the station.

Nothing could hold back the misery. She was done. She buried her face in her palms and wept. What had she seen? It was more than anyone should witness: murders, suicide, and that *thing*. Was it the same thing she thought she saw in Frank's? That coffined shadow she pushed aside like another of her childish fantasies or nightmares? Or was it one of those things people called her a silly little girl for even though she was twenty-three? It was there. She knew it was there, and it was outside the station, above Ruth's body. It wanted her to see the body, but she refused, so it forced her.

"Why?" She leaned against a tree, and an old broken branch stabbed her, drew blood. She looked at her wrists free of scars. She couldn't go forward anymore. She needed an end. Eddie had done this to her. Done everything to her and to the others. She could have ended everything on that balcony if he hadn't arrived. If she had just jumped, Eddie wouldn't have come here, wouldn't have been here with her to do those things. No one, even the dead, deserved what he did to them. It was all her fault. She knew it. She wanted to leave Montana, so he followed.

She pulled away from the tree, which tore a hole and ripped her jean jacket even more as she turned. Shivering rage filled her body and sprouted through her limbs as she strangled the trunk like it had taken everything from her. Its bark was white, smooth. It flaked like skin drying after the sun crisped it red. It was the same tree where Amos had left her. She hadn't walked away, but maybe she pushed him away?

And, because it was her story, she kept it hidden from him. Hidden from him when he needed it most. And maybe that's why these stories were told. Maybe they were told when others needed them. When others would find a way to move forward in a life filled with wrong.

Could she move forward? Who else had she turned away? Who else had she led to a life of need and suffering? A breeze crawled up the hill carrying the crackle of the lake's waves with it.

Leaves squelched under someone's feet. "Have you seen enough?"

Rhea released the birch tree. Didi stood on the path to Amos's dock. Bare-legged and in a black hoodie, she was made small by the hill that kept her far lower than Rhea.

Didi tugged on the hoodie's hem and shrugged. "Cold."

The trees hissed with the wind. Rhea shook her head. "I can't . . . no more."

Didi offered her hand. "Come on. I can help."

Rhea took it, and her body fell into a place where hope and comfort were lost to cold rain and dark waters. Like living clay, Rhea's body moved with Didi down the path and onto the dock where the old dining chair waited for Amos. Didi held the canoe, and that same body—Rhea's body—stepped in. Didi followed and paddled into open waters.

"Rhea," Didi said with feathery grace.

"Yes," Rhea said with barely enough force to let the words escape. Her body turned, and Rhea lounged there like a sofa centerfold she saw in the cabin's smut.

"Long ago, you told me you'd stay," Didi said. "Will you?"

In that cold place, Rhea saw the past, saw what she had done, the stories she'd heard, and the time she'd been in Saint Andrew. "Long ago," Rhea said. That *ago* spanned like the blood around Amos's body. Her time within Saint Andrew was more than her mind could hold, yet it was there before her. She nodded. "Yes, I'll stay. I want what you have."

"What do I have, Rhea?"

"Yourself."

"How?" Didi crinkled her freckled face, letting her child-self surface, then glazed it like placid ice, cut with a smile made by a skater's wild blade.

"You do as you please, as you want."

Didi set the paddle on the boat's keel and crawled over the canoe's ribs. Her cold breath washed over Rhea's cheek. "I do as I please."

Rhea nodded.

"I've killed, Rhea. Do you want to hear?"

Rhea nodded again and forced the word, *yes*, through her lips with a rush of breath.

"The Old Man. You've heard others say those words? I had no family. In the Manor, he took me and others. He hurt us. So I sharpened a silver butter knife on the Manor's stone. It took months. He hurt many. Others helped, but they died too, in the lake. Then I killed him. Understand, Rhea?"

Again, Rhea nodded.

"He's there." Didi danced her head toward the Manor. Her hair swung like dead limbs. "He has Eddie."

"How do you know?"

Didi moved closer and whispered, "Eddie and I shared a bed."

Rhea swiveled her head like a broken doll.

"He knew it wasn't you, but—"

Rhea pushed Didi's shoulder with the power of a child. "You didn't."

Didi held Rhea's shoulders and pushed her into the rails. "Don't blame me, Rhea. Eddie knew. He'll say he didn't, but he was too willin'. He wants more than you. Just like when he wrapped his legs around your sister. He'd take her, too, and your mom. But you were convenient. Can't you see?" Eddie took Didi's place. He held a syringe and grinned. He brought that needle down into Rhea's neck. It wasn't a pinch like nurses say. It melted muscle. It burned. Didi returned and said, "She screamed."

Tears fell, and Rhea said her sister's name again and again: "Clara. Clara. Clara."

"You're the only one who can make him understand how he makes others feel."

Rhea quivered. "How?"

"He needs you. You need to show him. Show him you don't care. You don't love him. You don't need him. That he is useless. Then his Hell will begin."

Like that hot needle, Rhea's chest surged with hate. Her ribs ballooned. And with that rage came the word, *yes*.

"I can help, Rhea."

"Clara," Rhea said.

"You want her?"

"Yes."

"We can bring her back. Bring her here. Want that?"

The words fell freely from her lips. "With me? Forever?"

"Yes, any time you want. Just wander, and you'll find her. But we, I need you. Eddie knows." Didi caressed Rhea's cheek with her knuckles. "I need you."

Rhea nodded, slow and uncertain as if she weighed the choices she'd made.

"I may have you?"

Like a child stepping into a sicko's booze and sweat soaked van, Rhea nodded and gave herself to Didi. Allowed herself into her arms. Yet this time in her arms there was loneliness like the last ice melting at the center of a lake. And like that ice, Didi melted into Rhea until Rhea's *self* was orphaned by the most intimate touch within. And she knew her choice. Knew her future. Knew her past and saw what she'd become and had been in a pointless downward spiral fueled by loss and misery that lasted no time and yet forever until loneliness consumed her.

She screamed, but the scream never reached the air around her body, never reached the ice follies that held their blooms toward the gray sky as Didi pulled the boat up to the Manor's shore. And Rhea watched herself inside her mind like a specter inhabiting another. It was Didi's plan. Now, it was Didi who had donned her body like a tight, red dress while flashbulbs popped.

Didi stood Rhea's body with a mechanical pose, and the yellow and white flowers bowed with the wind at her feet.

"I need ta tell ya somethin', Rhea," her body said. Except it wasn't completely her voice so distant and pitched with a cocktail twist of the South. "I need ta tell ya—" Her body froze, and her eyes filled with Didi's being, with Didi's *self* that was defiant and powerful like the surge of a wave yet dead and uncaring. "You did this to yourself."

Rhea shook her head. Her mouth gaped. "I . . ." No, Didi was right.

"Just like you brought death to your family. You could have stopped it, but you hated your sister for what she was. For being that pool-side princess you could never be."

Rhea—her shadow *self*—nodded.

"And you hated your mother for loving someone like your father. Someone who used and abused. But you're just like your parents. You feigned weakness to get what you wanted. You used people just like Eddie uses you. You're no better than he. And you're no better than your mother, bending to your dad's will like you and Eddie."

Rhea clenched her fists and trembled, then wrapped her

arms around her chest that should not be there, could not be there, and squeezed. Again, Didi was right. How could she have acted that way? How could she have used people the way she did? Rhea seized and screamed through clenched shadow-teeth. Her eyes were wild with hate and despair. She was lost, and she had brought herself to this moment where she'd become one of the lost, one of the ghosts who haunted this town of the damned. Everything she had done. All the choices she had made brought her to this point of solitude. She was a lonely speck, unwanted, unloved, unneeded. Didi. She was right. And her need to be with her body stretched and thinned, grew distant as her *self* faded.

Rhea's body stepped around the corner of the Manor and past an ash tree where a noose swung. At the tree's base, a clot of children in white gowns and bloody ankles stood greedily waiting as though a day's single meal had been served.

A small girl, a white cherub made wicked by a slim grin and a nest of blonde curls, stepped out from the group. It was that same girl from ages ago just outside the school. She asked, "Now, Didi?"

The other children giggled.

"No," Didi said, but it was Rhea's voice.

"May we hang her?"

"No, she's weak."

"Oh, please, Didi," the child said with a shrill plea. "Please let us kill her. Drown here then? Like you did to us?" The girl raised a tiny finger blackened with soil, reddened by rust under the nails and pointed where the boat scraped the shore.

"Not yet. The Saint wants living pain. Come, it's Eddie's turn."

The children's faces sagged, and they hung their arms limply at their sides while they slid their feet along the ground like lead waits slowed them. It was a parody of life and family with Didi forcing compliance through some deadly will or power over a clutch of the dead.

Didi grinned and said, "They're hungry, Rhea. Hungry for you. But we need to feed the Saint first. Then I'll take what I want." Didi shuffled Rhea's body toward the Manor, and the children followed.

CHAPTER TWENTY-EIGHT

Rain coated the grass in fine beads that bloated then fell as Eddie returned to the Manor. The black-haired child poled Eddie to the opposite shore where the flowers drowned in the rain and a noose hung from a tree.

The Manor was unlocked, and the door closed behind Eddie. In the foyer, dust curled around him like long hair wafting in dark waters, and yellow light flickered and fanned out from the balcony doors.

Look. The voice swelled like rage stoked in a furnace.

Eddie stumbled under its weight. The Old Man, the hunched horror, was there curled at the far end of the foyer next to a dark door. The room dimmed. He surged, grew, bloated into a shadow of stretched tendons like ink in muddy water, and wrapped himself around Eddie, crushed his will into a pitiful remnant of himself like a single piece of garbage buried in a landfill of hate. Like a dead god, the hunched horror was everywhere and nowhere and Eddie understood the Old Man's power.

Yes.

"No, please," Eddie said, but the Old Man slid his tendrils around Eddie, violated everything he was until the world gaped in shadow.

Eddie hobbled up the stairs, clasping a cane that was not there. Waves echoed off stony shores into the ruined hallway and sitting room where a log burned yellow and blue in the fireplace. And yet a chill soaked all through the open French doors. He had left her body below, forgotten, unknown, but the image of her through that thin gown remained.

Look.

Eddie stumbled onto the balcony and bent over the baluster like a drunk heaving liquor bought on another's dime.

There was no body.

Rhea was gone.

The Old Man's whisper became a growl ground into a slow-mo splat of base. *She stays.*

Rhea, she was taken. She tempted him to the Manor and to that room because she was taken. Something had possessed her just like Eddie was now. She'd heard a voice just as Eddie had and gave in.

Yes.

She was weak, had to give in to her silly ideas of being alone but always needing others.

Worthless.

Yes, she was worthless.

No. The Old Man tore at Eddie's every muscle, pulled on every tendon.

"No." Eddie forced the word through his teeth.

You. He pushed Eddie's body away from the baluster and hobbled down the central staircase and stood below the grand gasolier staring at the double doors between the two staircases. The horror burgeoned, filled Eddie with cold dread, wrapped his body in shadow. Eddie's vision receded, faded to a pinpoint of light as though he was being dragged down into water where only the merest glint of sun could reach. Then that too was gone, and the horror warbled like a submerged bullhorn.

Eddie, the horror said. Eddie's lips shook and seized. *Eddie,* he said again as if calling him from distant shores. *You are mine.*

In the blackness, hinges creaked, and a metal door closed with hollow finality that echoed in a cold room accompanied by children who shushed and giggled. One child, in a voice as thin as frozen spider silk, said, "Eddie. He's here."

Metal clattered, and the Old Man unwrapped Eddie in a titanic instant, a sick gift of sacrifice.

For you, my Saint, the Old Man said as its cane and heels tapped up wet steps.

Within Eddie, the pinpoint of light grew like a Valentino fade-in. But no movie played. Eddie's cotton-swab professor hadn't stopped the projector. Instead, Eddie was balled inside a tiny cage bolted with a brass crucifix and locked with an iron padlock. Huddled around the cage were those dozen children in white gowns. Lace hems hovered above a hay-bedded floor. Around Eddie's right ankle was an iron manacle chained to the cage. Each child had their own chain and cage in a granite-walled cellar lit by a single candle held by the black-haired demon-boy, made even more wicked by a slim grin.

"Eddie," the wicked boy said as the children parted. "You are bad."

Eddie pushed against the flat-iron bars. "No," he said as he strained. "I didn't—"

"Yes, you are, and you did." The boy's voice was as thin and sharp as a straight razor. "You lost your worth long ago. Since that moment, you've become something worse than most."

Eddie shook his head, but he was silent, frozen by the

child's presence. Yet he forced words from his throat. "I don't—"

"No, you don't. You lie, Eddie. You always have."

"No, I—"

"Why, Eddie?" The child leaned close to Eddie. His gown hung loose from his small shoulders like a discarded dish rag stained by years of abuse. The child's breath and words were shared only with Eddie. "I know," he whispered like it was a burning secret kept from parents. "I've lied, too, Eddie. But I lied first. That's why you're here."

Eddie wet his throat with what saliva he had. "No, not true. I-I've done things, but I've never lied."

"You know that's not truth: a lie spoken right here and now, to me." He shook his head, and a lock of black hair grazed his gown's lace collar. "Eddie, why are you here?"

The child's eyes, black as they were, hid all they knew. Eddie was lost. He had no control. He'd lost it all. Simple was best, so he said, "I—I drove here, in the Vega."

"That's true. Now, why do you think I brought you here?"

"You? No one brought—"

"Lie."

Eddie twisted in the cage. The manacle dug into his ankle and grew wet with blood. He breathed through his teeth. Hell no. This child couldn't control him. Fear wouldn't control him. He was Eddie. He chose. He had control.

"You know that's not true either," said the boy, cocking his head to the side. "If you had control, you'd have left, freed yourself, but you couldn't. You were weak. You needed me. And you need me, the Saint, now."

"Saint?" No, fuck that. Child. Thing. That's all it was. Like Ruth and Amos, it twisted words with its psychobabble bullshit. Whatever this kid was couldn't be what he'd hoped for. Or what he wanted. Or *where* he wanted to be. This town.

That's what he wanted. He didn't want this child. And yet, there he was. Where *it* was. Not just now and in the boat but with Saul, his house.

"That's right, Eddie. Altar boy? Hardly. Like you, Saul's easy."

"I don't need shit. This town, *you* need me. Need what I am."

"More lies. Or you're just stupid." The Saint giggled. "Which is why you need Rhea."

"No, I don't need her."

"Yes, you do, liar." The boy wrapped his fingers around the flat-iron bars, so his knuckles chilled Eddie's shoulder. "You don't have worth. You know you don't. You know. Rhea knows too. She wanted you, but not anymore. She knows what you've done, and she suffers now because of it. She'd have been yours, but you couldn't overcome your worthlessness. Couldn't overcome what you really are: useless."

No, he was more than that. He must be. The Saint couldn't keep him. He could leave. On that road, beyond the sign, he chose not to. It was his choice. It was all his choice. Eddie pushed himself against the back of the cage. Spattered welds dug into his back. He kinked his head to the side close to the child and pulled on the bars that had no desire to give.

"You think you can get out of this cage, Eddie?"

"I-I can't move, can't breathe."

"That's right. You can't breathe. You're trapped. Trapped inside yourself, in your dark room where you thought you were safe."

"Please, let me go." Eddie's chest heaved for breath.

The Saint reached around Eddie's shoulders and touched his neck just below his left ear. "Right there."

Again, Clara struggled between Eddie's legs. The needle bent just below her left ear and broke from the syringe. *Eddie, stop*, were the last words that fell from her lips. Inside the cage, Eddie shivered and choked as tears fell.

"Already, Eddie? You're pathetic. But now you know. Now you know Rhea, how she felt and feels. Now you know Clara, how she squirmed and fought." The Saint pressed his white cheek against the cage. "How you grew hard, wanting her. No, how you grew hard, wanting death wrapped in your legs. You're rotten. You have no use. You don't deserve to be here. Here with me."

"No, I want to stay. This is what I've wanted. I'll stay. With you. Serve you."

"You think I care? I don't need or want you. I want Rhea. I need her life. I need the ruin she'll become because of you. And it was all you, Eddie. You're the one who brought her to this point, to this moment where she wants nothing, wants an end."

"Wants?"

"Yes, Eddie. She's here. She's chosen. Unlike you who have no life to give. And no real life to live."

Eddie buried his face in his jeans that drank his tears. There was no hope for him, no worth. That seed of self-hate grew inside him, overcame him like so much pain he'd caused. Eddie looked at the boy. "You're right."

The boy smiled and held his tiny finger against his pale lips as if pondering solutions to an infinite problem, mimicking Rhea and the snide shit she pulled in the Vega. "What, Eddie?"

"You're right. I—" A door at the top of worn-lumber steps creaked opened.

"Whoops, too late," said the Saint. "She's here."

CHAPTER TWENTY-NINE

DOWN THE STEPS twitched Rhea with marionette grace in her babydoll gown flecked with mud and blood. Her left arm was cocked at her hip like some cartoon cowboy pawing his pistol and her other was raised palm-up like a trayless truck stop waitress. It was a senseless pose. Had she been acting in a play, delivering lines, the director would have spat and told her to get the fuck off his stage as he shook his crumpled, sweat-stained script. This was no stage. The fourth wall was broken or had never been, and within, Eddie's lies were exposed. Her hair blazed around blank doll-eyes and licked her shoulders. He wanted to say, *Jesus, Rhea, what the hell did you do?* But he knew: the Saint had tempted, and she accepted.

The Saint smiled and backed away. Then a moment was lost like a skipping projector, and Rhea crouched next to the cage's bars, framed like a living painting. "Eddie," she said, tempting him with a voice that was a cocktail of lyrical and quaint with a strange twist of Alabama. Where the fuck did that Alabama come from? And yet it was something he secretly yearned for, unknown to even him until this moment.

Somehow, she already knew, lured and subdued him with a hot needle of lust, with her nakedness beneath the gown, and through words that had nothing to do with sex. "I need ta tell ya somethin'. I need ta tell ya, I did it to myself." The southern lilt of her voice and a glint in her unblinking eyes emphasized *self* as though she was confessing yet justified in what she had done. Or was she searching for forgiveness and understanding? Or pity? Some semblance of her original *self* breaking its way to the surface?

She held a palm out to the demon-child who gave Rhea a key. She unlocked Eddie's cage and manacles then held out her hand like a white-feathered lure speckled in red.

Eddie took what she offered, and said, "Rhea.

But she turned, and Eddie followed her up the stairs.

"Rhea," he said again.

Curls stuck to her shoulders, when she shook her head.

From a paneled door under the staircase, they entered the foyer and slunk upstairs to the corner bedroom. She backed herself against the door, closing it while pressing a finger against her lips.

Eddie shook his head. "No, Rhea, I've lied."

"I know, Eddie." She cocked her head to the side as if questioning or judging. On the balls of her feet, she stepped toward him. "Give," she said with a tone that was dry and parsed out to the same dull note.

She pushed, and he fell on the mattress cocooned in sheets not from a lack of will, but from a lack of anything. There was nothing left of him. He'd lost Rhea. He'd lost himself. He looked back on what he'd done, who he was, who he could have been and knew there was no sense in his life. He'd become what his parents were, what Rhea's father—no, *his* father—was, and he hated it all.

Rhea stood above him. She was a fine-penciled silhouette

against the meager fire. Yet those fine lines became violent strokes of charcoal as she hefted her gown and nuzzled down where, even in this room, Eddie hardened.

"Rhea, I can't."

When she forced his boots and pants free, his knife hit the wood floor. He was bare, naked with only his unbuttoned shirt made bloody by others. She slipped back over him, her gown loose around her body as if she molted into something new, something she had never been. Curls fell from her shoulders and lapped his cheeks. Veins pulsed at her neck.

He began to say no but could only shake his head. Fuck it. She was gone. Just like Eddie's will was gone. He laid back in that bed, a slack-jawed idiot entranced by the horror she had made with her body, wanting her even more.

She took him on that bed as she dumb-stared at the ceiling's tin tiles, her body giving with each thrust, knowing it wasn't what he needed. He wanted, lusted, and gave while she took in her own way, indifferent without love, intent on hurting him as she curled her fingers around his neck and dug into his skin and muscle until his blood warmed the Manor's cold. And that taking was her right, his sentencing for all he'd done.

When she was done with him, she rolled onto her side and did not touch him, did not talk, did not look, cringed from every motion he made. The new evening gloom crawled through the cracked siding and stained windows, inviting the roaches and rodents that crawled in the walls.

Ruth's words filled his mind. *This place takes, reminds, but never gives or forgives.*

He nodded, knowing hopelessness. "I can never forgive. What you took wasn't enough." He turned toward Rhea who lay fitfully next to him. "I loved you."

Tears, red from others' blood, fell from Eddie's eyes. He

clawed them from his face. What had he done? What had he done with his life? Up to this moment, there was nothing he could lay claim to. Nothing he could pride himself on. Nothing that amounted to worth. He—the husk he'd become —was useless, worthless, a thing that destroyed because he needed.

Giggling children pattered down the hall and through the door. At the center of the flock of horrors was the hollow-eyed boy, the Saint, dancing tree-root fingers above his head in an evil game of itsy-bitsy spider. A slight, blonde girl followed close behind with a wicked grin splitting her lips.

Eddie elbowed up, grabbed his blade, and wrenched the sheets from Rhea's body over his own.

In a choreographed stream, the Saint drew the children around the bed where they stood like a funeral company above an open grave. Lil' Blondie clung to the Saint's gown. The giggling faded when the boy dropped his puppeteer hands and waded through the clot of children to Eddie's side where he kneeled on the hardwood floor grayed by time.

The Saint's breath was glowing steel in Eddie's ear, his lips, ice. "Rhea's ours, Eddie. But you're free."

Eddie, with his sweaty fist wrapped around the blade's haft, turned toward the child who was so close their breath mingled. "Free," Eddie said.

"Yes," said the Saint.

"I can go?"

"If you want. It *is* what you want, isn't it."

"No." In a tumble of faces and pain, the time he'd had in Saint Andrew snapshotted in his mind. Owen plucked at lures. Josh spat at his feet. Cal squatted and chugged beer in the ditch. Amos swaggered into the church. Saul stretched on the altar. Ruth judged behind the bar. And Rhea, her body was cold. "I don't want this."

"Then leave." The Saint's eyes like unblinking pools held Eddie's.

"But Rhea."

"She's ours, Eddie. Never yours. You gave her to us long ago."

"No, Saul said I can . . ."

The child cocked his head. "The priest was selfish. He saved himself. Murderers, *you*, can't be saved. Leave."

Eddie searched the child's eyes, its skin without pores, its unrestrained words delivered like practiced lines, so certain, so deliberate as if a stagehand whispered the lines off-stage.

Eddie murdered. He damned Rhea. Ended her family. They'd never return nor would she. The child, the Saint, was right and would let him go, but he'd never be free of his guilt, free of his sins, free of his loneliness, even if he left Saint Andrew.

He turned toward Rhea who had succumbed. And yet, the Saint wanted him to leave, told him to leave. Why? Saul, the man, the priest, whose body lay bloody on the altar, had sacrificed himself. He'd ended *his* torment and gave forgiveness to Eddie. There *was* an end. He could leave by saving just as Saul had. The priest had promised. The child must be lying. The Saint who lied first.

They, the Saint, *it*, didn't want murderers. It wanted torment. It wanted to take, to remind. But there was nothing of Eddie to take. Eddie would never forget, but Rhea would. She'd fade, and the Saint would remind, bringing her back to her moment of guilt.

In his worthlessness, Eddie was immune to the Saint. He must be. He was special. He would take her from the Saint.

Eddie turned. The child hadn't moved and still held their intimate distance. "You want her," Eddie said.

"Yes," said the Saint. "I want her. We want her. The town wants her."

Eddie said one word, "Truth." He looked into the Saint's black eyes where his reflection was distended and horrid in two black rooms rebuilt inside the child. Both Eddies, spattered with the blood of the murdered, stared back at him. He was a miserable waste, hollow and ruined like the Manor. But Saul saved. And his will surged, for he knew he had one thing to give. "Rhea," Eddie said into her hair. "I need you."

She turned. Tears fell. Yet those eyes drank life when she asked with hope, "You need me?"

He closed his eyes and wrapped his hawkbill blade with her hands. "I need you to help me save you."

She nodded, just once as he brought her hands and the blade to his neck and pulled. The pain was quick and the blood hot as he spat out a scream where his neck split like the Cheshire Cat's grin.

"Remember, Eddie. Remember your choice," the Saint said with a slash of a smile. Eddie fought the dark clouds of death as blood danced from his neck, pooled at his shoulders, and speckled the child's smiling face. "You, at the town's edge, decided you were special. But you're worthless, and now you'll suffer like all the others having saved nothing. Having saved no one."

Then the Saint and children scuttled into the hallway where the Old Man walked in, stood over Eddie and said, *Mine*.

Rhea looked down on him and smiled. And for a moment, Eddie saw something inside Rhea, through her eyes before his blood became a single brushstroke across the Manor as the Old Man dragged him by an ankle off the bed and down the hallway.

Eddie's head smacked each step that led to the basement

as if Clara had scripted her own death for Eddie, and he hated her. And it was that same blood that soaked his bed of straw in his crucified cage.

CHAPTER THIRTY

Rhea screamed in her own dark room when Didi rolled Rhea's body off Eddie. Rhea wiped away tears that could not be there and yet were, little dust motes of shadow that crawled down her fluttering face. She was the soul of a broken doll—discarded, unloved and unwanted by the dead woman who'd taken her body. Sick with what had been done and could be done with her body. Didi laid next to Eddie with a toothy smile Rhea had never felt or seen in mirrors.

In that room, Didi's eyes blazed like a lantern submerged in green waters while Rhea huddled in a dark corner. Her will was crushed by her choices. Crushed by whom she told her story. Crushed by what she had seen. Not only did she not have the strength to stand, but she didn't have the will to witness any more of what Didi had planned for her body. Or was it even a plan for her body? Maybe it was just a plan for her *self*, for whatever she was now. Her soul?

It didn't matter. Rhea was spent. She was a struck match, a useless burnt stick searching for purpose. But she was already that smoldering match, hardly held as a brief memory tossed into a blazing barrel to waste away in so much ash, discarded on a field of shared pain.

Then the children entered, and Eddie slit his throat or had Didi do it for him. His blood soaked the mattress with that same impossible amount that blanketed Amos.

Why? The child said he'd saved no one. Even after what he'd done, he thought what? That he could save her? Sacrifice himself? For her? That he could release her from this hell? Rhea shook with rage, with hate as blood dripped and drained through floorboards. Did she have that much blood? Not anymore. Didi had that blood. It was hers to do with as she pleased, and Rhea stood watch over the horrors Didi wanted, maybe even needed. Not once had she heard Didi's story, not truly, not the real story, not a story that had weight, that held suffering or joy, the story that led her to this place, in that same field of pain over which Rhea had been scattered.

Then that wicked, ripped shadow that stood over Ruth and hunkered in the corner of Frank's stood over Eddie's corpse. It paused, rolled its shadow-shredded eyes over her body like a slick pimp monetizing flesh, pointed at Eddie, and said, *Mine.*

For a moment, Eddie's eyes that had lost life met not Didi's but Rhea's, accompanied by the wet skidding of his hair and bone on wood. Rhea looked at her own shadow-hands and clenched them together in one fist, but her moment of misery wasn't over, nor did she know if it would ever end.

Didi stood Rhea's body in that blood-spattered gown, worn so many times to tempt Eddie. Why? Why had she? She should have known. She should have seen through his lies. Through Didi's lies. But it was too late. She was ruined, and she was the cause of that ruin. *I've done this*, she said inside.

"That's right, Rhea," said Didi through Rhea's lips. "You're here with me, until . . . Well, just until." Didi smiled and shrugged Rhea's shoulders in the way she did when she was no taller than her parents' dining table and truly didn't know her cuteness would melt the will of those around her. She shuffled Rhea's body toward the fire and said, "It's cold."

Didi, Rhea said. Her voice was a whisper through cotton-filled ears.

"Yes, Rhea?"

Why?

Didi tugged the fireside chair to the hearth and sat. She stared into the fire's light that licked her freckles lost in blood. She held her knuckles under her nose as if pondering her next words. Rhea'd struck the same pose after Eddie had said something stupid. She knew it annoyed him and wanted that. Didi shook her finger and said, "No, Rhea. That answer is mine. And you know that."

Didi still wouldn't share, still wouldn't give what Rhea wanted or thought she wanted. Maybe even needed. If she could understand Didi, understand why she was in Saint Andrew, maybe there was a thread of hope. Maybe she could twist Didi, use her to get her body back, use her to escape Saint Andrew. If there was hope. But her hope was dwindling. It was

—*Gone,* was all Rhea could force through her shadow-lips.

Didi nodded.

No.

"Yes, Rhea."

No.

"There's no leavin' for you. Not anymore. You're lost. You're weak, and you'll fade then return. This place takes then gives. It'll use you just like you've been used and have used your entire life. And it'll bring you back. Just when you find peace, it'll bring you back. It'll remind."

Rhea set her chin on her knees that had just enough substance to support what she was and wrapped her arms around her legs. She could feel the house and its impossible age. It breathed. It stretched and yawned as though it was older than the timbers and stone from which it was constructed. And, somehow, it knew. Knew what? Rhea wasn't sure, but there was something there, something that called to her.

"You can feel it," Didi said. Didi touched the stone hearth of the fireplace and wall. The plaster walls flaked like a sun-parched desert. The Manor throbbed, pulsed. Didi's voice was distant like it was shrouded by a shawl. "A long time, I've felt it, this place. It's old, not special, just wood, iron, and granite. Sometimes I think we made it. Us and those who came before like gods of our own hell. But you, Rhea. You've given. I won't be trapped in what I've created anymore."

How? The hearth's heat fed Rhea and warmed her *self*.

Didi shook her head. "We've all made choices, Rhea."

Tell. It was the merest of whispers that even Didi could not and did not hear. Yes, Rhea had made choices, but she hadn't done this to herself. Not entirely. Others had forced her down this path, twisted her reality into what they wanted. Her parents, her dad, her sister, Eddie. They had all changed her life without Rhea truly having control over the outcome. Now, at this moment, she was alone. No, not alone. She was with Didi who, too, was alone but had answers. Rhea forced the words from her will: *Tell me.*

"No."

What was it she didn't want to tell? Why? The children had said she killed them all. Was that what she kept close, kept secret? That made no sense. Rhea's end was near. Her body was taken and would end up like those children. The thought of it, hanging from that tree while Didi shivered with need and smiled while Rhea lost what she could become, a future lost.

Again, Rhea screamed, but not from the horror of what she had seen and heard, but from the uselessness of it all. A part of her cracked in that moment. And the Manor shook with the hatred and anger of that scream. No, not shook. Drank as though starved for misery. And Rhea's need to be bound to Didi weakened. Rhea slid her thinned and faded hand into the arms that were once hers but were now Didi's and wrenched them away from the hearth and hobbled to the window.

"Rhea, no," Didi said through lips she still possessed, yet for a brief moment, she could not stop Rhea's will.

Look, Rhea said. There, in that window through Rhea's—now Didi's—eyes, the cabin hid near the shore licked by the purple haze of the setting sun, and the dock stretched into the black waters trimmed in silver. To the south of the cabin, near the sunken boat where Rhea had struggled against whatever clawed her legs, was a break in the tree line crossed by branches. Under those branches, she had chosen her path that led to terror, and that terror led to truth.

Next to the window, Didi stood her ground. Her defiance had returned. Yet Rhea had just enough control to look into those panes of glass at what she had become like a double-exposed photo of herself over the distant shoreline. Rhea leaned in close, looked into her eyes that did not blink, did not move, did not give to Rhea's will. In those eyes, Rhea saw herself twisted and stretched.

Yet it was not just herself. It was her *self* she had seen in mirrors so many times before. Mirrors that seemed to want her and yet tell her what she was with an honesty she had never understood before. Mirrors that seemed to need something from Rhea. Or maybe it was Rhea who needed something. There was nothing in those mirrors that could take from her. Was there?

It was Rhea who had taken from herself, taken the paths set before her in indifference, in apathy, maybe even in hatred, loathing, or anger. Why did she do the things she had done?

Why had she muled so many drugs? Yes, she was guilty. She had done terrible things, but they weren't things that warranted what she now felt, had now witnessed. And they weren't things her family deserved.

She stepped back and took in her whole body. Never once was Didi with another until she had Rhea. On the dock. In the cabin. She was alone. Rhea backed toward the door.

Over the years, she looked in those mirrors because she knew she needed something and what she needed was what she had become. Something separated from her body, something lost in a world where pain and misery were commonplace, so commonplace she became desensitized, and all care fled. She'd give up the past. It had only the merest connection with whom she had become and who she'd be.

She took another step, and the warmth of the fire filled what she was. And, in that moment, she decided there would be a future Rhea, unconnected to what had happened in the past because there was only the present. How had she forgotten so quickly? That moment behind Frank's with Owen. She reclaimed that moment when he said, *Rhea, be yourself.*

And it was the belonging of *self* that her future self had, solitary and free, that Didi did not. Didi was stuck in this town. Held by the Saint to be reminded of whatever it was she had done or could have done yet no longer could. Whatever that was, whatever Didi's story was, didn't matter. There were no answers there. There was only a dead end, a termination of life and a future.

For Rhea, there wasn't even what was yet to come, because it hadn't been written. Her story had not yet been written. And that was something that didn't need to be shared, couldn't be shared. Yes, there was the past, but those words, that part of her story was penned by others. Rhea turned and stopped at the door.

"Where are you takin' us?" Didi asked. Something had changed in Rhea's voice through Didi's will. Yes, there was Didi's Alabama, but something had weakened, had been lost.

Rhea looked at Didi in the black room but said nothing. There was nothing to say. The game of half-truths and gifted words lacking value was over. Rhea knew the truth, knew this town. This town didn't matter. It didn't have power over her. It couldn't hold her.

She was not bound to her past. She wasn't even bound to the future. She was bound to herself and only herself. She was bound to *the now* in a flood of time and experiences which she controlled, which she perceived, which she drew power from. She wasn't even bound to her body that had been abused and used not only by others but by herself. It was just a thing.

And there was Didi. Yes, she had Rhea's body, but Didi— she, not even a she, *it*—also wanted Rhea's *self*, needed a future with someone. But Rhea would no longer give freely. She would no longer give to others. She'd harden. And with that will, Rhea held the cold brass of the doorknob and closed the door behind her.

"Rhea, don't leave. I'll tell you," Didi said in that shadow of power she once had in her personal hell that lived in that room of beds and lies.

In the hallway where a layer of chicken wire caged the bones of the house, Eddie's blood stained the rotted floor to the double doors above the foyer. Rhea shuffled like a toddler battling against Didi's will.

"Wait, Rhea."

Rhea did not stop, did not hesitate even though her palsied body fumbled down the steps and to the front door upon which she set her palms.

"Rhea, stop. There's nothing for you out there. Don't." Didi's voice shook.

Are you afraid, Didi? What do you want here?

"Nothing. No, please, Rhea, stay."

Rhea spoke into the door with ease. *Nothing? What's in this house?*

Didi's lips shrunk to a thin line weighed down by her thoughts. "Memories. I can give you memories."

Yours?

"No. Yes! I don't . . ."

I don't need memories. Under the grand gasolier, a knife of light cut across the foyer as Rhea opened the door, her hand like a gloomy Picasso saturated in blue.

"Rhea, stop. You can't do this to me. You can't leave me. I can't be alone. Not anymore. Alone in my suffering." Tears fell from her eyes—Rhea's eyes.

"I need you, Rhea. I've needed you longer than I know. Alone. Never with another. Abandoned, here in this house with that. That thing who was once the keeper. A life taken from me."

Lies. And you abused me. Used me.

"I-I don't."

You are that thing.

"No." Didi's voice muffled, weakened. She drew ragged breaths. Her shoulders trembled and jumped. "I'm here, Rhea because"—she smudged tears from her face—"of what I've done."

That's why everyone's here.

"I've hurt people."

Everyone has, Rhea said. *And you continue to hurt.*

"No."

Yes. I'm done. I'm done because I don't care. I'm done because you are the one who's lost. I'm done because I know who I am, and you never will. Rhea turned and opened the doors where the Manor's yawning height shadowed daffodils and the swamp's shore where a flat-bottomed boat rested. Before she took that first step out of the Manor, shadow Rhea turned one last time toward miserable Didi and said, *I'm sorry. I was wrong, Didi.*

Behind them, a door creaked.

"What?" Didi's voice shifted to hope like a crystal goblet filled with water then wine.

I'm not leaving, not yet.

From that dark door under the stairs the children shuffled, all but that wicked boy yet led by the blonde devil who asked, "Now, Didi?"

A power churned inside her and exploded in a sound that reached the Manor. It was her voice. The voice she had known when she was small but had lost in all the years she'd been hammered down by others. It was a voice she had imprisoned through submission as she lingered through life with as little defiance as she could muster. She had what she had never had before. She had a voice that lifted her above what she once was, a little girl who tagged along with her sister. That little girl who held Eddie's hand. That little girl who looked to her mother for support.

She was her *self*. She was Rhea and knew she'd be that Rhea at that infinite point of *the now* that all people lived. She had the will, and she willed her voice through the body Didi had taken and revealed what she knew. "Yes, now. She's weak."

The children giggled and clustered around Rhea. Inside, Didi groaned, cried, shivered, grabbed Rhea's self, yet her hands clutched nothing, simply swiped through what Rhea had become, a new *self* that controlled.

No, Didi said inside. *You can't. I won't let you.* But her voice was distant and hollow.

And in a body that once resisted, Rhea walked upon granite that stung her feet—her feet, not another's. Yes, there was pain that prodded and explored her skin that had become ribbed and wrinkled with water and blood, but it was a pain that reminded she was alive and whatever was inside her was not, was something that should be forgotten, something that should fade into the past like millions of others who deserved more. Under the hanging tree, where roots spread like clotted veins, Rhea took the noose.

Through Rhea, Didi screamed but that scream was cut short, and its echoes fell dead on the Manor's shores. Rhea clung to the rope. Inside, she held Didi at bay then pushed with her hands that could not be. Didi struggled against wisps of Rhea's *self* like leaves refusing to fall from a dying tree.

Didi scratched, screamed, *You can't. Not like this!*

Rhea's *self* ripped at Didi with her nails that faded back to yellow. The more she shredded, the more hateful the spirit of Didi became. The more Didi howled, the fainter she appeared. Rhea clutched Didi's neck and split her from the body beneath that tree. Didi contorted to escape in a grim pose as Rhea wrapped the noose around Didi's neck, and the laughing, dancing children tugged her above them. Didi, silvery in the newborn night clutched the rope and stabbed out her feet like a fawn's first steps. Her eyes bulged. Her teeth glistened.

The wicked blonde girl tied the rope around the trunk and through a concrete smile said, "You'll do, Didi. We'll get her later."

And Rhea walked from that scene of misery, despair, and rage in that frigid night in her ridiculous babydoll gown. Her abused body wanted death's chill that branched through being, and it took nearly all her will to overcome. But she did not stop. She defied the pain of a body nearly empty of life, reached the boat and opposite shore before a scream rang from the Manor so beastly that the sickness of fear swelled within her.

"No, you bitch," Didi yelled. "I hate you. Hate you! You're

mine. My gift to the—" Like a twig snapped over a knee, her voice ended.

And the vision of Didi hurling over the swamp and tearing into Rhea's body never happened. Over her shoulder, the Old Man walked from the Manor, dropped Didi's twitching body from the hanging tree, and dragged it inside toward that dark door.

CHAPTER THIRTY-ONE

Rhea ran past the lake houses that slept with only the merest of TV flicker or faint laughter. On the highway, Luke and his pickup were gone. Only a smear of black remained, yet Luke's corpse refused to do anything but struggle in Rhea's mind. She closed her eyes and continued like an inmate on her final walk.

When she reached the station and Ruth's body, she stepped into the office's billowing warm air, closed the door, and tossed her gown into the trash, covering Eddie's plastic bag of dope. She put on one of Amos's uniforms and clown-sized boots from a broom closet. In that uniform, she became a frayed photograph of a parent's cherished moment, yet she was pale and threadbare and still shivered. She wrapped herself up in Amos's badge-clipped bomber jacket and fur trooper cap.

She sat in the chair Eddie had when Amos grilled him. Blood spattered the window and stained the floor. Eddie and his stupid hawkbill blade murdered Ruth here. He'd said his dad gave him that knife when he was a kid. Was that even true? He probably picked it up at some truck stop or swiped it from a dollar store. Now Eddie was in that Manor, in the basement where Didi forced Rhea's body, forced her *self* to see just enough of the children and those cages.

She shook her head. How horrid. How awful. How could those children be trapped in this place? Were they all the same children on the playground? Did it matter if they were?

Didi had said *Sometimes I think we made it. Us and those who came before like gods of our own hell.* Was Ruth one of those gods? Did she have her own personal hell in which she lived? Probably. And where was it?

Frank's. Ruth stood behind that bar like a mother to all those who suffered in Saint Andrew. Above her hung that singed dress and bra, a constant reminder of what she had done: that boy, that pretty boy, with a bullet through his face. But there was more to her than that. It was what she thought she had done to what that boy and his child could have become.

Yet, it was her choice. Ruth's choice. She had control of her body, of her future, and yet she didn't, perhaps even couldn't, see it that way. For her, the guilt was dead weight. Yet, if she was a god . . .

Rhea stood, warm once more in the heavy clothes of the man who truly wanted to help her. She grabbed Amos's truck keys. Outside the station, the sky had cleared, and the stars shone through the ragged limbs spreading new leaves. The air was crisp yet tainted by the lake and moldering leaves carpeting the ground.

She opened the Bronco's hatch and dragged Ruth's body to the truck and apologized before hoisting it inside with less care than she'd hoped. She drove to Frank's, unlocked him with keys stashed in Ruth's hoodie, and dragged her inside.

Rhea kneeled next to Ruth on that mopped, hardwood floor, yet Frank's stayed silent. There was no life in the bar. The jukebox stood in the dark corner. The pool cues lay on the green felt. The tables were stacked with chairs. The liquor stood watch. It was unalive without Ruth as though everything knew the building had no heart and therefore could not live. Rhea locked the front door and hefted Ruth's body up the stairs to her apartment.

It was a simple layout: one bedroom with a bathroom connected to a great room that led out onto the balcony overlooking the highway, The Store, and the lake. It was comfortable, and yet there was no sign, other than clothes, that anyone truly lived there. There were no photos on the wall, no artwork, no knickknacks to serve even as a disguise of personality. And, of course, there were the yellow and white flowered sheets spread just enough over the French doors to reveal the night outside.

So Rhea brought Ruth to her bed. She undressed her, cleaned and bandaged her wound, even though the life had drained from Ruth entirely, and dressed her. Rhea changed out of Amos's uniform and into Ruth's gray sweats, yellow hoodie, and flipflops. And waited. She waited because there was nothing else she could do. Yes, she could take Amos's truck and drive out of Saint Andrew, but she needed one last thing. She wouldn't retreat into solitude. She wouldn't become a selfish solo-show of Rhea. She'd be what others needed, and those others would add to her life, not take. She needed that solitude when she defied Didi, and she still needed it now, but she couldn't just abandon Ruth.

Maybe life wasn't one choice or another, but all the choices and people who surrounded her. And if Ruth truly was damned and a god of her own hell, maybe there was hope in Frank's, and maybe there was hope for Amos and Saul if they wanted it. But first Ruth.

Rhea took a chair from the dining room just off the balcony but stopped at the French doors. It was the sheets, the flowers on the sheets. They were the same that had grown outside the Manor and the same that were printed on Didi's nightgown: white saucers with a yellow teacup, ice follies, daffodils.

"Who are you, Ruth?" Rhea asked Frank's. When no one answered, she pulled the dining chair next to the bed and held Ruth's hand. It was cold yet remained worn, well-used as it had been when she was alive. And even though their lives had just crossed, Rhea said, "You deserve better, Ruth. And I'm sorry I brought Eddie here. No, that's not right. I'm sorry Eddie did what he did. I didn't know. I should have, but the lies were thick."

But that wasn't enough. There was more she wanted from Ruth. No, not wanted *from* her, wanted with her and for her, so Rhea said, "I want you free, Ruth. I want you free from this place, from Saint Andrew." She kissed those hard knuckles. "You don't need to be here anymore. Whatever it is that brought you here, it can't keep you." A tear rolled down Rhea's cheek then soaked into Ruth's skin. "And I'll help, even if I have to stay."

In an impossible moment like those that had happened time and again in this town, a vein under one of Rhea's fingers pulsed. Ruth drew in a breath, opened her eyes, and smiled.

"Rhea," Ruth said though dry lips. "I'm in Frank's."

"That's right," said Rhea. "I'm here with you."

Ruth closed her eyes and slept. Outside, a car growled by and crickets sawed on. When Ruth came to, she pursed her lips and said with renewed strength, "Rhea, you shouldn't stay."

"I know, Ruth. And I know his place won't keep me. It can't keep me. But I won't let it keep you, not any longer."

"Rhea, Eddie—"

"No, Ruth. I know what he did. Your hell, it's Frank's. Why?"

Ruth looked up at Rhea. Tears pooled in Ruth's eyes and, like a newly struck well, broke free. "Because Frank's was hers. Didi's." Ruth pointed at her vanity near the foot of her bed. "Bottom drawer, find the indenture, the deed to Frank's."

The vanity's mirror was shivered into a dozen shards that somehow remained frozen within the frame. Mounted to the drawers were plates shaped like a thistle's flower upon which handles mimicked stems. Rhea pulled the stem and slid the drawer open. Inside was a hard envelope with the texture of old skin. Rhea untwisted the black string that held its flap shut and pulled out a frail piece of paper folded a dozen times on worn lines. Unfolded, weak light bled through those lines. Like a shawl, Rhea spread the indenture over Ruth's legs.

The property where Frank's came to stand was marked in fine, black lines forming a deep trapezoid surrounded by numbers and markers. At the top was flowery script indicating the original owner's term of indebtedness in lengthy legalese. Ruth pointed at the very bottom of the document and said, "There's my name." It was struck in fluid cursive fit for an elementary classroom's wall: *Ruth Hughes*. The names went back to a child's lower-case scratchings looking something like *al* or *alphonse* like Ruth had said what seemed so long ago, but Rhea couldn't be sure. It was smudged, stained by water. Unreadable.

Beyond that were the names Ruth had mentioned on their way to the cabin, and just behind those, nearly faded to nothing was *Deirdre*, or at least its first few letters followed by a watercolor smudge of black that may have been *Brendon* or *Brennan*. Her script was beautiful with flourishes and scrawls that varied in thickness and elegance like calm ripples made by lazy fingers in a cool pond.

"There were others before her," Ruth said as she pointed at other names that had been lost to time. Ruth sat up in bed and sieved breath through her teeth as she held her stomach. "She was hauled on an orphan train of sorts from Alabama to the Manor. I'm sorry I wasn't honest."

Rhea paused and looked at Ruth with a tilt of her head. "When I asked on the road?"

"That's right, Rhea. Didi did terrible things in that house. Things that should never be done to another."

Rhea paled and trembled as her voice came out dusty and dry. "I know."

"Rhea?"

Rhea shook her head. "I was there. She took me, abused me." Rhea closed her eyes and her body flinched with the memories of the boat and room. Her stomach churned with the knowledge of what was inside her. She couldn't let that moment rob her of this one, the one with Ruth. "But you weren't there. You were dead. Or . . ." Rhea shrugged.

Ruth reached for Rhea, and Rhea held her. She'd grown warm, softened. "Rhea, I'm sorry, hon'. I should have told you earlier." Ruth's eyes had been drained of tears and now held nothing but compassion in their lake-green glow.

"Ruth, it's okay. You couldn't have known when I first came. We were just passin', *passing* through or so we thought."

"I knew better, that he'd want you to stay." Ruth pursed her lips as if severing words that could not or should not be told to others.

"I'm not, Ruth. I'm not staying. And I want you free."

"I don't think—"

"No, I know. I know I can leave."

"Have you tried?"

"Yes, but things have changed." Rhea looked from the indenture back to Ruth. "Have you?"

Ruth opened her mouth, nearly spoke, inhaled, and finally whispered, "No."

"Then why are you here?"

"These people."

"And why haven't you tried?"

"Same," Ruth said and coughed blood onto her closed fist.

"Ruth. You're staying here for others."

"You don't know that." She wiped the blood on her sheets. "No, I'm here like the others."

"They're here because they think they need to be. They think they deserve to be. You can't help them."

"No, I can make it easier."

"Why?"

"Because I never did. Not before I took Frank's."

"When? When you took that boy?" Rhea looked at Ruth's bandages and the blood peppering her fist. "When you buried that boy?"

Ruth flinched and released Rhea. "You don't know. You couldn't know how that felt."

"Ruth, please." Rhea's voice leaped back a decade or two to when she was a child smeared with tears. "Ruth, I'm sorry. You're right. I don't understand. Why won't you try?" Rhea shook her head and turned toward the vanity's mirror.

In that mirror she was shattered into a dozen Rheas, all the same, unchanging. But that was an illusion. When she moved, she was severed then reformed in the next shard yet remained in the previous like separate Rheas trapped in multiple presents, alone in their chosen cell. "I can't leave you here, Ruth. I can't let you suffer."

"Rhea, I'm dead." Tears wet her knuckles. "I can't leave."

"Others have said there'll be suffering, pain, a hell. Do you want that?"

Ruth's lips tightened into a single, parched line, and her reflection slipped from the bed to join the dozen Rheas. She wrapped her arms around each of them. "I'll try, Rhea. I'll leave."

Frank creaked. He groaned. A radiator hissed. And echoing up the staircase, the jukebox crackled Cline.

CHAPTER THIRTY-TWO

STRAW CLUNG to Eddie's bloody shoulders. When he tried to yell, his throat fluttered and spat. No air touched his tongue. Instead, it wriggled like a dead root. Muck or sleep sealed his eye. Even if he could open them, no light hid beyond his lids. The room—or wherever he was—was steeped in black. Only his heart—yes, it still beat—and the crunch of straw let him know there was a world beyond the dark. It was his reality. His world. It was a place he knew like his black room where he watched himself hate and hurt. But this new room was washed clean of all that. A place where there was nothing. No others. No thought. No *self*. All he had was the pain at his throat where he did . . .

Did what?

Ah, there it was, his voice. But it wasn't a voice that touched the room he was in.

Where?

Right, where? Where was he?

No, why?

Why? Why was there?

This pain.

In. Around.

Through.

His throat through his neck. Something had happened, and he did not want to remember.

Not yet.

Of course, not yet. Because he would remember. He knew he would remember. It was something that had to be done, but the fuck if he'd remember right then and there. Where was he? Wherever he was, there was peace. His body was drained. His mind was empty. And everything had stopped. Everything except the manacle that bit his ankle.

No.

And cold bars that scratched his legs.

No, stop.

The bars he'd felt before. Felt in the—

Cage.

God, yes.

There is no God.

Not in his cage that was more than just bars. It was a memory.

No.

If he had a voice, he would have screamed.

No. Not yet.

A memory of Rh—

No!

Rhea.

I-I can't.

Memories of Rhea toeing down steps toward his cage.

Fuck her.

That'd never happen again. Especially since she was probably prancing out there in those tight jeans.

Slut.

Prancing while Josh licked his lips and tugged at his zipper.

Kill him.

Oh, good, right. That was the solution to all his problems: death, murder.

Wrench.

He planted that wrench in Josh's skull like it was a terracotta pot.

Terracotta. Tiles. Desert.

That's right, there was so much more. Josh's skull, just like those tiles that tempted Rhea down in the desert. Down in that desert where he, Eddie, lied and killed.

Good.

Good? That was another lie. So many lies. There was nothing good about what he had done, and he knew it, but he wanted it. Wanted it bad.

Give it to me.

Somewhere Ruth—

God damn her, that potato sack, Oompa-Loompas mother fucker.

—delivered sermons no one wanted.

She got it good too along with that cop.

Amos *and* Saul got it good. Their blood spilled in that—

Church.

But that was all in the past: memories. A time that would never be again, because his new black room consumed, faded all until time vertigoed minutes into years. Or was it years into minutes?

Too long.

Solitary. Like a scarecrow, crucified in a deserted field. Hopeless and alone. Useless. Even spoken words left him, would not touch his barren world. A world where all that remained was the hiss of air through—

Pain.

It was his first friend in that eternal time of nothing. It started in his thigh that folded then yawned like a cat's jaw just to snap shut again with his heel on his ass. Then his other leg folded. Then, impossibly, his gut clenched, twisted, released, only to seize again. He'd have screamed, but this time little air escaped his throat, and the flesh there buzzed dry. As if his world listened, a new sound knocked on stone. A steady tap that grew into a spatter that touched his shoulder like a tongue licking his dry skin. Water. Conjured like a gift from—

The Saint.

Had it been that long? Had his body somehow lasted those minutes made years made days? How could he have forgotten that simple thing? Just one drop. One fix. One taste. It's all he needed. He shuffled across the cage. The water tapped his neck. Then it tapped his cheek and nose, but the bars kinked his head and shivered his spine. His ear met his shoulder and only then did the water touch his swollen tongue.

Mine.

It was acrid, tainted by mud or whatever fed it to him. But when he swallowed, his Adam's apple slipped through the thin paper of his throat like a pool ball through a net.

Need it!

Inside, he yelled, but even that wasn't release enough. Only the water mattered. Like dried meat across razors, he unfolded his arm through the cage bars. Bits of skin fanned like French pastry. It was nearly enough. He'd feed himself what he needed.

Thank God.

Beads of water tapped his chin. Cartilage crunched where he dug his knees into the bars. Beads tapped his apple. Just one thrust and the water would be his. He pushed. He shoved until that water dropped into the gap in his throat.

No.

In that slit, the water fell.

No.

Yes, through that slit he had made with Rhea's hand.

Rhea.

That's right, Rhea. In that room, she abused him.

Then, when it hurt most, Rhea laid next to him, licked his ear lobe and said, "I love you." When he turned, she was gone and so too was the water.

Gone. No, she'll stay.

Of course. She needed to stay. She needed to be with him. She needed him. It was the only choice she had. What else was there? Inside, his heart burned. Outside, a match was struck and a candle lit.

That little bitch.

No, not Rhea.

That little blonde bitch.

That's the one, Lil' Blondie. Those neat curls and smug grin slicing her face. She leaned near the bars and said, "I like knives, Eddie. I hear you like knives too and needles. I'm out of those, but do you like *this* knife?" She held his hawk-billed blade.

It was stupid, but he nodded.

"May I use it, Eddie?"

He shook his head: another stupid thing. Straw crunched.

The girl pouted. The candle flickered. Thin stitches of saliva bridged her lips when she whined, "But I want to." She leaned closer. Her breath, cold and dead, touched his ear. "And I will."

His muscles had hardened, dried to wrinkled jerky, so the first touch of that blade was like a single playing card's edge across hard leather. But when that card bit, the splendor of pain rainbowed through his chest and starved brain. It was horror. It was hate. It was terror. It was Eddie split between the past and the now, convulsing with every slice, stab, and saw. He wanted his black room. The black room of the past, but it had been robbed, so all he had was pain as his body was butchered, limb by limb, bone by bone, and tossed into a little brass basket fit for—

A fairy tale.

God, yes. A fairy tale. A fairy tale where Lil' Blondie skipped with that basket cradled in her arm stacked with Eddie like so much kindling as she hummed a pale nursery rhyme with his head nestled under her other arm. Somehow his eye saw her skip through woods to the cabin's boiler. And when that iron door was opened with the broom handle, and his bits were tossed in, the flames licked pain like he was whole. The rubber of his boots melted into his missing eye. The cotton of his collared shirt seared to his chest. And he joined the ash of his *Sisters* shirt.

Sisters.

That's right, sisters.

Clara. Rhea.

He remembered, didn't he?

Remember.

But, oh, the pain. The flames licked, clung, filled him. Consumed him as he tried to move, wriggle, anything, but he was no longer whole. His body the sum of his parts plus the pain that torched him until . . .

Until?

Death.

"Eddie?" the Saint said.

He didn't want to say it, but he did: *Yes?*

With an iron hook, Lil' Blondie stacked Eddie back in the basket, skipped to the cabin, and placed his charred head on the bed's pillow. She kissed his lidless right eye that twitched and gathered enough of the candle's light to see the black-haired boy, the Saint, with his hands folded at his waist, standing like an apostle over a tomb.

"Remember this place, Eddie?" the Saint asked. "I'll let you remember."

Yes.

"This is where Rhea left you. Stopped loving you. If she ever did."

No.

"This is where you chose to stay in this town, in this place, with me. And it's here where you chose to be what you've become. You chose this hell, Eddie. And now it's all yours. Again. And again. And when you've forgotten or made choices of pain, I'll be there now and forever."

No.

The Saint nodded, and the girl set to work, humming as she puzzled Eddie's body together, fed and dressed him until he was again whole.

"You want her, Eddie?" Lil' Blondie asked.

He nodded.

"Frank's," she said and stepped aside.

Like Karloff shuffling for the first time, Eddie left his time-less hell, left the cabin and walked to Frank's.

CHAPTER THIRTY-THREE

THE MUSIC GREW LOUDER. It filled the bar and hummed through the floor and Rhea's feet. The voice returned and said, *Rhea.* Except, it had changed. It was no longer a single voice. It was something worse, something she had heard once before. It became that chorus of a thousand voices when she first kneeled before the jukebox shrine. Yet those voices were ripped from the choir and became a harsh whisper of few.

"Do you hear it?" Ruth asked through her teeth.

"Yes," Rhea said. "It's changed."

"You've heard it before," Ruth said less as a question and more as an affirmation of what she already knew, had already witnessed.

"It's worse now." Rhea cocked her head to the side. "There's a new voice." She shrugged Ruth from her shoulders, turned, and held her hands. "Eddie."

Ruth nodded. "Where is he, Rhea?"

"The Manor. The Old Man took him. Took Didi, too, after the children hanged her."

"The children."

Rhea nodded. "Before she was taken, Didi was in me and with him, Eddie." She touched just below her stomach and brought her eyes to that spot where she ached with hate and disgust. "He killed himself, slit his throat to—I don't know—save me, maybe. The basement, he's there, or was."

Ruth shook her head. "I'm sorry."

"No, Ruth," Rhea said. "The death of Eddie, that doesn't—"

"I know. I'm sorry about what happened, what Didi did to you, what the Old Man meant for you to do. What Saul . . ." Ruth dropped her head then looked up as if reeling in the past to the now. "Saul lies. The Old Man lies."

"Yes." Rhea closed her eyes and washed the memories clean of the voice that had terrified her, pushed her to do things, to make choices she knew she shouldn't. She hadn't given in to that voice. And she wouldn't now, even if it was Eddie. Especially if it was Eddie.

"Rhea, Saul will come back, they—we always do. And Eddie, he'll come back too."

"I know. I can't help him. I don't want to help him. He chose, and he'll remember—and should."

"We need to leave. The balcony," said Ruth. "We can jump. It's not far."

"No, I can't." She wouldn't put herself there again. "And you can't. Not with what he's done. We can go through the bar, the kitchen, out the back. Will you be okay?"

Ruth nodded and leaned on Rhea as she held her wound. The steps and walls were steeped in red that breathed with Cline's quavering contralto as she hoped for a new life and an end to sweet dreams. With enough room for a single set of shoulders, Rhea led the way. The staircase creaked and cracked like an old spine and kinked at the corner where there was a tiny landing. Below, just a few short steps away was the bar where, for days unending, Ruth had served.

"Ruth," Rhea said.

"Yeah, hon'?" Ruth's breath was somehow stained with coffee.

She couldn't admit it. She didn't want to admit it.

"I'll go," Ruth said.

Rhea shook her head and took the next step followed steadily by the rest until the bar and all its rows of booze, twisted lines, and brass plaques hidden behind the dark mahogany came into view before she twisted into the kitchen.

"Eddie," Rhea said.

Eddie stood terrible and defiant, drenched red by the jukebox's bubbling lights as the record crackled and started Cline's song anew. Blood stained his *Sisters* T-shirt where braided scars throbbed along a gash that licked his neck like a splash of hot oil. The shirt's hems were charred, and there was a hole over his ribs where flames had burned through. He squinted his one remaining eye, the other was covered with braided scars. "You left me."

Rhea shook her head. She didn't need to say it. Or did she? Did he need to hear it from her? At the cabin, she just left. He hadn't truly been with her at the Manor. She never said to his face, *No, Eddie. I don't need you. I am leaving.* Did he need—No.

Why the fuck did she care what he needed? What the hell did he do to deserve anything from her? Hell? He'd made it for himself. She turned to Ruth and said, "We're leaving."

Rhea held out her hand, and Ruth took it.

"You're leavin'?" Eddie asked. "Leavin' me? Leavin' us all? Leavin' just like you left all the other places we been."

"No. That's not . . ." For a brief moment she had slipped back to who she once was. It was hard to abandon all that had happened. She shook her head. "You know, you're right, Eddie. For once, you're right. I'll leave, and you'll stay. Here. In this place. You'll hurt, and you'll keep hurting because—because I know you. I know what you are, and I know what you deserve."

Rhea stepped toward Eddie and the door. Eddie slid just enough to keep her near the stairs with Ruth sandwiched between the walls. He shook his head and said, "Ya ain't leavin' without me."

"Ruth, we need to leave." Her voice trembled.

Ruth garlanded her arm around Rhea's shoulder, and said, "Power. You don't have that here, Eddie, not yet."

Eddie shook his head. "No." He took three, quick steps and grabbed Rhea's throat with a hand that was bloody and cold.

Rhea squeaked. It annoyed her. Not Eddie's hold on her, but the way she squeaked. She hated it. She was more than that squeak. That couldn't be her last sound. She wouldn't allow it. She wouldn't allow him to reduce her. There was no pity when she strangled his wrist and pulled. "Eddie, stop." Gasps broke each syllable, but it was enough—better than that pathetic squeak. Under Eddie's fingers, her bruises from that moment in the cabin burned.

Ruth stepped next to Eddie and held his wrist, touching Rhea. Maybe Rhea had let her last breath out in that moment. Maybe she had started to give in to the black cloud that shrouded her sight. Maybe her body, in that moment, had resigned to death. But also in that moment, together, they pulled Eddie from Rhea's throat.

It was a strange act. There was no violence. There was no hate. There was no contempt. There was no vengeance or revenge. There was only the smooth embrace of one soft with youth and hope and the other hard with age and regret.

And in that act that held nothing, nothing of the past, no care for what would come and no care of who they touched and that person's choices, Eddie's arm grew limp and fell to his side. Eddie stumbled back into the be-back sign that read the same time as when they first arrived. He shook his head, and tears ran down his cheeks and fell on his chest. He pleaded to Rhea with his eyes alone.

She wanted to look away. And almost did. Instead, she stepped forward and held his attention with eyes she made soft with sympathy that quickly turned to concrete certainty when she said, "Sit, Eddie."

Eddie nodded and sat on his stool, fourth from the door. He knitted his fingers into a single fist on which he set his forehead.

Ruth pulled from the wall a bottle of Johnnie Red. She poured thick fingers into a rocks glass and slid it on a cocktail napkin across the bar with the bottle in tow like the glass's big brother. Eddie pulled a pack of camels from his pocket and lit a bent cigarette.

"Wait here, Eddie," Ruth said.

He nodded and sucked down the glass and poured another. Ruth went upstairs.

Eddie swigged whiskey. "You think you deserve to go?"

Rhea said nothing. There was nothing to say, not in that moment. Eddie tempted, lured Rhea in with his half-truths and empty words that bore nothing on what Rhea was about to do and would do in the days to come.

Eddie answered himself. "You do. You think that. Know this, Rhea"—Eddie leaned back in the stool and pointed at the ceiling then Rhea—"none deserve what this place gives."

Eddie sucked down more scotch. Smoke slid around him like lake weeds. He didn't look at Rhea. Instead, he looked into the mirror framed by booze. Eddie's confidence fed Rhea's anger and hate, sickened her heart. Moments before, he was nothing. His knuckles whitened next to the glass, and smoke washed over his lips like a tide of lies.

Rhea picked up the bottle of Johnnie and poured. "Drink, Eddie," she said, and he did.

Ruth came back holding the indenture and a red duffel, packed sausage tight. She looked at Eddie then Rhea. Rhea hardened her eyes, twitched her brow, and shook her head. Ruth nodded and for a moment closed her eyes, before she set the indenture next to Eddie's glass.

"Eddie," Ruth said, "Frank's is yours, if you want him."

Eddie looked up from his glass, snorted a laugh, and twisted his lips into an asshole sneer.

"You do want him," Ruth said, "don't you?"

"Yeah, I want him." He shrugged and took a drag. "Ain't much else, is there?"

"For you?"

Eddie nodded.

"No, not much else. And it's better than what's out there." Ruth nodded toward the lake. Eddie reached for the indenture, but Ruth swiped away and tucked it into her sweats pocket. "You need to do something, first, Eddie. Sign the Vega to Rhea."

Eddie laughed. It was a harsh cackle like a charred branch cut by a dull saw. "It's broke. Registration's expired." He scratched the scar just below his Adam's apple.

Ruth shrugged. "Then it don't, doesn't matter." She looked at Frank's and all the memories frozen on the walls. "And you won't need it."

"The cabins too?" Eddie asked and twitched.

"Yep. Stay here, Eddie," said Ruth. "You have the Vega's keys?"

"Nah, Cal, in the garage."

Ruth turned toward Rhea. "You ready?"

"Let's go," Rhea said.

Ruth unlocked the front door, but before she closed it, she turned and said, "If we don't come back, stay here for the night, my guest. Bed's upstairs." Eddie raised his glass and set it back on the bar. "Locked?" she asked and dipped her head toward the door's lock.

"Nah. Town's been dry today," Eddie said.

Ruth nodded and closed the door. As she left, the lights inside flickered, and the floods on the sign below the balcony glowed yellow. Together, Rhea and Ruth crossed the highway to the garage that was lit up in the late night. In the shadows behind the garage stood the tow truck. Latched to its back was Luke's charred pickup. Rhea stopped. Ruth kept going. Inside the garage, the Vega was on the hydraulic lift, and Cal's head was shrouded by the undercarriage.

"Cal," Ruth said.

Cal cracked his head on the Vega. "Da fu—" He dropped a socket wrench and stepped from under the car while wiping his bald head with a greasy rag. "Wha?" he said then looked at Rhea.

"Cal," Rhea said as she pointed at Luke's pickup.

Cal shrugged. "What?"

"Where's Luke?"

"He's fine," Cal said.

"Fine?"

"Rhea," Ruth said. "What about Luke?"

Rhea, through her teeth and shaking lips, told Ruth about Luke's last moments.

Ruth pulled a curl from Rhea's wet cheek. Their eyes met when she said, "It'll be all right. He'll be all right." She tapped her chest. "Like me." Over her shoulder, Ruth asked, "Give him to his dad?"

"Hell, no," Cal said. He wiped his nose. "The farm."

"Good," Ruth said. "Cal, we're leavin'."

"I figured. Car's good. Take it."

Rhea wiped the tears from her freckled face and said, "Just like that?"

Cal shook his head as if Rhea had insulted a dead relative. The piston hissed and the Vega creaked as it took on its weight. Digging the keys from his pocket, he tossed them at Rhea's feet. "Take it. Get outta here."

Rhea said, "Just like that?"

Ruth pursed her lips, inhaled, and said, "If we stay here longer, you'd know. Luke? It was bad. He'll come back. The car? That's Cal. Take it or leave it."

Rhea nodded and picked up the keys. "Cal—"

"Forget it," he said and sat at Josh's desk with his arms crossed.

Rhea walked into the shop and said, "Thank you."

Cal waved the greasy rag like a dilettante flunky.

The Vega's door squawked, and Rhea sat behind the wheel. It was a strange seat. Eddie had done the driving, and it was contoured to his body. That seat made her sick. Eddie somehow seeped into her from it. It was a closeness to him she didn't want nor need. Yet, the Vega was a necessity, a thing. Just a thing that'd get her out of this town but be a collection of stories open to the pages of her years with Eddie. She clenched the steering wheel. Her knuckles whitened. She inhaled, held, and exhaled.

Outside the window, Cal leaned and said, "It'll start."

Rhea looked at Cal, nodded, and fired up the Vega. It growled as she goosed the gas.

Ruth sat in the seat next to Rhea and said, "Amos."

"Yeah," said Rhea.

"I can't leave him like that."

"I know. I've got his truck. We'll bring him back to the station."

"No, the dock," Ruth said.

"The dock?"

"His dock."

"Why?" said Rhea, but Ruth shook her head. Rhea nodded, just once, and her body grew heavy with grief. The dock that must have been his to keep, to remind him of what he'd done and could never undo. Poor Amos. What had he said to Eddie before he died? She decided on calm reason, no blame. That was Amos. "Does he want to come back?"

"Probably not, but somehow it'll happen. Saul most likely. Josh or Eddie could figure it out and bring him back. It's best if it's us."

"All right," Rhea said.

It was grim work. Saul was still on the altar. Amos was stuck to the floor in his own blood, and he was heavy, so they backed his Bronco up to the church and loaded his corpse in the back. "Ruth, can he see what we're doing?"

Ruth shook her head. "No, well truth is, I don't really know. Probably different for everyone."

"You never saw?"

"No," said Ruth.

"Ruth, when Didi took me, I could see."

Ruth stepped next to Rhea and held her shoulder. "It'll be okay, hon'."

Rhea closed her eyes. "Maybe." That living house, the Manor, would never be gone from her mind. It'd linger in memory's haze until it needed to feed. "I'm afraid, Ruth."

"Of?"

"What'll happen when we leave. What'll happen to-to you. And this place'll always be there."

"Hon', you can only be where you are. You know that. I now know that. It's what helped us get to where we are." Ruth pointed at Amos's body. "Sooner or later, we gotta move forward."

She was right. They both were right. She looked at Amos, poor Amos ragged in the back of his truck. "Ruth, can we get him down to his dock?"

"With help, but I don't want no one's help with this."

"What'll we do?"

"After . . ." Ruth lowered her head and pinched her nose as if fending off an old pain.

"Ruth?"

"It's hard, Rhea."

"What?" She touched Ruth's shoulder as she leaned against the Bronco's tailgate.

"Giving this place up." She opened her eyes and looked at Rhea. "I thought I could just leave, but I've been here longer than I know."

"Leaving any place is hard, even those you hate."

Ruth's lips turned down into a firm arch. "I don't hate this place, hon'. I hate what it does."

"You said, after. After what?"

"After I sign over Frank's to Eddie and grab the Vega's title, we'll head to the cabin and canoes. We can take Amos to the dock that way. Then-then we'll leave."

Inside Frank's Eddie sat on his stool and a gang of anglers smacked pool balls while swigging beer. Rhea and Ruth stood behind the bar. Eddie signed over the Vega and looked up from the indenture. "Just sign, and it's mine?"

"That's right," said Ruth.

"Free and clear," said Eddie.

"Free and clear. Just like I did."

"The hell's this?" Eddie pointed at the scrolling script and plat drawing.

Ruth shrugged. "What's yours is yours. The rest you owe."

Eddie looked at Rhea, down at the indenture, back up at Ruth. He took the pen next to his empty glass and set the tip on the parchment. Over Eddie's shoulder, Rhea could see the jukebox. It was silent. If there was any time it'd strike up the next tune, it'd be now, but it didn't. The walls stood still yet powerful. A sigh of a gust rolled down the street, and Frank's leaned with it, creaking just enough to let Rhea know it was still there, still alive, still a part of Saint Andrew.

She looked at Eddie and said, "Sign." Eddie signed the contract and set the pen down. "Leave us alone, understand?"

"You're not leavin'?"

"We're leaving, but we've got a last bit of business," said Rhea. Ruth leaned against the beer fridge with her arms crossed. Had something changed in her after the signing? Rhea couldn't tell. "Ruth?"

"Sorry, hon'."

"Eddie signed."

"Good. Let's get out of here."

In the Bronco and at the cabin, Ruth was silent. They stoked the stove and boiler and showered. In the cabin bedroom, Rhea touched thin ashes staining the sheets before stuffing the rest of her clothes and two thick coins in her duffel. Ruth tossed together a meal, and they sat at the table near the potbelly stove like an old couple who had words that didn't need to be said. On the table was a leaf. All its flesh was gone. Only the veins remained. Its stem was stained with blood. Rhea pinched the leaf between two fingers, spun it close to her face, and tossed it in the kitchen's trash.

Getting Amos into the canoe was a chore, but the lake was calm as they dipped their oars into the water and flowed past the Manor that slumped like a sleeping hound. At Amos's dock, Ruth held him on the dining chair with her fingers curled through his beard. She was a mother or an old lover in that moment fit for the tragic stage.

Soon, he drew his first breath, or, rather, his next breath in what might be a life of unending breaths. He pursed his lips and laughed through his nose. "I'm here."

Ruth said nothing. Instead, she brought his head down on her shoulder and held him close. Amos looked up from Ruth's shoulder. Tears fell.

"Amos," Rhea said. "What happened?"

"Why here, you mean?"

Rhea nodded.

Amos opened his mouth and raised a finger. "I could go back to that trail where we stood. I could tell you what I'd've told you then. Hell, I probably should've given what happened." He leaned back and kicked a heel over his knee and said, "But, I won't."

Rhea stepped back, just a nudge, and held out her open palms. "Amos, I—"

"Don't say it, Rhea. Well, let's just say, there ain't no use. Not no more."

"Well," Rhea said, "I'm leaving. Leaving this town. I know I can."

"That's somethin' special. Like you. Eddie?"

Rhea shook her head.

"That's all right. I'll handle him."

"I'm leavin' too, Amos." A bit of the lazy Saint returned to Ruth's voice.

"I figured."

Ruth leaned near Amos and whispered, and they held each other tight, Amos with his head over Ruth's shoulder looked up at Rhea.

Rhea pointed up the path. "You should come with us."

He shook his head, released Ruth, and scratched his auburn beard still flecked with his own blood. "Nah. I'm not ready. I still need this place. You don't. Not anymore." He stabbed a meaty finger at Ruth. "And don't go blabbin' neither. She don't need to come back."

"I know, Amos," Ruth said.

"Leavin' soon?" He looked up at the dark sky clear of clouds where stars winced. The wind settled too. Waves tapped the shore as if to make sure it was still there. The redwing blackbirds had picked up their warbles, and the crickets hushed their electric strumming.

"Walk with us," Ruth said.

"Nah," Amos said. "I think I'll stay. There's somethin' I need to remember."

"I understand," Ruth said. "Goodbye, and I—"

"Don't you say it," he said. "Just go, Ruth."

Ruth smiled and stepped ashore.

Rhea tugged Amos to his feet. For the first time, tears fell from Rhea's eyes that weren't of misery or regret. They were a thing better than the words she wanted to say but couldn't find, so she held Amos close. He held tight and let go.

He pursed his lips, and his beard rolled with them. "No need to say nothin'. Go like she done."

Rhea nodded and stepped off the dock. The path was clear.

The Store and garage were open, but no one stood inside. Instead, most gathered at the pumps and guzzled beer while Saul and Josh stood on the church steps. Eddie had set up a ladder against the front of the bar. Most of Frank's name was scraped off, and in its place, he painted the first few letters of his name in yellow.

Rhea and Ruth slipped behind those who looked on. In the Vega, Rhea fired up the engine, looked at Ruth, and smiled. Ruth nodded just once then pointed down the road. The Vega eased forward as Rhea released the clutch and drove past the playground where children laughed and screamed.

Past the sign, Rhea sighed. She'd left. The Saint released her. The road forward was clear. She reached to touch Ruth's thigh but felt vinyl. In that seat, Ruth cried satin tears down gossamer cheeks stretched thin in a world that did not want the dead and said, *Goodbye.* Rhea slowed the Vega and touched Ruth's face that faded into smoked light and ribbons then nothing.

Rhea did not say goodbye. She smiled, cried, and drove down her own road.

THE END

JOIN THE CURSED DRAGON
SHIP NEWSLETTER

Want more just like this one? Sign up for our newsletter so you don't miss out on the adventure. You'll get:

- A free book for signing up
- Advanced notice of new releases
- First word of books on sale
- Opportunities for free books
- Most up-to-date information on author appearances.

We're busy and know you are too. We won't send more than one newsletter a month.

Register below.

ACKNOWLEDGMENTS

It's hard to write alone.

A writer needs people.

I wrote those two simple statements four years ago. This book is due to those who are with me, no matter how distant, while I write. Thank you.

Tony D'Souza, you said you forget you're reading my writing as if it's "a dream and it all feels so real. Just keep going and get to the end." Your words inspire and remind me of why I write.

Kali Van Balle, your support and guidance within, without, and even after the classroom made me understand what a true teacher, writer, and colleague can be.

Kevin J. Anderson, your mentorship gave me confidence and joy in the words I write. This novel may have never seen the published page if our lives hadn't crossed.

Sara George, with you as my editor, I never write alone. Thank you for making this novel complete. Both you and Kelly Lynn Colby, took me on at Cursed Dragon Ship right when I had nearly given up.

Samantha Yarbrough, Adam Gushwa, JJ Johnson, and Mary Jurney, as my beta readers, you read this book with patience and gave me a true reader's perspective.

Bob and Audry Lang—mom and dad—you let me play D&D every weekend since the sixth grade in that small,

Midwestern town. Those endless hours with friends in different worlds let me grow.

To my wife and sons, Michal, Julian, and Elliot: Every day with you brings hope and happiness. Without you and your patience and support, I would not be a writer.

And finally, aunt Marie, over four decades ago in Eyota, Minnesota, I sat behind your couch playing with my Star Wars action figures while you and my mom talked about Middle Earth like it was a real place filled with heroes doing incredible things. That moment made me a writer. I wish you, Marie, were still here to read these words. Thank you.

Photo by Tiffany Olsen Photography; "Chuck Lang, Author;" Tiffany Olsen, Photographer.

Chuck Lang is a horror and science fiction writer influenced by his years as a carpenter, four years in the US Navy, and two decades as an English teacher with an MFA in Creative Writing from Lindenwood University. He lives and writes near the frequently flooded Red River in Fargo, ND with his wife and two redhead sons.

instagram.com/chucklang_

facebook.com/chuck.lang.421904

bsky.app/profile/chucklang.bsky.social

ANOTHER TITLE BY CURSED DRAGON SHIP

Blinded by a past bathed in blood,
Gabrielle can't see a future without more
of the same.

ANOTHER TITLE BY CURSED DRAGON SHIP

When a girl is brutally murdered, the sherif has no idea what's really at play. It falls on Leona and Jewel to dig deeper into the mystery. If they fail their town will fall to darkness along with everything they hold dear.